MAD MONEY
& MURDER
A POND INVESTIGATIONS MYSTERY

Book 1

Jenni Stand

POND INVESTIGATIONS MYSTERY SERIES

Laughing Owl League LLC

First published in the United States by Laughing Owl League LLC.

MAD MONEY & MURDER
by Jenni Stand

For further information, visit laughingowlleague.com

Paperback ISBN: 979-8-9898881-0-8
First Edition

Cover Design: Jennifer, Robert & K. A. Standridge

Pond Investigations Logo designed: K. A. Standridge

Laughing Owl League LLC Logo designed: Jennifer, Robert & K. A. Standridge

Contact Information

jenni@jennistand.com ✉
facebook.com/jenni.stand92
@Jenni_Stand 𝕏

Dedication

I dedicate this book to my wonderful husband and daughter, Rob and Katy, for both their support and someone to bounce ideas off as I work my stories out.

Acknowledgements

Ellie Alexander and The Tech Guy for creating the fantastic writing course, Mystery Series MasterClass, https://courses.elliealexander.co/.

I can't recommend the course enough.

Glenda Mills, developmental editor and beta reader, for some fantastic suggestions—I used them all.

Beta Readers: Sabina Orzari, Tish Bouvier, Rob (my amazing hubby) for their ongoing support and great feedback.

Advanced Readers: Sally Jackson, Darlene Wallette, Rebecca Perkins, and Christine Paradis

My Fantastic Copy Editor: Shannon McKelden Cave who taught me so much with all her edits and notes.

To my fellow students of the Mystery Series MasterClass and the Author Academy group.

To my neighbor, Stacey, I made sure a certain word was spelled correctly. You know, the Irish way.

To Cindy at Office Depot, you can read my book now.

Location Notes

Restaurant note: While the restaurants mentioned in this book are real, the employees and situations I created for my series are not.

The Bijou was a real movie theater. It offered a full menu, wine and beer list, besides the traditional movie theater fare. Sadly, it closed before I got to see a movie there. I've continued as if it still exists. This is a work of fiction, after all.

Chapter One

"I quit!" Elizabeth Susan Pond said aloud for the first time.

Liz stared down into the murky, receding waters of the San Antonio River below her. She and her lifelong best friend were standing on one of the many limestone footbridges connecting the walking paths that made up the historic San Antonio River Walk.

"What?" Pam Whitlow asked.

"I quit. I'm not going to be a private investigator anymore," Liz replied, studying her reflection in the river water. Her shoulder-length dark brown hair pulled back into a ponytail. She looked tired. The dark circles under her green eyes were obvious, even in her distant reflection.

"What? Why? You can't. I won't let you." Pam crossed her arms. Her long, striped, knit sweater swished around her knees. Her long brown hair flowed around her shoulders.

Liz smirked at the woman she loved like a sister, and she may as well be since they were born on the same day, in the same hospital, only one room apart. "And how are you going to stop me? Stopping someone from doing what they want isn't very Zen of you."

"You're right. But stopping someone from making a huge mistake is. You found what you love to do."

Liz opened her mouth to interrupt.

Pam held up a finger to stop her. "Normally. I was going to say that. Normally, you love your work. And you're good at it. Great at it. People dream of being that lucky."

"Yes, I know. And fine, I'll admit it, I'm good at it, but Regina Masterson..." Liz turned back to look at the river, wiping away the single tear as it rolled down her cheek. The memory of her last case, her first real failure as a private investigator, brought tears to her eyes.

Pam's voice softened. "Regina would have been grateful that you found her body for her family. You started looking for her, even when the police saw no reason to believe anything was wrong. You did right by her, regardless of the unfortunate outcome."

"I know, you're right. I keep telling myself that, but it's not been enough to get me back into the office."

"Of course, I'm right. I'm the wise one in this friendship, remember?" Pam teased, bumping Liz's shoulder with her fist. "And you should, you know. Get back into the office, I mean."

Liz filled her lungs deeply, released a loud rush of air, and resumed staring down into the dark waters below. It was that time of year again. Every January, the waters were drained from sections of the man-made river that ran through the heart of San Antonio, Texas. The sophisticated lock system designed to help prevent flooding when it rained needed routine maintenance. While the water was drained and filtered, the concrete riverbed and locks received a thorough cleaning and inspection, and any necessary repairs were completed. Locals had even created a weeklong party to celebrate the annual event, called the Mud Festival. Complete with a king and queen, a mud pie-eating contest, and a pub crawl of the many bars and pubs along the River Walk. A wide banner hung high between two tall cypress trees bordering the river, advertising the festival to begin the following Sunday, the day the waters returned.

Liz enjoyed this time of year. Since she lived, worked, and jogged next to the San Antonio River, she appreciated the city's efforts to take care of the landmark. This year was different, though. Liz was too distracted to enjoy either the annual draining or the preparations for the upcoming festivities.

"Liz?"

Her best friend's voice drew Liz back to the conversation at hand. "You don't understand. I've lost all faith in my investigative skills. Look at me! I'm a trained and licensed private investigator with a Bachelor's Degree in Criminal Justice, and neither helped me find Regina before it was too late!"

"No one blames you for that. No one expects you to be perfect. And no one has a perfect record! Regina's parents don't blame you, do they?" Pam asked, placing a hand on her hip.

Liz could feel her friend's firm gaze on her as she shook her head. "But that doesn't stop me from feeling guilty. Right now, I don't feel like I could locate a ream of paper in an office supplies store without a map. And that's just part of my worries!"

She pushed away from the cool limestone parapet of the bridge. The pair of friends walked off the stone footbridge in front of her building and turned left. It was early evening and the Walk was busy. The crisp January night wasn't keeping people from enjoying a diverting night out at the bars. Someone bumped into her, and besides an offhand, "Excuse me," Liz's disappointment came to the forefront, because she *saw* nothing. And therein lied her other problem.

Aside from being a trained private investigator, Liz had another skill, one she was born with. Elizabeth Susan Pond was a psychic. As she grew up, she learned the names of her various paranormal abilities. Clairvoyance allowed her to see the future and the past, while psychometry enabled her to know the history of an object. She also had a smidge of empathic ability, a skill that helped her sense the emotions of the people around her. Even to Liz, this sounded unbelievable. But she stopped fighting disbelief in her abilities a long time ago. As a rule, Liz didn't tell anyone. She could count the number of people who knew about her unique talents on one hand. Five. That was all the people who knew her deepest secret, including the woman beside her.

"You still aren't *seeing* anything?" Pam whispered after they broke free of the crowd.

Liz shook her head. "Nothing. Meditation isn't helping, mostly because I can't do it."

"What do you mean, you can't do it? You've been meditating since we were kids, when Aunt Audrey figured out it could help with your visions." Pam's voice dropped to a whisper with that last word.

"I mean, I can't do it. Every time I close my eyes—" a shudder spread across Liz's shoulders, "—all I see is what I saw the night we found Regina. The barn, Regina dead on the floor, and candles everywhere. I've thrown out all my candles. I can't stand the smell or sight of them anymore."

Pam cringed at the description. "I can't imagine. Are you still having nightmares?"

Liz nodded. Nightmares for someone like Liz were especially torturous, since sometimes they came true.

"So, you aren't *seeing* anything. Nightmares are the mind's way of helping you deal with trauma. You can't meditate. Wow! Let's tackle this one at a time. First, I know it's weird for you not to have your—" Pam paused as a large group passed them. "—*crocheting* work anymore."

Liz looked at her friend, her eyebrows crinkled, then she remembered. *Crocheting* was the word they used when they were kids whenever they talked about her visions in public. She smiled at her friend.

"You've been very stressed for the past month, and everyone knows how stress can affect all kinds of things in the human body and mind. Maybe, just maybe, for you, stress can also affect your *crocheting*."

More people bumped into them as they walked.

Liz's bottom lip popped out as she considered the idea. "That's reasonable."

"As for meditating, you have access to not one, but *two* yoga and meditation teachers. Your mom and I can help you overcome this hump. You don't have to close your eyes to meditate. You can simply focus on a single object, or even a blank wall. I've never done it, but I'll find information on it, and we'll learn it together. What's next?"

Liz smiled at her friend's direct approach to problem-solving. "Work. I'm considering a career change. Maybe focus on my locksmithing job instead? Part-time brings in extra money, and the change to full-time wouldn't be that difficult."

"One tragic case doesn't mean you should give up what you enjoy doing. You've told me you've never fully relied on your, um, other skills in your investigations, so you can still do the work. Except, of course, when you go after one of your hobby cases."

The mention of her hobby cases brightened Liz's face. Even though she had lived her whole life with ESP, she was a dyed-in-the-wool skeptic. She had met no one like herself in all her twenty-eight years. The "psychics" she came across were frauds. Nothing more than criminals milking innocent people of their life's savings and trust. This infuriated Liz. If a client came through her door, talking about how they were bilked by some con artist claiming to be psychic, Liz took the case pro bono.

"I would miss taking down those criminals."

"I'm sure. And the victims appreciate your hard work on those fraud cases. Let's put a pin in that for the moment. What would you call this new locksmith endeavor?"

"Pond's Locks?" Liz offered weakly.

"Dr. Pick!" Pam grinned brightly.

Liz laughed. "That sounds more like a banjo-playing dentist!"

"Pond Security? Nah, that sounds like a bodyguard company. No one would believe you as a bodyguard, even with your boxing skills." She dismissed her own suggestion before Liz responded.

"Pond's Picks?"

"That's a good one!" Pam raised her hands, as if she was framing it on a billboard. "Pond's Picks. You lock it. We pick it!"

"That sounds like a tongue twister!"

The two friends tried saying it five times fast. They both failed miserably, laughing at their failures. Memories of reciting tongue twisters when they were little girls flowed through Liz's mind. Of course, then, there was usually a mouthful of crackers involved.

As their laughter subsided, Liz looked around, noticing that the crowds had thinned. The pair passed under the Presa Street bridge and stopped.

"Wow!" Pam and Liz said in unison. They were standing in front of the newest addition to the River Walk, a new hotel.

Liz's eyes followed the beams, admiring the handiwork. She respected the people who created a building like that—everyone involved, from the architect to the construction crew. The ability to go from an idea to a completed structure fascinated her. "I hear they are getting a five-star chef to run the restaurant," Liz commented, not taking her gaze off the structure.

"Really? I've heard they are creating this whole Zen garden greenhouse experience on half the roof next to the pool!"

"Cool. I can't wait to explore during the grand opening!"

As local business owners, they were invited to such events, especially along the River Walk. While Liz had her investigation company, Liz's mom, Audrey, and Pam co-owned the popular yoga studio called Alamo Bells Yoga next door.

"Me too! Brrr! I'm getting cold," Pam commented, turning away from the skeletal structure.

"It's dropped a few degrees since we started our walk, that's for sure." Liz crammed her icy hands into her jacket pockets as they walked past Marriage Island, a tiny heart-shaped islet in the river that has hosted many unions. Tall trees hid the night sky, but with thousands of twinkle lights dangling from the branches along the river, it was easy to imagine you could see the stars.

"Do you want to go up and over or keep walking?" Liz asked as they wandered in the direction of the next bridge.

As she walked along, something in the river—what remained of the river, anyway—caught her eye.

"What's that?" she spoke aloud, as curiosity got the better of her.

Liz stepped off the sidewalk onto the limestone gravel, passing metal planters and solar lights. A black chain attached to decorative wrought-iron posts created a safety line under the bridge's shadow—the city's way of keeping pedestrians from tumbling into the river. Liz stopped at an opening in the low chain fence and looked down into the riverbed. The water was much lower now and vertigo threatened Liz's balance as she leaned precariously over the edge.

"What *is* that?" she repeated as she crouched down.

"Probably another coffee maker, like last year. I'm freezing. Let's go up and over. We can make hot chocolate at your apartment."

"Just a second."

The waters continued to recede as she watched. The cold air settled around Liz in her stillness.

A muddy, bloated, deformed face stared at her out of the murk.

A scream lodged in Liz's throat. Liz fell onto her backside in shock, crab-crawling her way to the sidewalk, the gravel hard against her icy hands as she scrambled away from the eerie sight.

Chapter Two

"Pam, no!" Liz jumped to her feet as Pam stepped toward the river's edge to look. "Don't! You don't need to see that!"

"What's going on? What is it?" Pam asked, her eyes round.

Liz took a jagged breath before answering. "Wait. Just wait. I have to make sure. Stay here. Promise me?"

Pam nodded, her lips pressed together.

Liz turned and crept back to the edge. She had to be definite about what she saw before calling the police. No muffled scream this time. Just a wave of sadness. Someone's daughter laid dead about twenty feet below, staring at her with milk-clouded eyes. Her mud-caked blond hair was plastered to her cheeks. Most of her body was submerged in the silty mud on the river's bottom.

Something else caught Liz's attention. She kneeled, hung onto the cold iron post with her free hand, and studied the odd-shaped items next to the poor woman's waist.

It took her only a moment to recognize them. She had a similar set at home. A pair of neoprene-covered barbells were tied to the dead woman's slim waist with a thin cord. The number displaying the weight, while dingy, was still visible. Each barbell weighed fifty pounds. Someone wanted to ensure this body stayed out of sight for as long as possible. If it hadn't been for the annual draining, who knew how long it would have lurked below the surface.

Liz's gaze moved to the woman's clothing. The color of her dress was almost imperceptible, and one shoe was missing. She realized the dress was, in fact, a uniform. A frigid chill ran down her spine.

"Oh no!" Her hand flew to her mouth as her gaze flicked to the top left of the uniform, trying to avoid looking directly at the woman's face again. She recognized the logo. She knew who the victim was.

Liz stood up and stepped back onto the sidewalk, taking Pam's elbow to keep her from satiating her curiosity. Liz looked further down the river at the next hotel they had been about to approach on their walk. The matching logo from the grimy uniform, lit up in glowing red neon, adorned the side of the hotel high above the lights of the River Walk.

"We have to call the police," Liz told Pam.

"What's down there? You should sit down. You're as white as a sheet!" Pam attempted to lead Liz to the stone bench nearby.

Liz refused to move while she dialed 911 on her cell phone, keeping her eyes on the San Antonio River Suites logo, the body of Brittany Cabot out of sight behind her. "Hello? I have to report finding a body."

"What?" Pam gasped as her hand flew to cover her mouth.

Liz tightened her grip on her friend's elbow to keep her from moving. "Yes, I'm sure. She's in the San Antonio River. She's under the Navarro Street bridge." A pause. "My name is Liz Pond." Another pause. She recited her cell phone number.

The dispatcher's reassuring voice came through the speaker. "I've dispatched a squad car to your location. Are you all right? I can stay on the line with you while you wait."

A grim smile crossed Liz's lips, even though the dispatcher couldn't see it. "No. I'll be fine. I have a friend with me. But thank you." Liz hung up and turned back to her friend.

"A body, really?" Pam looked slack-jawed toward the gap in the iron chain.

"Yes. Please, you don't want or need to see it. Trust me."

Pam shook her head, even as she couldn't take her gaze off the gap in the chain, knowing what was beyond. "I'll take your word for it." Pam returned her focus to Liz. "Are you okay? You're still dealing with the effects of the *last* body you found."

Liz nodded, hugging her arms around her chest. She rubbed her arms for warmth. The air around Liz felt colder than it did only minutes earlier. She stepped farther from the edge of the river. And, as a result, they stood farther from the body. Pam followed her without argument.

"I wonder who it is?" Pam asked quietly.

"I already know," Liz answered, her voice barely above a whisper.

"You do?" her friend asked, her eyes the size of saucers.

"As far as I know, there's only been one staff member who has gone missing from that hotel," Liz pointed to the hotel just beyond the bridge, "and that person is Brittany Cabot." Even thinking about the name caused Liz to experience pangs of guilt. "Her roommate, Rosemary, asked me to look for her when she disappeared in early December. I couldn't take the case, though." Liz paused.

"Because you were already working on Regina Masterson's missing person case. You did nothing wrong," Pam consoled, rubbing her best friend's back. "You only work on one case of that type at a time. If I remember correctly, you referred her to someone else. It's not your fault the other investigator didn't find her before it was too late."

Liz knew her friend was correct, but that didn't keep the guilt at bay. She led Pam away from the river's edge, putting more distance between them and the gruesome sight below. After only a few minutes of waiting, Liz was shivering. The temperatures weren't so bad, but standing still reminded Liz that it was still winter, even in Texas.

Bouncing on her toes to stay warm in the cold January night air, Liz pulled her thin green jacket tighter around her torso, hugging herself with her arms tight across her chest. She looked over at Pam and saw her friend mirroring her movements in an attempt to get warm.

"I hear sirens," Pam commented through chattering teeth.

"I hope they're for us."

A young couple approached the friends, their arms around each other as they walked, hands in each other's back pockets. Their heads were down and almost touching. They were so engrossed in each other that they ignored Liz and Pam.

"Hurry up!" Liz said out loud as the sirens continued to echo among the buildings. The words came out louder than she expected.

The young couple stopped and turned toward them.

"Excuse me?" the young lady asked, attitude in each syllable. Her fingers tapped on her left hip with three-inch-long acrylic nails painted bright fuchsia.

Liz raised her hand with a smile of apology. "Sorry, I was talking to my friend." She gestured to Pam. "Our friends are taking forever to get here."

The young man smiled at Liz and Pam, running a hand through his dark, close-cropped hair. "Are you okay waiting by yourselves?"

His girlfriend's jaw dropped as she turned on him.

"I can't believe you're hitting on her! Or is it the skinny one?" She gestured to Pam with a jerk of her head. She crossed her arms, tapping her foot on the sidewalk.

Liz could swear flames shot out of the young woman's eyes.

The poor young man stammered, "No. No, baby, of course not. I was just being polite. You know I'd never do that to you."

The angry young woman spun on her heel and stomped away, not glancing at Liz and Pam again.

The boyfriend looked at the two women. "Will you really be okay waiting? We can wait with you."

Liz shook her head.

Pam smiled. "We'll be fine." The sirens were getting closer. "Our, uh, friends will be here soon."

Liz nodded. "Yes, thanks. You better get going. Oh, and good luck!"

The young man relaxed and gave them a crooked smile. "She's not that bad. Just jealous over, well, everyone."

"Matthew!" The screech echoed from beyond the Navarro Street bridge.

He waved and turned. "I'm coming!" he called out.

Liz smothered a giggle as she turned to Pam. "Poor guy. He is *so* running in the *wrong* direction." She could hear them arguing, his voice deep, hers shrill, their voices faded as they got farther away.

Pam snickered as she let out a quick breath of air. "Whew, I was worried they'd see the body! Can you imagine?"

Liz shivered as she nodded. "I know I wouldn't want to be the one dealing with her if she had an *actual* reason to be upset."

Sirens drew her attention to the street overhead. Red and blue lights flashed off the buildings and through the stone parapet of the bridge above.

"Whew!" Relief washed over Liz. The police were there.

An officer stuck his head over the edge. "Are you the person who called the police?" he called down.

"Yes." Liz waved.

"Be right down." The officer disappeared from sight.

A few moments later, she saw the tall, uniformed officer emerge from the bottom of the stone staircase next to the bridge. His gleaming white teeth flashed brightly against his dark skin as Liz and Pam approached him under cover of the dimly lit bridge.

Liz held out her hand. "Hi. I'm Liz Pond, and this is my friend, Pam Whitlow."

At least six inches taller than Liz, the handsome officer accepted her hand, giving it a gentle squeeze in greeting. "Officer Marcus Sanders," he replied. "Wait." He wrinkled his brow and turned back to Liz after shaking Pam's hand. "Liz Pond. The private investigator?"

Liz's eyebrows shot up.

Officer Sanders smiled kindly. "I helped on the Regina Masterson case last year. Don't worry. I won't be offended if you don't remember me. A dozen officers showed up at that crime scene, but there was only one private investigator. And, well, a lot happened that night."

Liz nodded, shaking off the memory of that horrible night for the second time that evening. "Well, sadly, it looks like this missing person's case didn't end any better."

She led the officer to the fence opening at the river's edge and pointed.

Pam stood near the stone wall by the bench to wait.

Officer Sanders leaned over the edge and grimaced. He straightened up. "So young. What a shame." His hand reached for the radio handset clipped to the shoulder of his black uniform. "We got a live one here, Mike. Call it in." A short crackle of static followed when he released the handset.

He led Liz over to stand next to Pam. He pulled a pen and notepad from his chest pocket and flipped the pad open with a practiced flick of his wrist. "From what you said, Ms. Pond, you think you know who she is?"

Crap, Liz thought. *No backing out now*. She nodded. "Yes. I suspect she is—was—Brittany Cabot. She worked at the San Antonio River Suites." Liz gestured with a nod to the hotel past Officer Sanders's broad shoulders. He turned and looked up. The vivid logo glowed on the side of the building. Stepping over to the river's edge to take another look, the officer nodded when he saw the same logo that had captured Liz's attention. He returned to the women.

"Excellent memory." His pen flew across the notepad.

Liz bit her lip before speaking. "Her roommate approached me to find her when she first disappeared. But—" Liz paused, her gaze drifting to the nearly empty river, grateful she couldn't see the body from this vantage point.

"But, what?" Officer Sanders asked, his pen poised, his gaze steady on her face.

"But I was already working on the Masterson case. And I'll only work on one active missing person's case at a time. I referred her roommate to a different investigator. I don't know if she ever went to see him."

The officer jotted down more notes, his pen flew across the small pad. "We can't save them all. That's the hardest lesson of police work."

Liz frowned. "For private investigators too."

He turned to Pam. "Did you notice anything when you found the body, Ms. Whitlow?"

"Pam, please. And no, I didn't. I haven't even seen it. Liz wouldn't let me after she realized what it was."

Officer Sanders nodded. "Good. You don't need that kind of thing in your memory. Trust me. I'll need your contact information if there are other questions."

The women each recited their full names and phone numbers for the officer.

He closed his notebook and put it away. "A detective-investigator will be here—"

A high-pitched scream interrupted him. The trio whirled around toward the scream's source.

"Oh no!" escaped Liz's lips. The harried young man and his high-strung girlfriend were on the other side of the River Walk, and they'd seen the body. Scream after scream escaped the girlfriend's mouth.

The sound reverberated off the buildings bordering the river.

Liz squeezed an eye closed and turned her head away from the sound.

"Wow, she can hit those decibels!" Officer Sanders flinched and grabbed his handset. "Mike, we have civilians

on the other side of the river. Where's that backup?"
Before his partner could answer, more sirens and flashing
lights drowned out the other officer's response and the
young lady's screams.

"Excuse me, ladies. I've got to get them moving before
they draw a crowd. Will you be okay waiting here for a
minute? The detective will want to speak with you both
when he gets here."

Liz nodded. "We'll be fine. Please, try to get her to
stop screaming."

"Yes, please." Pam agreed, covering her ears with her
gloved hands as yet another shriek floated across the
river.

Officer Sanders jogged back to the stone stairs. He
disappeared and reappeared on the other side of the river
moments later. A few more curious onlookers had arrived,
drawn by the young woman's screams. The officer stood
at least a head taller than the small crowd of gawkers.

Liz heard him politely, but firmly, ask people to move
along and stop taking pictures. She nodded when she
heard him.

"Please, allow the victim some dignity. Don't share
those pictures. Just delete them."

In today's age of social media and technology, it would
be only a few minutes before pictures of the crime scene
were all over the internet, and not long after, the news.

Officer Sanders finally reached the young couple and
the first request out of his mouth was: "Please! Stop
screaming!" loud enough that even Liz and Pam could
hear him.

The young lady was so shocked at the officer's demand,
she stopped screaming immediately. "Oh my!" she said,
turning her tear-streaked face to his stern one. "Will you
please take me home? I just can't handle this!" She placed
a manicured hand gently on his arm.

Liz snorted.

Pam giggled.

The officer gingerly removed the woman's hand from the black sleeve of his uniform.

Her bottom lip puffed out in an obvious attempt at a sexy pout.

He looked at the nervous young man next to her. "Cadet?" Marcus Sanders asked with all the force of a drill sergeant.

The boyfriend jumped to attention and stopped the movement of his right arm mid-salute. "Yes, sir!" His arms snapped straight to his sides.

Officer Sanders's lips twitched. "Are you responsible for this young lady?"

"Yes, sir!" the cadet replied, still at full attention, chin up, eyes forward.

"Make sure she gets safely home, then!"

"Yes, sir!" The young man saluted this time. He grasped his girlfriend's taloned hand and dragged her reluctantly away from the officer.

Officer Sanders shook his head.

More uniformed officers arrived to break up the growing crowds on both sides of the river.

Officer Sanders returned to Liz and Pam. "I can spot a cadet at fifty paces. You two were no help, though," he commented under his breath.

"I'm sorry," Liz apologized. "If you'd seen that couple earlier, you'd laugh too. Let's just say a double standard is alive and kicking in their relationship."

Pam muffled a giggle.

Liz's gaze drifted across the river now that the screaming had ceased. Dozens of people were milling around the river's edge. Some were taking pictures, some with their mouths covered in shock. One person stood out, though.

It was Rosemary Travers, the victim's roommate. It didn't look like she'd noticed Liz.

Rosemary whispered into the ear of a man next to her. They moved through the crowd without a second look at the grisly scene.

Liz watched them leave as more uniformed officers arrived to secure the scene. Bright yellow police tape was draped across the sidewalk, drawing onlookers like flies to honey.

Officer Sanders drew the ladies into a hushed conversation about the upcoming mud festival and a debate over which bar would win the "mud pie"-eating contest ensued.

Liz knew it was the officer's attempt to take their minds off the matter at hand.

It wasn't long before they heard a deep voice demand, "Who was the first officer on the scene?"

The change in Officer Sanders was immediate. He went from relaxed to standing at attention. He raised his thick arm and gestured toward the detective standing under the bridge.

Liz turned in the direction of the wave and saw Detective-Investigator A. J. Sowell striding out of the shadows toward them, his worn brown leather jacket zipped to his neck, the faintest trace of a white shirt underneath.

"Officer Sanders." The men shared a firm handshake.

Detective Sowell turned to her after nodding at Pam. "Liz? What are you doing here?"

"Hi, A. J. I found the body," she replied quietly. A wave of gratitude at the sight of a familiar face washed over her. This was the first time she'd seen the detective since Regina Masterson's funeral. Before that, they'd work together daily for a week trying to find her and her kidnappers.

"Really? I'm sorry to hear that. I'll need to speak with you both. Do you mind waiting over here while I get a handle on this situation?"

Liz nodded and turned to the uniformed officer. "Thanks for your help, Officer Sanders." She smiled up at the tall man, offering him her hand.

"You're welcome, Ms. Pond. Pam." He squeezed each of their hands before stepping away with the detective.

"That's A. J.?" Pam whispered when they were alone.

"Yes," Liz whispered in reply.

"Wow, he's cute!"

"Pam, not now!" Liz rolled her eyes as she chided her friend. She resumed rubbing her arms and shoulders for warmth. Her whole body felt as cold as ice. "Aren't you freezing?"

Pam shook her head. "I'm cold, but I think I'm getting used to it." She held her sweater snugly around her torso with her crossed arms.

"Lucky you. I feel like there is no warmth left in my body!" Liz commented, rubbing her legs. As she straightened up, Pam placed her hand on Liz's forehead and studied her face.

"I think you might be going into shock. I'll ask someone for a blanket. Be right back."

Pam left her alone and disappeared up the staircase. Liz watched as officers and crime scene professionals streamed through the area. She overheard someone requesting a ladder so they could reach the body. They were wearing standard black rubber boots on their feet that came to the knees of their blue coveralls, meant to protect both the technicians and the crime scene's integrity.

Liz watched A. J. speak with Officer Sanders for a few minutes, ending with the pair stepping to the edge of the emptying river. She was grateful that she didn't have to look at Brittany's remains again. There was absolutely no doubt in her mind of the body's identity.

A. J. shook his head and took Officer Sanders's hand again. The uniformed officer walked away, giving Liz a last wave before disappearing up the staircase to the bridge above.

Running his hand through his short brown hair, A. J. returned to Liz. "I hate it when they're so young," he whispered when he reached her side, the corners of his mouth turned down.

Liz didn't need her empathic ability to recognize the sadness he felt. She nodded. "Me too." Liz studied his face while she resumed rubbing her arms for warmth.

"You okay?" A. J. asked. "You look pretty pale."

Liz grimaced as she looked into his warm brown eyes. "I think so. Just freezing. Pam thinks I'm in shock."

"Do you want a blanket? I can ask Officer—"

Liz stopped him, placing her chilled hand on the sleeve of his jacket. "Pam already went to ask for one."

A. J. leaned against the cool stone bench, his gaze moving to the controlled chaos by the river. "You know who it is, don't you?" It wasn't a request for information but agreement.

Liz nodded, looking at her hands, "Brittany—"

"Cabot," A. J. finished for her.

Suddenly, Liz couldn't control the emotions slamming into her soul. Her hands shook, and her gaze locked on them. *Why can't I make them stop shaking?* was her last thought before time slowed, her mind spun, and the world went dark.

Chapter Three

When a thick gray wool blanket draped around her shoulders, Liz came out of her stupor, blinking unevenly as the world around her gradually came into focus.

"Liz?" A. J. was kneeling in front of her, rubbing her shoulders briskly.

She looked around before focusing on A. J.'s handsome face, only inches from her own. *When did I sit on the ground*? She thought, but out loud, she asked, "A. J.? What happened?"

He stopped rubbing her shoulders, pulling the blanket tighter around her body. One hand went to her cold cheek. "You're in shock. We'll talk more tomorrow."

Liz shook her head. "No. I'm okay. Let's do this." She ran through a quick breathing routine. She felt her heart rate slow, and the mental cobwebs disappeared. Mostly.

A. J. placed a firm hand under each elbow and helped her up.

"If you're sure." A. J. kept one hand on her arm.

Liz wiped a hand across her forehead. "I'm good. I promise." She stared at the blanket for a minute, as if noticing it for the first time. Shrugging, she pulled it tighter around her chilled shoulders.

"Okay, I only have a couple of questions. What were you doing when you found the body?" A. J. pulled his pad and pen from his dark cargo pants pocket. He kept his body between Liz and the activity by the river.

"Pam and I were just walking. I've—" Liz gulped, "—I've had a lot on my mind lately. Where's Pam?" A shiver ran through her body under the heavy woolen blanket.

"She's up on the bridge with Officer Sanders. They threw down the blanket for you. She'll be back in a minute." A. J. rubbed the back of his neck, grimacing. "I'm sorry I haven't called to check on you. Things have been busy at the department lately."

Liz gave him a small smile. "It's okay." Their eyes met.

A. J. broke eye contact and cleared his throat. He glanced down at his notepad. "Did you notice the time when you found her?"

Liz shook her head. "No, but it was only a minute before I called 911, if that helps." She pulled out her phone and brought up the list of recent calls. She told him the time.

A. J. nodded, stating that he'd get that recording from the 911 central office.

A uniformed officer walked up to A. J. and whispered in his ear.

The detective nodded, mumbled, "Thanks," and turned back to Liz. "Look, they're bringing her up soon, and you don't want to see that. I'll call you tomorrow. Okay?" He looked around. All the officers were busy as more curious pedestrians showed up.

Liz didn't argue. What she had seen already was more than enough for her. She started to take the blanket off, but he stopped her.

"You're freezing. How about you drop it by my office at the station tomorrow? I'll make sure it gets back to Officer Sanders." A. J. readjusted the blanket around her shoulders.

"Thanks, A. J." Liz turned, keeping her gaze away from the river.

Pam jogged toward them from the staircase. "Sorry, the officers wouldn't let me pass until Officer Sanders intervened. What did I miss?"

A. J. answered for Liz. "She's in shock and needs to go home. Pam, a quick question. Did you see anything?"

Pam shook her head. "No, Liz wouldn't let me near once she realized what she was seeing."

"Lucky you. Are you okay? No symptoms of shock?" he asked, studying her face.

"No, I'm fine. But that's probably because I'm the only one here who hasn't found a murder victim twice during the past month."

Liz and A. J. shared a look and frowned.

The trio walked to the yellow police tape that crossed the sidewalk, holding back the crowd of curious onlookers. A. J. raised it so Liz and Pam could duck under and step to the other side. "Are you okay getting home? I can have an officer escort you." He placed a hand on Liz's elbow.

Liz smiled genuinely for the first time since he arrived. "We're good, but thanks."

A. J. ignored her response.

Liz straightened up and A. J.'s hand moved to her back. His hand massaged her back in slow circles, distracting Liz.

The detective's gaze scanned the crowd. "Murphy!" A. J. called out and waved to a tall man standing in the middle of the throng.

William "Mac" Murphy, a local reporter and crime blogger, elbowed his way through the crowd until he stood next to Liz and Pam. "Sowell." He greeted A. J. with a handshake. "Hi, Liz. I thought that was you. What's going on?" He nodded to Pam as he pushed his glasses up his nose, pulling out a pen and notepad from the dark leather satchel by his hip.

"No comment," A. J. answered reflexively. "Sorry, habit. Look, Murphy, I've got a lot to do. Can you see Liz and her friend home? Oh, Mac, this is Pam Whitlow." A. J. gestured between them by way of introduction. "Liz is in shock, and I don't want them to walk home alone. I'd ask an officer, but they're all pretty busy."

"I am not!" Liz argued weakly, even as she pulled the blanket tighter around her cold frame. She looked between the two men and Pam. She could tell she'd already lost this battle.

A. J. ignored her protest, his serious gaze focused on Mac. "And don't ask her any questions, please. Call me later, and I'll see what answers I can give you. Deal?"

Liz muttered next to them.

Mac nodded. "Sure, I have your number. Come on, Liz." He stepped to the side, holding his arm out to allow her to move ahead of him. He shoved the pad and pen back into his messenger bag simultaneously. "Pam, it's nice to meet you."

"Likewise," Pam responded, stepping past the tall blond, blue-eyed reporter.

"But, I…" Liz shivered from head to toe. "Fine!" She gave up. She turned to the detective. "Bye, A. J. I'll talk to you tomorrow."

"Get some rest, Liz." Their eyes met.

She nodded as he moved away.

Liz, Pam, and Mac turned their backs on the busy crime scene.

The detective shouted orders to uniformed officers to get the crowds under control, his voice echoed off the buildings behind them.

Their progress was slow as they wove their way through the crowd. Questions flew from every direction when onlookers realized the women had come from the other side of the police tape, but they were left unanswered. Mac pushed his glasses up onto the bridge of his nose again when they finally broke through the crowd to an empty sidewalk.

Liz squinted up at him. "Since when did you wear glasses?"

"Since I was three," he replied automatically, running his hand through his wavy blond hair. "Oh," he grinned, "I'm waiting for a new contacts prescription, so in the meantime...." He tapped the frames with his index finger.

"Oh, okay. You don't need to walk us home, but thanks. Bye!" Liz walked away from him, pulling the blanket up before it trailed on the ground, grateful she could move unimpeded at last.

Pam chuckled as she followed her friend.

Mac hurried, his long strides allowing him to catch up with the pair with little effort. Reaching out, his hand dropped onto her shoulder, stopping her in her tracks. "Wait. Come on, Liz. Detective Sowell asked me to make sure you got home." He tightened the woolen cover around her shoulders. His expression changed to one of concern, and his voice softened. "Hey, are you okay? You aren't hurt or anything, are you?" His gaze ran over her blanket-wrapped form before looking at Pam.

Liz looked up at the tall man in front of her. She bit back a retort when she saw he was genuinely concerned. "Thanks, I'm okay. Crap. Fine!" A huff escaped her mouth, and a puff of mist reminded her how cold it was. "I found a body in the river. Apparently, I'm suffering from a touch of shock." Annoyance tinged the last words out of her mouth. She hadn't meant to tell him anything. Her petulance toward the reporter diminished. "Look, I'm sorry, Mac. It's been a long night."

She turned away when she spotted the hotel's logo over Mac's shoulder. *Poor Rosemary*, she thought. Liz remembered the victim's roommate worked in the same hotel and probably wore the same uniform. A wave of sadness washed over her.

"Liz?" Mac's voice snapped her out of her musing.

"Yeah?" She looked up at him and then around. Relief flooded her body. At least she hadn't found herself on the ground this time.

"You kind of spaced out for a second." His jaw stiffened, and he straightened the leather strap of the satchel crossing his chest. "Come on," he took her arm through the thick blanket. "I promised I'd get you two home. Which way do we go?"

Liz gestured meekly down the river. "That way." And just like that, exhaustion slammed into her, and suddenly she was grateful for his help. It took all she could muster to place one foot after the other. A yawn stretched her jaw to the point of agony.

Mac matched his normally long stride to Pam and Liz's slower pace.

The blanket drew curious looks from couples walking along hand-in-hand, but the trio ignored their stares.

After several minutes of walking in silence, the reporter asked, "Liz, are we still going in the right direction?"

"Okay. Just tired," Liz responded vaguely as a yawn overtook her words. Her eyes watered. And she wiped the tears away with a corner of the scratchy wool blanket.

Mac shook his head. "That must have been one hell of a shock you received. Are we still going in the right direction?" he repeated. He looked to Pam, raising an eyebrow.

"Yes, we won't go up out of the River Walk until we get through Casa Rio," Pam responded helpfully, taking Liz's other elbow in her hand.

Liz nodded, not bothering to cover her mouth as more yawning followed the first one. She massaged her cheek, cursing under her breath as more tears flowed down her cheeks. She wasn't crying, but her eyes always watered when she was exhausted.

"Do you know who it was?" Mac asked quietly.

More yawns. Liz shook her head. "Police will identify her," she replied when she could finally speak between yawns. *For crying out loud*! She thought, when she realized she just told him the victim was a woman.

A broad smile crossed his face at her slip-up. "It's okay. I'm going to find out. I promise I won't ask any more questions. Tonight anyway."

Liz stopped walking and made a motion of locking her lips and throwing away the key.

Mac stopped and laughed. "You know, most of the private investigators I know *want* publicity. Why don't you?" He wiped tears away from her cold cheeks with his ink-stained thumb.

A little surprised at the tender gesture, she ignored it. Irritated at not sensing anything from Mac's touch, Liz shrugged, pulling the blanket tighter about her chilled body.

The reporter's hand dropped to his side.

"I want my work to stand on its own merit. Not on how much publicity I get. Besides, I don't know if I'll be a private investigator for much longer. Dammit! I didn't mean to say that." Liz squinted up at Mac. "How are you getting information out of me?"

It was Mac's turn to shrug. "It's a gift. Why don't you want to be a PI anymore?" he asked as they took the bypass behind the white adobe and limestone Arneson River Theatre stage with its well-known backdrop of three stone arches. The arches housed five iron bells, known as "The Hugman Bells," named for the architect of the San Antonio River. Each bell represented one of the five historic San Antonio Missions, the most famous of which was the Alamo.

Liz fell quiet, biting her bottom lip as they walked, not answering his question until they returned to the sidewalk on the other side of the theater. "I'm...oh, I don't know. I'm just thinking about making a change. Maybe. That last case..." Her voice trailed off. She knew he didn't need her to elaborate further. Mac had been at the barn the night Regina Masterson's body had been found, with all the other reporters drawn by the lights, sirens, and calls for backup through their police scanners.

He nodded. "That was a rough one. But how does that affect your career? From what I saw, you did great. The police wouldn't have jumped on the case so quickly if you hadn't found her car the way you did." Mac's eyebrows wrinkled as he pushed his glasses up the bridge of his nose with one finger. "I've been meaning to ask you. How did you find her car so fast? It was abandoned in the middle of nowhere."

A vision. Liz's eyes flew open wide. *I didn't say that out loud, did I?*

Judging by Mac's calm exterior, she hadn't. Whew.

"I put the word out with some tow truck drivers I know. I asked them to let me know if they saw an abandoned vehicle matching the description of her car."

That was mostly true. In reality, Liz got a vision while at Regina's apartment when she touched the spare keys to her car. The vision showed the vehicle hidden behind a low billboard advertising the Natural Bridge Caverns. She described the sign to her tow truck driver contacts, and within a day, one of them called her when they spotted it.

Luckily, Mac accepted her lie readily. Nice and simple.

Pam listened to their exchange quietly.

Thankfully, this side of the River Walk was quieter, with fewer pedestrians, while the bars on the other side were overflowing. Music and laughter drifted on the chilly night air. They were making good time, not slowing down until they reached one of the many restaurants along the River Walk.

Liz led the way as they passed the umbrella-covered tables of Casa Rio, a long-standing fixture in San Antonio. Like many food-service businesses along the river, the restaurant had tables set along the river's edge, so their patrons could soak in the river's scenery and the city around and above them as they ate. Strings of lights brightened the exterior tables for nighttime eating and additional décor for the upcoming festival. Brightly colored umbrellas covered each table year-round, and Liz found they gave a festive feel to the River Walk. The only difference for this time of year was the addition of outdoor heaters. Tall, shiny, aluminum propane heaters were scattered among the tables to help keep brave customers comfortable in the cooler temperatures.

Several waitresses called out greetings to Liz and Pam, stopping short when they saw Liz wrapped in a blanket.

Liz returned a small wave, but the movement sent a corner of the blanket flapping. She caught it before it fell into a large bowl of salsa on the only occupied outdoor table.

"Sorry," she apologized to the couple sitting there. The man, who had short, dark hair with a smattering of gray, smiled at her. "It's all right." He resumed his conversation with the woman who was his dining companion. "Did I ever tell you about the time I hid from spies under *that* table? The one with the red umbrella." He pointed to a table at the edge of the river.

A musical laugh floated from the woman. "Oh, Davey! You tell the best stories. You really should be a writer!"

The man shrugged, popped a chip into his mouth, and winked at Liz.

Liz smiled sleepily and turned away, wondering if the man was telling the truth. If her abilities were working, she'd shake his hand in a heartbeat to satisfy her curiosity and see if he was telling the truth. If her psychometry returned, she planned on sitting at the table he mentioned.

A teenage server, wearing black slacks, a bright white blouse, and a black server apron tied around her slim waist, an order pad in hand, stopped next to Liz. "Hey, are you okay, Liz? Pam?"

Liz smiled sleepily, rubbing her aching cheek with the blanket. "I'm fine, thanks. Tell the others that I'm okay, please." As more restaurant staff looked her way, she smothered a yawn.

"She's in shock, but she's not hurt," Pam explained gently.

Mac picked a few business cards from the outside pocket of his leather bag. "It'll be in the paper tomorrow. You can follow the link from my blog." He smiled charmingly, his blue eyes sparkling. "Ladies, shall we?" He gestured to the stairs on the other side of the restaurant.

Mac and Pam followed Liz as they came up onto Commerce Street. After a few minutes, Mac looked at the tall building to their left. "Hey, Liz, I thought I was walking you home. Do you need to go into the police station?"

The concrete and steel structure that was the downtown substation of the San Antonio Police Department, and a parking structure loomed high above the restaurants nestled on each side.

A yawn escaped as Liz shook her head, wiping her eyes with the corner of the blanket. She gestured across the street, the blanket flapping in the breeze. "I live over there."

Mac looked across the street and saw a liquor store, its entire storefront nothing but green-framed windows, a dancing neon sign spelled out "Open" repeatedly. Next to it was an open passageway with reddish-brown ironwork filling the top portion of the short breezeway and a popular club with high-arching windows that reached the second story above the double doors.

A serious-looking muscular bouncer stood next to the open doors with a short line of hopeful customers waiting to get inside behind a bright red velvet rope.

"Where?"

Liz put her hand under his scruffy chin to make him look higher. "Up there."

Sure enough, above the breezeway, there was a door blocked by a short wrought-iron railing, bordered by two tall, thin windows and a bright blue-and-white awning.

A large picture window and matching awning filled the space above the door.

"Really? I didn't know there were any residential spaces in this building."

Liz grinned. "There weren't. The building owner was a client when I first started out as an investigator. He made an exception after I helped him out with a problem." Another yawn escaped. "Excuse me!"

Not caring in her current state of exhaustion, Liz jaywalked across the quiet street to the passageway.

Pam rushed to catch up with her.

The reporter, more cautious, looked both ways before following. Mac trailed behind them through the short walkway. They were greeted by loud music, clinking glasses, and people dancing among the tables, umbrellas, and tall outdoor heaters on an elevated patio just above his head.

Liz turned left at the end of the passageway, oblivious to the bar's noise, and stopped at the bottom of the open wrought-iron stairs that ran up the wall to her left. "This is me."

Mac rubbed the back of his head, glancing around them. "Liz, you took me to your office." He looked around, his eyebrows drawing together. A simple painted, wooden sign adorned the wall next to the gate. It said "Pond Investigations LLC" and included her phone number. Below that, a doorbell and speaker were mounted onto the stone wall. A tall wrought-iron gate blocked access to the stairway.

Liz gestured up the stairs with her blanket-wrapped hand. "My apartment is behind my office."

"No way!" Mac looked up. A small balcony and a blue door were at the top of the stairs. A large, brightly painted ceramic sun hung on the wall above the entrance. "I've never noticed a second door before."

Liz fished her keys out of her pocket and unlocked the gate. "Thanks for walking us home, Mac. I really appreciate it." She held her hand out to him.

He wrapped Liz's icy hand in his, shaking it and rubbing it tenderly. "Are you sure you're okay?" He turned to Pam. "Is she okay?"

Pam shrugged, shaking her head.

Liz nodded, extracting her hand. "Nothing that a hot shower and a good night's sleep won't cure."

The ladies stepped through the gate, closing it behind them. Liz still had to look up to see his face from her position on the first step. "Really. Good night, Mac, and thanks again for getting us home."

"I'm spending the night," Pam told him. "I'll keep an eye on her."

Liz looked at her friend in surprise. "But you have to work in the morning!"

"I'll be fine! It's not like I have far to go for work." She gestured to the Alamo Bells Yoga Studio next door up a short flight of steps only a dozen feet away from where they stood. Pam pressed her lips together and stared at Liz, unwavering.

Mac grinned at their exchange. "Night, Liz, Pam. Hey, I've got to stop by the police department before I go home and write my story. Do you want me to return the blanket for you?"

Liz hesitated before removing the blanket from her shoulders and dropping it to Mac over the railing. The cold cut through her thin jacket like a hundred razors. "Thanks. Tell the desk sergeant it belongs to Officer Marcus Sanders, okay?"

"I will. Night!"

Liz and Pam jogged up the stairs to the safety of Liz's sanctuary.

Chapter Four

Nervous sweat poured down Liz's back as she ran toward the dilapidated barn in the overgrown field. Her focus stayed fixed on the structure. Her heart pounded as her feet struggled to find a footing on the uneven ground, slick with late-night frost. Frozen weeds crunched underfoot. Her gloved right hand moved to the gun holster at her hip to prevent it from bouncing as she ran. Without looking, she knew that Detective-Investigator A. J. Sowell kept pace with her on the run from his police vehicle. The SUV sat far behind them on the other side of an old barbed-wire fence surrounding the untended field. The nearly full moon high overhead lit their path as they ran.

They'd only been running for a couple of minutes, but fear made it seem much longer. Fear for the young woman they'd come to rescue. At least Liz hoped they were here to save her, and not—a shiver ran down her spine at the thought.

She slowed to a walk. Her breath escaped in white puffs of vapor as they reached the large, open door. Pitch darkness greeted them as A. J. stepped to the right of the oversized opening. He gestured for Liz to go left.

Liz nodded and dodged to the side of the doorway. She struggled to slow her breathing, to reduce the visible sign of her location, a trick she'd learned as a private investigator. They still didn't know who else might be here.

Fiddling with her right glove as she waited, she pulled back the fastener on her gloved trigger finger to expose her fingertip, freeing it to handle her weapon more safely. She took the gun from its brown leather holster and held her firearm in both hands, safety off, right index finger resting along the cold, dark steel frame of the gun. Just like she did at the shooting range. Ready and waiting. Tonight, its weight in her hands quieted her nerves.

Liz and A. J. shared a look across the gaping darkness. Neither knew what they were about to find. They entered the abandoned structure after a final breath of biting, frosty night air, and a nod of agreement.

Liz slipped around the doorframe and moved to the left, crouching low. A. J. stayed high and moved to the right, hugging the wall. Liz kept the detective in her peripheral vision as they crept through the dank building. A musty, mildewy smell wafted from the stacks of old straw bales leaning precariously against one wall. Moonlight fell through the open doorway, glinting off the neglected farm equipment around them.

The soft hooting of an owl echoed among the rafters. Ahead, lights flickered beyond a row of double-stacked, round hay bales forming a dividing wall.

A. J. touched Liz's arm, and she flinched, her nerves on edge.

He showed the direction he wanted them to take with a quick jerk of his head. Liz fell into step next to him, wishing they didn't have to go further.

This place was quiet. Too quiet. A weight formed in Liz's chest, but she didn't know if it resulted from a concern for herself and A. J. or the young woman they came to find.

Liz cinched the zipper higher around her neck, grateful for her warm coat. The chilly December air made each exhalation come out in a puff of soft white cloud, while each inhalation sent a chill through her body.

She forced herself to take a few calming, deep breaths. She felt her heart rate slow. Liz didn't want to let A. J. down, knowing she was his only backup. He'd called the station for support when they were still in the SUV, but neither of them believed waiting was an option.

The flickering lights grew closer, brighter. The deafening silence was nerve-racking.

They hesitated only a moment before they stepped around the stack of bales into the light.

"Police! Freeze!"

Liz's shoulders jerked as the command roared from A. J.'s mouth, his voice deeper than usual. Nothing. No movement.

She squinted as her vision adjusted to the light. There were candles on paper plates, hundreds of them all around the open space. Some were on the floor, and others rested precariously on bales. There were even some in the bucket of an old rusted red tractor. What in the world is going on here? Liz thought.

Her eyes followed the candles briefly until something else caught her attention. In the center of the room, a chair laid on its side.

"A. J.," Liz whispered hoarsely, her throat dry.

A. J. turned to face her after checking behind them, his weapon gripped firmly in his hands.

She nodded to the chair. They crept forward together, and A. J. took the lead. The wooden armchair would have been more at home at the head of a dining room table. It was dark brown and polished to a high sheen.

While A. J. stepped around to the other side of the chair, Liz turned her head, checking their surroundings, trying to avoid tunnel vision. She sidestepped closer to A. J. and looked around the open space, not knowing if anyone was in the barn watching them.

She turned back toward the detective. Her gaze started to drop.

"Liz, don't." A. J.'s voice cut through her focus.

Suddenly, he was right next to her, trying to stop her from looking down, but it was too late. Her gaze was already low enough, and she saw the worst thing imaginable for any police officer or investigator.

Regina Masterson, the young lady they'd come to rescue. The young lady they'd spent two weeks trying to find laid dead on the ground by their feet.

Her wrists were tied to the arms of the chair with rough rope. From the raw scrapes covering her wrists, she had struggled. A lot. Her clothes were torn at the arms, legs, and chest. Blood stained each rent of the fabric. Had she been tortured? Her eyes were wide open, just below the gaping wound in her forehead, the result of a single gunshot. Dark red blood pooled below her head. A single, dark blood line ran down from the wound to the floor.

A scream caught in Liz's throat and...

Beep, beep, beep!

Liz sat up in a cold sweat, her mouth open in a silent scream. Her alarm continued to ring as she caught her breath, her hand rested on her heaving chest. Her breath came out in heavy pants. That was the first time in weeks that she'd dreamed so completely about the conclusion of the Masterson case the month before. Obviously, finding Brittany Cabot's body the night before had triggered the memory she had been trying so hard to move past. Her friend's words came back to her. Nightmares are the brain's way of dealing with trauma. Well, deal with it already. Liz thought crankily.

Slapping off the alarm, she stretched, knocking her pillows to the floor. The extra blankets she had piled on her bed the night before now felt too hot and heavy. A crocheted blanket and light lavender satin sheets were tangled around her legs. She swore under her breath as she disentangled herself from her bedding.

Sighing, she twisted until she was sitting on the edge of the bed. A yawn escaped her as another stretch forced her to stand. She would crawl back under the covers if she didn't get up.

Groaning audibly, Liz dragged herself to the bathroom. The sky blue and white bathroom décor was soothing to Liz's tired eyes. A note was taped to her oval bathroom mirror. *L-, I've left to get ready for work. Call if you need to talk. Later. -P.*

Leaving the note where it was, Liz got ready for her day.

Before long, Liz was standing on her soft yoga mat in her home studio, dressed in black leggings and a fitted black t-shirt. Barefoot, Liz eased through a few yoga poses to warm up her muscles before her morning run. After she finished, she pulled on thick socks, put on a thin, blue, hooded jacket, and zipped it up. While light, it effectively blocked the cool morning breeze and offered a thin layer of insulation for warmth. She pulled a colorful granny square hat, her mother's handiwork, over her brown hair, tucking unruly strands under the crocheted fabric as she walked over to the shoes abandoned next to the door the night before.

Stepping onto the small balcony, Liz locked the door behind her. Pausing, she propped each foot on the arm of the wrought-iron chair on the balcony and adjusted the laces on her shoes.

The club next door, The No Name Bar, using the humorous slogan "Where no one knows your name," showed no sign of the crowd from the night before. Tables were clean, stools flipped over, resting upside down on the tables, umbrellas closed, and the floor swept. They kept a tidy business.

Liz let herself out of the gate at the bottom of the stairs. Walking up a short flight of metal and tile stairs, she stopped in front of the Alamo Bells Yoga Studio. The darkened windows told Liz her mom and Pam weren't there yet.

Initially, Liz's mom's business partner was Susan, Pam's mom. After she died, her husband, Tom, became a silent partner. Pam worked there throughout high school and later, while receiving her certifications to teach yoga and meditation classes. A few years ago, Tom transferred his share of the business to Pam so she could become a full, active partner.

Liz headed down the green metal staircase to the river level. Zigzagging around tables and chairs in the open space used by various restaurants and shops, she took deep breaths as she crossed the red-tiled common area.

"Morning, María!" Liz called out to the convenience shop owner.

María looked up from the bundle of newspapers in her arms. "Morning, Liz! Did you hear about the body they found in the river during the draining?" The faintest hint of a Hispanic accent in her voice.

"Yes," she replied, jogging in place. Liz bit her tongue. She didn't want to get caught in a whirlwind of questions. Especially when she didn't know if the police had identified the body yet.

María shook her head sadly. "What is this world coming to?" The middle-aged Hispanic woman shifted the bundle of newspapers in her arms, shaking her head of short salt-and-pepper hair. "Well, have a good run, *mija*!"

"I will. Bye!" Liz jogged over and tapped the copper-colored sign pole for the ice cream shop, advertising Texas's favorite ice cream brand, Blue Bell, which she counted as the official start of her route.

She slowly jogged alongside the thoroughly drained San Antonio River. Soggy trash and leaves were scattered among the puddles and mud, but after last night's gruesome discovery, Liz avoided looking too closely. The stone staircase to the street level loomed next to her. She walked up quickly and continued her slow jog along the bricked sidewalk of the Crockett Street truss bridge. Low, heavy, iron fences protected her on each side, one from traffic, the other from falling into the empty riverbed below.

Gradually increasing her speed, she passed more restaurants and a favorite entertainment location, The Magician's Agency, before turning right onto Alamo Street. Across the plaza sat the most famous mission in Texas, the Alamo. Typically swarming with tourists and the occasional historian, Liz welcomed the quiet sidewalks that running in the early morning hours gave her. The only people she saw at this time of day were employees of restaurants and shops opening for business.

Liz hit her stride before she was through the plaza. Cool air struck her face as her speed increased. The rubber soles of her shoes silently hit the concrete sidewalk. The route she used for jogging was so ingrained, she didn't have to pay attention to street signs or turns anymore. Her feet automatically navigated for her. Even though she didn't look at the surrounding buildings, she knew every location she ran past. Some were historical sites, like the Alamo and the Menger Hotel. Others were restaurants, ice cream parlors, and the Shops at Rivercenter, which was the mall at the head of this section of the San Antonio River. The shortest part of her route finished swiftly, so it wasn't long before she ran down a second staircase and was on the opposite side of the river from her apartment. She could have jogged over the footbridge that allowed pedestrians access to both sides of the river, but there was something about running through the plaza that appealed to Liz's sense of history.

Two staffers carried a table across her path. "Morning, Liz!" they said in unison as they lugged the heavy table.

Liz ran in place as she waited. "Morning, Sarah. Ben."

Typically, Liz chatted with a riverboat captain or maintenance men cleaning trash from the water, but no river meant no boats. Liz's thoughts wandered as she passed yet another restaurant. The scent of bacon, pancakes, and coffee wafted to Liz's eager nose. She fought off the urge to abandon the rest of her run for breakfast. She waved to the hostess, Isabella, at the restaurant door, waiting to greet the hungry, early morning breakfast crowd.

As her run carried her along the River Walk, she wondered if A. J. had confirmed their suspicion about the body's identity. Matching a single set of fingerprints would give him an answer relatively quickly. Identification would take longer if it wasn't the missing girl. However, there was no doubt in Liz's mind that she had found Brittany Cabot last night, but it was only proper that A. J. confirmed it. *At least Brittany's friends and family will have closure.*

And just like that, the roommate came to mind. Rosemary Travers. *Why did she take off like that last night? And who was the man walking with her?* When other people were walking *toward* the crime scene, Liz found it odd that Rosemary was practically running away from it.

Liz ran along the sidewalk at the bottom of the outdoor theater's semi-circular concrete and grass seats. Unable to fight morbid curiosity, she slowed to a walk when she approached the Navarro Street bridge. Her gaze drifted across the empty riverbed. She saw litter, rocks, the occasional crushed beer can, even a metal chair, scattered among the mud and muck in the concrete basin below. She couldn't stop looking at where the body had been weighted down. Thankfully, the grisly discovery was long gone, taken away by the city's morgue officials the night before. The only sign that anything untoward had happened was the bright yellow police tape tied between two trees on the other side.

An officer stood nearby, sipping coffee from a disposable cup displaying the name of a popular local coffee shop. A. J. must have ordered a watch to protect the crime scene's integrity. Probably hoping they would find more evidence in the light of day. It was a slim chance. Nevertheless, it was police procedure, and Detective A. J. Sowell was all about following procedure.

Tearing her gaze away, Liz resumed her run to the footbridge past St. Mary's Street, where she crossed over to the other side of the river. She slowed to a walk as she approached the expansive San Antonio River Suites Hotel. The hotel towered fifteen stories overhead, filling an entire city block. Benches sat empty under the shade of tall cypress trees.

Memories of Rosemary Travers stopping Liz at this same spot a month earlier collided with the present,

as Rosemary approached, her tear-stained face told Liz
all she needed to know. The police had confirmed the
identity of the body. It was official. Brittany Cabot had
been found.

Chapter Five

Dressed in a light pink dress with a black server apron tied around her waist, Rosemary Travers threw her arms around Liz. The embrace surprised her, as it was the first time Rosemary had ever hugged her. They'd stopped and talked loads of times, too many to count, and visited over coffee, but their budding friendship never went beyond those chats.

Liz staggered a bit, stunned, both by the force of the embrace and by something else.

She felt a sudden and intense weight in her chest and a brief wave of sadness came from Rosemary.

Just as quickly, the weight was gone. A single tear rolled down Liz's cheek from the fleeting rush of empathic ability.

Liz struggled to keep her euphoria in check at the sudden, albeit brief, resurgence of at least *one* of her psychic abilities. *They aren't gone. They're just waiting,*

Liz thought. She forced her mind back to the moment
at hand.

Leading a crying Rosemary to a nearby pair of benches,
they sat facing each other.

The other woman's distress pushed Liz's concerns into
the background. She waited, allowing Rosemary time
to collect herself. Liz reached out and placed her hand
on Rosemary's arm in support, and to be honest, out of
curiosity. Nothing. *Oh well.*

She studied the young woman sitting opposite her.
Rosemary's black hair was pulled into a thick braid that
hung like a rope down her back. Her mascara ran in dark
rivulets over her olive cheeks. She dabbed at her eyes with
a tissue she pulled from her apron pocket.

"Liz, do you remember my roommate, Brittany?"
Rosemary sniffed loudly. She took a deep breath and let
it out slowly while waiting for Liz to respond.

Liz nodded. "Of course."

Rosemary took a deep breath and let it out in a loud,
audible rush. Her shoulders dropped, and her bottom lip
quivered. "She's dead. The police just called me."

Liz didn't bother trying to fake surprise, but the young
woman beside her didn't notice.

Rosemary leaned toward her. She looked around, but
no one was within earshot. "They said she was murdered!"
she whispered.

Liz nodded, patting her arm. "I know."

Rosemary's gaze flew to Liz's face. She moved away
from Liz, sitting back in the highly polished wooden
bench. "You know? How do you know? I just found out
a few minutes ago!"

Liz half-smiled at the reaction. "Rosemary." Liz reached
for the young woman's hand, holding it lightly. "I know
because I found her, uh, body last night. I'm the one who
called the police."

Rosemary's jaw dropped at that bit of news. She pulled her hand away from Liz and grabbed a fresh tissue from her pocket. She wiped her eyes and dried her cheeks. "I don't understand. Were you looking for her? You told me you couldn't take the case when I came to you. How?" Rosemary bent toward Liz.

Liz took Rosemary's hand gently. "Shhh. I wasn't looking for her, but I found her. The police didn't tell you where she was found?" Liz's eyebrows knitted together. *How odd*, she thought.

Rosemary sniffed and shook her head. She wiped away the tears that continued to flow, reaching for a fresh tissue in her apron pocket.

Liz stood and walked away from the benches. Rosemary followed, dropping the massive wad of damp, mascara-stained tissues into a trash can as she passed.

"I found her over there." Liz pointed down the river toward the bridge just beyond the hotel.

Rosemary's gaze followed Liz's pointing finger. There, in the distance, past the trees and curving staircase to the street level, stood a police officer, and more lines of police tape than were there when Liz passed by earlier. Now, most of the sidewalk was blocked.

Rosemary's jaw hung open. "I walked by here last night. That's what—?" She shook her head. "I don't understand. How could she have been there?"

Rosemary didn't mention the man she was walking with. Interesting. Liz turned back to Rosemary and placed a hand on each shoulder. The heavy weight in Liz's chest returned. It spread quickly to her limbs as the young woman's sadness, mixed with confusion, flowed through Liz. "The police didn't tell you anything?"

Rosemary shook her head, pulling out another tissue. "Only that she was found, and they suspect murder.

That's it." Rosemary stepped closer to Liz. She lowered her voice to a whisper. "What happened?"

Liz took a deep breath, preparing to filter out at least the worst parts of what she saw the night before. They returned to the benches and sat down, next to each other this time.

Clearing her throat, Liz struggled to find the right words. "My friend and I were walking along the River Walk last night while the draining was happening. And—" she paused, gathering her inner strength, "—I noticed something in the water. When I looked closer, it wasn't a thing. It was Brittany. Brittany's body. At least, I suspected it was her. The police detective-investigator who came to the scene thought so too. That's how they identified her so quickly."

Rosemary shook her head. "I can't believe it. Do you know how long she's been there? Do the police know, do you think? How did she get there?" The pretty server seemed incapable of only asking one question at a time. "Wait. Why did *you* suspect it was Brittany? I've watched all the crime shows. I know a body in water doesn't look great if it's been there for a while. Identifying her face couldn't have been easy." Rosemary made a gagging expression.

Hating to add to Rosemary's distress, Liz felt she needed to tell her. "I thought it was her because..." Liz paused, looking around. No one was paying them any attention. The only staff nearby were huddled in a corner, a low hum extended from them as they were all talking animatedly. A busboy walked past, and a server reached out and pulled him into the cluster. There was no doubt in Liz's mind—the news was spreading.

Liz returned her focus to Rosemary. "I thought it was her because she was wearing her uniform." Liz nodded at the matching outfit the young woman was currently wearing.

"What?" Rosemary looked down at her uniform.

She looked back at Liz, her eyes huge. She took a sharp breath. "But that means..." Rosemary's distress turned to barely controlled panic. "Liz. Brittany *always* changed out of her uniform before leaving the hotel. Always! If she was wearing it when you found her, that means she was wearing it when she died."

The dots lined up for both Rosemary and Liz simultaneously.

"Which means..." Rosemary started as they turned in unison to look at the hotel.

"...she was killed here," Liz finished for her, her voice dropping to a whisper. Suddenly, the hotel she jogged past every day didn't seem so inviting.

Rosemary's eyes were wide when she turned to meet Liz's face. "But why? And who?"

Liz shook her head, maintaining eye contact. She knew where this conversation was going. "I don't know."

"Liz, please. I understand why you couldn't take the case before...but can you now?" Rosemary grasped Liz's hand, her eyes pleading.

"I don't..." Liz started to decline, but she knew she couldn't turn her down, not again. She had to know. Would Brittany Cabot still be alive if she'd taken the case? Or was it already too late by the time Rosemary approached her? Liz knew the answers would either make her feel better, or tragically worse, if she discovered that Brittany's untimely death could have been prevented.

Liz pushed her questions and concerns aside, tamping down her internal doubts about her investigative abilities. She looked Rosemary squarely in the eye and set her jaw. "I'll take the case."

Chapter Six

"Thank you! Oh, thank you, Liz!" Rosemary jumped up from the bench in her excitement. Wads of tissues fell from her lap and littered the ground surrounding her black, rubber-soled shoes. She crouched to retrieve them and walked to the trash can to discard them before returning to Liz's side. "What do we do first?" Her tears subsided.

Liz smiled at the change in Rosemary's mood. "How about you come by my office in an hour? Oh," Liz remembered where they were. "Is your boss going to make you finish your shift?" Finding out that your missing roommate was just found murdered was as valid a reason to go home as Liz had ever heard.

"I don't know. I hope not." Rosemary looked down at her uniform and the other employees, who slowly broke away from their cluster as hotel guests arrived for breakfast. She leaned toward Liz. "Am I safe here?" she whispered.

Liz hesitated. She wanted to say yes. She sighed. "Honestly, I don't know. If more employees had been reported missing, I'd be more concerned. It is only Brittany, right?"

Rosemary nodded emphatically.

"Then it's probably safe. Keep your eyes open, stay quiet about what you suspect, and follow your gut. If your gut says something is wrong, it's usually right." Liz found people would accept following a "gut instinct" more easily than psychic intuition as a general rule.

Rosemary nodded in response to the sound advice. "I will."

Liz stood. She silently cursed herself. She'd never been worried about carrying business cards on a jog before. "Do you have your phone?" Liz knew that was a silly question in this day and age.

Rosemary reached into her apron pocket and retrieved her phone without looking. "Of course."

Liz recited her contact information as the waitress deftly entered it into the device. "Give me an hour to reopen the office and clean up after my run."

"Um, reopen the office?" Rosemary asked, arching one eyebrow.

Liz opened her mouth to explain, then changed her mind. "It's a long story. An hour?" Liz looked at her questioningly.

Rosemary nodded and stood, hugging Liz again.

Liz sensed a tiny flicker of hope from the young woman.

"I'm going to go talk to my supervisor now. She'll understand. Hopefully, I won't need to speak with Mr. Moore. He'd convince me to work through this. I just know it!"

Mr. Moore was the very proper, uptight manager of the hotel. Even Liz knew he would show up for work in the middle of the zombie apocalypse.

Liz smiled, grateful she was her own boss—at least for now. "If that happens, call to let me know, and I'll expect you after your shift, okay?"

"Okay. Thanks again, Liz. Really. See you soon."

Liz started to walk away, but stopped after only a few steps.

Rosemary looked at her quizzically. "What's wrong?" She walked to stand by Liz. They looked down the river where police tape was blocking the way. Liz's way home was through the crime scene. "Oh."

The area was now buzzing with crime scene technicians studying everything, in the distant hope of a clue remaining. "Yeah, I think I'll take the long way around." Even though Liz knew the body was long gone, she didn't think she could face that particular part of the river just yet.

"Was it horrible?" Rosemary asked in a low whisper, unable to tear her gaze from the crime scene in the distance.

"It was worse for Brittany," she responded, her voice equally low.

A fresh tear rolled down Rosemary's cheek.

Liz placed her hand on the young woman's shoulder. "I'll see you in an hour."

Rosemary nodded, sniffed, and wiped her eyes.

Liz turned and retraced her steps. When she approached the area opposite the crime scene, she didn't slow down or even glance at the activity on the other side of the river.

Liz unlocked the door to her office and walked around the low dividing wall to her desk, past a row of tall, black, four-drawer filing cabinets against the wall. Filing cabinets were a staple in every private investigator's office, even in today's technological world. Files still needed to be kept, often with hard copies of photos and signed documents—all readily available whenever Liz testified at a trial, whether a criminal case or a messy divorce.

Perching on the edge of her desk, she picked up the phone receiver and quickly dialed her assistant's number.

"Henderson residence." The woman who answered the phone sounded like she'd just eaten something she didn't like.

"Hi, Mrs. Wells!" Liz said cheerily, knowing it would irritate the woman on the other end of the phone.

"Oh." It was incredible how much disappointment Claire Henderson's estate manager could squeeze into those two letters. "It's you. Hello, Ms. Pond."

"It's me!" Liz replied enthusiastically, getting a little too much satisfaction out of how much the woman disapproved of her. "Is Claire available?"

"One moment, please."

"Mrs. Wells?" Liz called out.

"Yes?"

"Can you tell her we have a case, please?" Liz could almost feel the estate manager's irritation through the phone. She smiled.

Liz heard the soft thud of the receiver as it was placed on the table. She knew it was a cordless phone, but she also knew Mrs. Wells left it behind in the hope of a private word with her employer. Possibly to plead with her to not take the call.

It didn't work.

"What?!" Liz heard Claire's exclamation clearly through the receiver. She grinned. What poor Mrs. Wells had to suffer through working for the improper and unorthodox heiress to the Henderson family's trust.

The clicking of high-heeled shoes on the tile floor followed the noisy exclamation.

"Liz! Do we have a case? Really?" Claire's sing-song voice was filled with excitement.

Liz couldn't help but laugh at the difference between the two women's personalities. "Yes, we have a case. No, this doesn't mean I've decided. So, Claire, when can you get here? Our client is either showing up in an hour or this afternoon. I don't know which yet." Suddenly, Liz felt flustered. This was her first case since—her mind drifted toward a cloud of despair.

The emotion dissipated quickly as Claire's cheers resounded through the phone.

"Ms. Henderson, please! A little decorum!"

Liz smiled as the solemn Mrs. Wells pleaded with her eccentric employer.

Claire laughed, a sound like the tinkling of bells.

Seriously, Liz thought. *This woman should have been a fairy.*

"You'll recover, Mrs. Wells," Claire responded pleasantly. "Liz, honey, I'll be right there. This is wonderful! I can't wait to hear all about it!"

And with that exclamation, Claire hung up on Liz.

"Bye, Claire," Liz said out loud before replacing the receiver, giggling. One thing's for sure. Her unusual assistant always made her laugh.

***

Within the hour, Liz was puttering around the office. She replaced her running clothes with a worn, red and black plaid, flannel shirt hanging open over a plain red t-shirt and jeans. The stainless-steel coffee maker gurgled on the small counter in the corner of the waiting area. With a half-eaten slice of whole wheat toast slathered with creamy peanut butter in one hand, Liz was opening the blinds in the tall windows that bookended the front door when Claire burst through the entry.

"Liz? Where are you?" Claire called out.

"Here." Liz replied from her place behind the door. She pushed it closed with one foot, the cords to the blinds still gripped in her hand.

"Oh, sorry. Did I hit you?" Claire dropped her oversized purse on her desk in the corner and crossed the room.

"You missed. You'll get me next time, I'm sure." Liz had just enough time to shove the last bite of toast into her mouth before Claire grabbed her in a tight hug.

Liz patted her friend on the back. She chewed, swallowed, and meekly mumbled, "Uncle!" through the cloud of curly red hair blocking her view.

Claire released her, laughing. "Sorry, I'm so, uh, at a loss for words. Can you believe it? I can't wait to work again. Tell me, what made you change your mind?"

Liz began to respond when a light tap on the door stopped her. She and Claire stepped out of the way before it swung open, and in walked Pam.

"Hi, Pam, what—" Before Liz could finish the question, she was pulled into her second tight embrace of the past few minutes.

Pam interrupted. "Claire called me. Did I miss anything? How are you doing this morning?"

Liz should have known that her enthusiastic assistant would call in reinforcements.

Pam released Liz and gave Claire a quick hug.

"How did I beat you here? Your apartment is only minutes away, while my house is outside of town," Claire teased gently.

Pam was perpetually late.

"Yeah, yeah, I know. Maybe I need a new watch?"

"I'll buy you *two* new watches if it helps you get to places on time." Claire grinned. "So, what made you decide to reopen the business?" The redhead looped her hand through the crook of Pam's arm.

Liz stepped around her friends and crossed the room. She busied herself pouring coffee for the three of them. Each woman had a personal mug, painted at a local ceramics store on a girls' night out last summer. Liz grinned when she remembered having a vision about the previous person who'd used her paintbrush, a young man who was obviously in love with the handsome, obviously gay, young man who managed the store.

Stalling for time, to gather her thoughts, she prepared each ladies' coffee exactly how they liked it before turning around.

She marveled at her friends when she turned, a mug in each hand. Both were strong, independent, fiercely loyal, and supportive. And that was where the similarities ended. Standing side-by-side, they each looked like they had just walked out of a magazine. Claire could easily be from the pages of *Vogue*. The heiress dressed in the highest fashion, and she was voluptuous. If Marilyn Monroe had been a redhead and had green eyes, she and Claire could easily have been mistaken for sisters.

Meanwhile, Pam looked like she stepped from the pages of *Yoga Journal* magazine. Tall and lean, her long brown hair was pulled back in a ponytail, she was dressed for work at her yoga studio next door.

This brief study of her friends made Liz feel frumpy by comparison. Liz was far from either voluptuous or a yogi. She stayed fit because of her jogging, yoga regimen, and boxing training for self-defense. Liz was not a girly girl.

"Liz!" Pam called out, bringing Liz's attention back to her friends.

"What? Sorry, I was just thinking how different we all are." Liz gave them each their mug before grabbing her own.

Claire sat on the brown faux leather armchair in the small waiting area while Pam pushed the reaching branches of a realistic-looking majesty palm in the corner and lowered herself onto the matching couch. Liz stayed on her feet, sipping her coffee for courage, and slowly paced the floor on the other side of the long coffee table. "So. Okay, try not to freak out." Her eyes flicked to Pam's serious expression before locking eyes with Claire.

"Well, that statement alone makes me *want* to freak out!" Claire exclaimed, sitting straighter.

Pam bit her lip.

Liz sighed. "You know I've been trying to decide whether I still want to do, well, this." She gestured to the surrounding office with her free hand.

"Yes, I assumed you decided when you called me. You said we have a case?" Claire set her sunshine yellow mug on a crocheted coaster on the small coffee table.

"Well, I haven't, not really. We, Pam and I, went for a walk last night to talk things over a bit, and—" Liz paused, taking another sip of coffee, sitting on the edge of Claire's corner desk "—I...uh, well, we found a body."

"What?" Claire's gaze whipped between the two women. "Wait? That was you. In the news this morning?"

Liz and Pam nodded in unison.

"It's made the news already?" Pam asked.

Claire gave Pam a look, *the* look. "Pam, I know you don't like to start your day with the news, but seriously, pick up a newspaper! The article said a couple of pedestrians found it. I assumed it was some poor tourists!" Claire studied her friends' faces. "Are you both okay?" she adjusted her cashmere cardigan after taking a sip of coffee.

Liz nodded. "Beyond the state of shock that hit me when A. J. started questioning me."

"She wouldn't let me see the remains. So I'm fine," Pam commented. She turned to Liz. "Are you okay now? You were sound asleep when I stuck my head in before leaving this morning. You shouldn't be drinking coffee. You need herbal tea. Have you been shopping lately?" Pam stood and walked to the kitchenette, her long forest green knit sweater swishing around her legs as she moved. She rooted around in the single cupboard, looking for tea and honey, stopping to plug in the electric kettle before resuming her hunt.

Liz smiled at the back of her best friend. Pam thought a cup of herbal tea and locally sourced organic honey could solve everything. "I'm fine. I promise. Other than a doozy of a nightmare reminding me of the night A. J. and I found Regina's body." Liz looked into her mug, biting her lip.

It was well-known among Liz's tight-knit circle of family and friends that she'd been plagued by nightmares ever since the murder of Regina Masterson in December.

"Well, that's to be expected. Finding a body will definitely remind your psyche about finding the other," Pam said. She turned away from the cupboard empty-handed, unplugging the kettle. Not being able to make tea didn't stop her from trying to pry the coffee mug from her friend's hand.

Liz smiled, refusing to relinquish her cup. "I'm fine. I promise." She opened her eyes wider and took a sip, staring at her friend pointedly.

"Pam, Liz is fine," Claire said, waving at her friend to sit. "I am curious about Detective Hottie, though. We haven't heard from him in weeks."

Liz and Pam both rolled their eyes.

"You and your nicknames," Pam said, giggling as she resumed her seat.

"Oh, come on, neither of you can tell me he's not a cutie!"

Pam shrugged. "He's nice, just not my type."

Liz responded with a faint blush warming her cheeks.

Claire giggled. "I'm sorry. I'll stop teasing you." She raised her perfectly manicured hands in mock surrender. "Back to the case, do...hey, does this mean your abilities are back?" As one of the few people who knew, Claire had been concerned about her friend losing such a rare gift.

Liz shook her head at the question, but her eyebrows lifted and she tilted her head slightly. "Well, that's not entirely true. This morning I had, I don't know what to call it. A flutter?"

"Okay. What's a 'flutter'?" Pam did air quotes before she picked up her coffee. Even though she preferred tea, she'd never turn down a cup of coffee.

Standing, Liz rolled Claire's desk chair over to sit opposite them, propping her stockinged feet up on the edge of the coffee table, bracing her elbows on her knees, and holding her cup in both hands. She breathed in the aroma of warm vanilla and toasted caramel of the flavored coffee.

"When I spoke with Brittany's roommate this morning," she began.

Claire interrupted. "Who's Brittany?"

"Oh, I guess that wasn't on the news this morning."

Liz and Pam quickly recounted everything that happened the night before.

"I met up with Rosemary, Brittany Cabot's roommate, during my morning run. That's when I found out that my suspicion was correct. And when she asked me to find out what happened to her roommate."

"And the 'flutter'?" It was Claire's turn to use air quotes.

"Rosemary hugged me. She'd just learned the news. I definitely felt sadness from her." Liz patted her chest, demonstrating that she had experienced an empathic episode. She felt an inexplicable weight in her chest as a result of that ability.

Liz's eyes burned. She fought back tears. She didn't fully realize until that moment how much she'd missed her ESP abilities over the past weeks.

"Wow!" Pam sat back, crossing her long legs in her typical black yoga pants. "That has to be a good sign, right?" She looked from Claire to Liz. "I mean, this tells me they aren't gone, just, I don't know, resting maybe?"

Pam had known about Liz's psychic abilities since they were kids. Ever since the family barbecue when Liz's parents brought Pam's family in on the secret when the girls were only nine. Claire had only known about Liz's gifts for about a year. But in Claire's case, she figured it out on her own.

Liz studied her assistant's face, remembering when they first met a year earlier. Claire had hired Liz to investigate the medium she had been paying to communicate with her recently deceased grandmother. After a few sessions, and several thousands of dollars later, Claire suspected he was a fraud. She found Liz in the phone book, and by the time the case was over, Claire was convinced that, while Liz was a psychic, the medium was definitely not.

When she confronted Liz about her suspicions, Liz had been shocked. No client had ever guessed before. Claire also told Liz that her investigation business needed an extra pair of hands. When she inherited sole control of the Henderson family trust from her late grandmother, Claire's mother suggested that, since she didn't *have* to work, she should find volunteer work to keep herself busy. So, Claire volunteered to help Liz. The heiress had a special skill of her own. As a certified public accountant, Claire had proven invaluable to Liz and the business.

Liz shrugged in response to Pam's question. "I don't know what it means. It felt good to *feel* something again. You know?"

Her friends nodded emphatically. Pam sipped her coffee, set the mug on the table, and glanced at her watch.

"Oh crap! I'm late! I have a class starting in five minutes!" Pam jumped to her feet and ran to the door.

Liz followed her. Sure enough, a crowd had formed at the entrance to the popular yoga studio.

"I'm coming!" Pam yelled from the balcony. "I'm sorry," she said to Liz and Claire. "I forgot it's Monday. Your mom doesn't come in until after lunch today, she's teaching yoga at the women's prison this morning. Bye, I'll call you later!" She hurried down the steps, letting herself out with her key, and jogged the short distance to the studio.

Liz smiled when the crowd of students greeted Pam with cheers and teasing.

As she started to close the door, she saw Rosemary walking over the footbridge. "Rosemary!" Liz called from the balcony, waving her entire arm to get her client's attention. "The gate's open!"

Liz stepped inside and pressed the button to release the lock.

Leaving the door open, Liz turned to tell Claire that their client had arrived, but her assistant was already all business. She placed Pam's mug in the small sink and the others on their respective desks.

Rosemary entered the office and smiled at Liz. Tracks of tears marred the makeup on her face. Claire hung their client's coat on the vintage wooden coat stand next to the waiting area.

"I am so sorry for your loss," Claire offered, enveloping the young woman in a quick hug.

Rosemary straightened her uniform, which looked out of place away from the hotel, sniffed, and gave Claire a watery smile before following Liz to her desk.

Chapter Seven

The wall around the desk did nothing for sound protection, but it offered a modicum of privacy when Liz visited with clients. Gesturing for Rosemary to sit, Liz walked around the desk, pushing past another tall, bushy, fake majesty palm in the corner, and pulled out a yellow legal pad from a drawer as she lowered herself into her mesh, black, ergonomic desk chair. She slid a wicker basket filled with a variety of padlocks on her desk to one side.

Rosemary raised an eyebrow at Liz. "I have to ask, why?" She picked up a smooth copper padlock.

Liz grinned. "I'm also a locksmith. I like to keep my skills sharp. See?" Liz plucked a lock out of the basket and grabbed a loose torsion wrench and hook pick tool from her desk drawer. Holding the lock in her left hand, she positioned the torsion wrench into the bottom of the keyhole keeping it in place with her thumb. With a practiced hand, she worked the hook pick into the keyhole with her right hand and seconds later the shank of the lock popped open.

Rosemary's tear-filled eyes popped open. "Wow, that's pretty neat."

Liz smiled as she reclosed the lock and dropped it and the tools into the basket. "Thanks. So, let's get to work. Do you mind if I record our conversation?" She gestured to her cell phone resting on the polished, mahogany-stained, wooden desk.

Rosemary shook her head, dabbing at her eyes with a tissue. "No, I don't mind."

Navigating to the app with a quick series of taps, Liz cleared her throat and began by reciting the date, time, and her and Rosemary's names. "So, Rosemary, when did Brittany first go missing?"

"December seventh," Rosemary answered promptly. "She didn't come home from work, that I could tell. I stopped and picked up food on my way home. I thought there was a chance—" She twisted a tissue between her fingers, unaware of the tears streaming down her face.

"That she may have come home and left again since you were late?" Liz finished for her, sliding a box of tissues to her client.

Rosemary accepted the box, setting it in her lap, pulling a fresh tissue from it as she spoke. "Exactly. She has so much stuff that I couldn't tell."

"So, you didn't know if she'd packed a bag and left?"

Rosemary shook her head, causing tears to splash onto her uniform's skirt. She wiped at the wet spot with her palm. "Brittany shops—shopped—a lot. I didn't think she'd leave any of her stuff. It was *all* important to her." Rosemary's bottom lip quivered as she attempted to regain control of her emotions.

"When did you file a missing person report with the police?"

"On December eighth and ninth."

Liz looked up from her notes, her brows knitted together. "Why twice?"

"I was worried about her. The police officer I spoke with on the eighth asked me if it looked like there was any kind of struggle in our apartment. He didn't like it when I told him I couldn't tell."

Liz looked up again, setting down her pen. "Why couldn't you tell?"

Rosemary shifted uncomfortably in her seat. She opened her mouth to speak but closed it again promptly.

"Rosemary, what's wrong?" Suspicion wiggled into Liz's thoughts as she watched her client squirm.

Rosemary twisted the tissue in her hands until shreds covered her lap.

Liz studied her client, wishing that her psychic abilities were back in top working form. "Rosemary?" She attempted to catch her eye, but her client refused to look up.

"My mother always told me not to speak ill of the dead!" The adage exploded from Rosemary.

Liz jumped back in her seat, her hand on her chest.

"I'm sorry." A sheepish look passed over Rosemary's face. "I didn't mean to shout like that. It's just that..." Rosemary looked around before leaning forward.

Liz scooted ahead in her seat.

"Brittany is—was—a shopaholic and a slob," Rosemary confessed in a rush.

Liz struggled not to laugh or smile. "That's it?"

"That's it?" Rosemary's voice rose. "You should see her room! So much stuff!" She raised her arms. "And all that shopping, she'd only remember to save money for her share of the rent and groceries half of the time!" She stopped talking, let out a loud breath of air, and collapsed back into her chair. "I'm sorry. I guess I've been holding that in for a while."

A faint smile ghosted across Liz's lips. "It's fine. It's usually better to get those things off your chest." On her notepad, Liz wrote, *Check finances.* She laid the pen on her pad. "I assume the officer asked you to come back after twenty-four hours had passed, in case she came home. That isn't uncommon, especially with a young adult with no local familial attachments, and there's no obvious sign that any illegal activity happened."

Rosemary nodded, throwing the mess of tissues into the trash can, conveniently sitting near the chair. Many tears had been shed by clients sitting in that chair during the five years Pond Investigations had been in business.

Rosemary pulled a tissue from the box in her lap. "That's what the officer told me. So, I waited one more night, but she still didn't come home. I was off the next day, so I would have seen if she'd shown up. I made a point of sticking around our apartment."

"But she didn't come home," Liz commented, studying her client's flushed face.

Rosemary shook her head. "I went back to the police department as soon as the twenty-four hours had lapsed, and they filed a missing person report that time. An officer came to look around the apartment."

"And what did the officer find?" Liz jotted a note to find out the identity of the police officer.

"Nothing. Well, the officer agreed that she is—was—a slob. But nothing stood out to him either. He told me an officer from missing persons would reach out to me with more questions." Rosemary's bottom lip trembled.

Liz reached for her black leather desk planner. She flipped to December ninth. In her own neat penmanship, she read: *Walk-in: Rosemary Travers.* "You came to see me that same day. Why so soon?"

Rosemary shrugged her shoulders. "I don't know. I was worried and tired of waiting. I didn't think the police would take it seriously." She turned her watery gaze to Liz. "I didn't know it was you when I found your number in the phone book. You jog past the hotel every day, and all those times we sat down over a cup of coffee, I never thought of what you might do for a living."

"The police *always* take missing person cases seriously. The difficulty lies in determining the *truly* missing people and those who have simply left. When there's no sign of a struggle, and they cannot determine if she packed a bag, it makes it difficult to confirm. Do you know anything about her finances? I'll find out, but I'm curious what you know." Liz watched as Rosemary struggled against her mother's words of wisdom.

When finally she spoke, her voice was calmer. "She had terrible credit, always used cash. Honestly, I don't know if she even had a bank account."

"That's unusual. Especially with so many people using credit cards to buy things online. Strange for a shopaholic to not take advantage of the vast market available to her on the internet."

"If she wanted something that badly, she'd give me the cash, and I'd order it for her." Rosemary half-shrugged. "But I'd only agree if she gave me the money first. She'd burned me on a purchase before."

Liz smiled. "Sounds like you make for a good roommate."

What Liz meant to be a compliment caused fresh tears to flow down Rosemary's cheeks while she dropped her head into her hands and sobbed.

"Oh, honey, it'll be okay." She reached out to Rosemary in an empty gesture as the desk sat between them.

Rosemary sniffed a few more times, blew her nose, and wiped the last remnants of eye makeup from her face.

Liz allowed her client a moment to collect herself. "So, when I couldn't take the case, did you go see the investigator I recommended?"

Rosemary sniffed. "No."

Liz didn't need her empathic abilities to feel the shame and guilt emanating from Rosemary. "Why not?"

"I don't know. I thought I was being silly, overreacting. You know?"

Liz nodded, a sentiment she'd heard espoused plenty of times before. "I know. Okay, here's how it works. Normally, I charge $250 for a retainer, plus expenses. But, considering the circumstances, and it still bothers me that I couldn't take this case last month, it'll be $150 for the retainer, plus expenses. After resolving the case, we'll settle up if there's anything else due."

Rosemary turned her tear-stained face toward Liz. "Thank you. What does all that mean though?"

"It means that anything directly related to investigative fees—database searches especially, go toward the retainer. Expenses include gas, if there's a lot of driving, or food and drink if I have to stake out a location."

Rosemary nodded, understanding, "Do I pay you or..." she drifted off.

"You can pay my assistant, Claire. First, can you fill out this questionnaire, please? It'll help if we know as much as possible about your roommate before we get started. Names of family, friends, significant others, social media accounts, passwords, you get the idea." Liz held out a clipboard with a detailed form attached to it.

Rosemary accepted the paperwork and took a pen from the cup on Liz's desk.

Liz excused herself to give the young woman some privacy. She walked to Claire's desk and filled her in on the change in fees in a low voice.

Before long, Rosemary joined them, clipboard in hand. "I've filled in what I can. I have never spoken with her parents, but I'm pretty sure their phone number is on the bill. I'll check when I get home and give it to you. Brittany called them at the beginning of each month. I guess I have to call and give them the news." Her lip trembled as fresh tears collected on her lower lashes.

Liz shook her head. "No. The police will do that. I'm sure they've notified them by now. Do they live in town?"

"No, Dallas."

Liz took the clipboard and set it on Claire's desk behind her. She stepped out of the way to allow Claire and Rosemary to handle the fees. After they finished, Claire slipped past Liz and retrieved Rosemary's coat from the oak coat stand.

Rosemary thanked her and draped it over her arm. She held her hand out to Liz. "Thank you for taking the case."

Liz took her hand in a gentle grip, smiling through her disappointment at the absence of psychic impressions from the handshake. "We'll do our best to find out who did this to her," she promised quietly.

"Thank you." Rosemary offered Claire a watery smile and left.

Liz watched her client walk down the stairs, pulling on her jacket as she went. The timer on the gate's security was set to open during business hours, so she pushed it open and walked out unimpeded. The spring on the gate swung it closed behind her with a metallic clang.

Chapter Eight

Liz released a big sigh. It was cold enough to see her breath in the chilly morning air. She rubbed her arms briskly for warmth. It's colder now than it was this morning during her run, but the drastic weather changes were one of the quirks of living in Texas. Especially at this time of year. One day you didn't need a jacket and were comfortable in jeans and a t-shirt, the next, it was freezing temperatures, and the winter coats, hats, and mittens came out!

"It's winter again!" Liz called out as she stepped back inside, closing the door securely behind her.

"That's okay. It's supposed to be spring this afternoon." Claire ran and hugged Liz in the center of the office. "We have a client!" Claire cheered.

Liz sputtered as her face disappeared in a cloud of Claire's flowery-smelling hair for a second time that morning. "Yes!" she patted her enthusiastic coworker on the back.

Claire released her friend and did a little cha-cha dance back to her desk.

Liz smiled at her antics. "How did I ever manage this place without you?"

"That's easy," replied Claire in her sing-song voice. "You didn't!" She teased as she scooped up her mug.

Liz marveled at how light her assistant was on her feet, especially in high heeled boots. Laughing, Liz retrieved her mug from her desk. She sipped, stuck her tongue out, and clenched her eyes shut. The coffee in her cup was now room temperature and unpalatable. She dumped the dregs down the drain in the small sink next to the coffee maker and poured a fresh steaming cup. In moments, she was holding the warm mug between her cool hands, breathing in the aroma of toasted caramel and vanilla as the steam from the flavored coffee warmed her face.

"Mmmmm," she mumbled as she sipped the hot brew, black and unsweetened, resting a hip against the counter.

In the meantime, Claire pulled out a notepad and got busy making a to-do list from Rosemary's questionnaire about her roommate.

"Okay, what's step one in a missing person's case?" Liz quizzed from her spot by the coffee maker.

"Get to know the missing person," Claire answered as her pen dashed across the page. Her head turned from side to side as she referenced their client's answers on the clipboard.

"Right."

"Although, she's not missing anymore. Thanks to you!" Claire added.

Liz lifted a finger into the air. "Thanks to the annual draining of the San Antonio River, you mean. With those weights on her, there's no way of knowing how long she would have been down there if the city didn't drain the river regularly."

Claire wrinkled her nose. "Yuck. That wasn't on the news broadcast." She consulted the list and questionnaire again.

"I wonder where the weights came from?" Liz wondered out loud, pushing away from the counter. "Are you done?" She gestured to the clipboard.

"I am!" Claire sat back in her black desk chair, sipping her heavily creamed and extra sweet coffee.

Liz picked up the clipboard and skimmed the questionnaire, slowly pacing the office while she read and sipped. Mentally, she realized she should rearrange the questions, so it was more organized for the division of their work. Later.

Claire's neat checkmarks, marking tasks she would do, ran down the left side of the page. Since she joined Liz in her work, Claire had taken on the research involving the general information available online. She completed general internet searches and visited online news sites, radio broadcasts, and newspapers. She also browsed certain paid services to access newspaper archives, high school student connection services, and multiple free services, such as dating sites, both reputable and, well, not so reputable. Plus, of course, all the current social media platforms. Last summer, Liz and Claire spent an entertaining afternoon creating fake accounts on various social sites to allow them to look at personal accounts without drawing attention to their true identities. All in the name of information-gathering.

It amazed Liz how much personal information people freely put online. That productive afternoon had provided endless information on many cases and forever changed how both women interacted with the online community. No more posts announcing trips in advance (translation:

Hello! My home is empty!). No more *I broke up with my boyfriend and am crying into my beer at so-and-so bar*-type posts (translation: I'm drunk and vulnerable!).

If they could find and use the information they gleaned from social media accounts to help their cases, so could other people with more nefarious intent.

Liz nodded as she reviewed the items Claire checked off. "This is great! I'll get started on the usual background check, driver's license check, finances." As a licensed private investigator, Liz had legal access to various paid services that unlicensed people like Claire shouldn't access.

"So, Claire. A little something to help guide our work. Rosemary and I realized something when we were talking earlier this morning. She asked me why I suspected it was Brittany's body before she was formally identified. When I told her that I recognized the uniform, she told me that Brittany never left the hotel in uniform. Ever. She *always* changed first."

"Oh!" Claire's eyes widened. "That means..."

"Either the killer works at the hotel and is still there or was a guest and is long gone," Liz finished.

"That's not good. Let's not worry about that right now. We can focus on the clues we do have. Oh, I have an idea!" Claire stopped talking and turned to her computer. She typed quickly. "The hotel's name was on the news this morning."

"The San Antonio River Suites," Liz recited, walking around the desk to look at Claire's screen.

Claire had the website for the hotel up on her screen. She navigated to *Amenities* and clicked on *Fitness center and personal trainer*.

Photos of a fully stocked fitness area with stationary bikes, ellipticals, and treadmills filled the screen. The gym also offered a collection of traditional free weights. A large, smiling, muscled man posed next to a rack of dumbbells. The caption told them his name: Jim Stephens.

Liz took control of Claire's mouse and used the browser's tools to zoom in on the high-quality picture. There they were. Slightly out of focus now, and a bit grainy, but Liz had no doubt. She pointed to the black neoprene-covered dumbbells. "Those look exactly like the ones that weighted down the body. I wonder if there are any other identifiable marks on the weights?"

Liz zoomed out again. Her gaze moved to the smiling trainer's rugged, handsome face. "Is that the face of a killer?" she wondered aloud.

"Do you think he...?" Claire asked, her eyes huge, sending the picture to the office's color printer.

"I don't know, but I'll want to talk with him, that's for sure."

Liz walked to the large, clean whiteboard on the partial wall that divided the room. She picked up a black dry-erase marker from the basket mounted to the wall and wrote *SUSPECTS* on the far left side of the board. Claire retrieved the picture from the printer and hung it below the header with a magnet. She wrote the trainer's name, *Jim Stephens*, neatly under the picture.

Their first suspect in place, the two women got to work at their respective desks. More notes and pictures joined the photo of the trainer throughout the morning.

By lunch, Liz pushed away from her desk and stretched. She padded around the wall in brightly colored stockinged feet, having kicked off her shoes an hour earlier. Grabbing a page from the printer, Liz added it to the growing collection on the whiteboard displaying Brittany Cabot's life and death. She turned to Claire, who was dabbing her eyes with a tissue. "Hey, is everything okay?" She studied her friend's face closely.

Claire nodded, dabbing at her eyes. "Are my eyes bleeding? Because they feel like they're bleeding. I *never* thought I'd see the day when I was sick and tired of reading about shoes!" Claire opened a desk drawer and retrieved eye drops, quickly dripping some into each eye. She sighed in relief.

Liz laughed. "Well, her roommate mentioned that she was a shopaholic."

"Oh, she was definitely that! No question. But, she was also obsessive about her shopping. I've read thirteen posts about how much she wanted a specific pair of shoes! Thirteen! Now, it's like, 'Who shot J. R.?' I *want* to know if she got them or not!" Claire looked at her screen as a forlorn look passed over her pretty face. "I'm not *that* shallow. Am I?"

Liz shook her head, wanting to tease her friend, but instinctively knew it wasn't the time. "No way! Do you like fashion? Absolutely! But, shallow, never. The first time I met you, you weren't concerned about the money *you* had lost to that charlatan who claimed he could speak to your deceased grandmother. But you were furious when you realized how many people he'd bilked over the years. That's really why you wanted him shut down. Shallow, no, definitely not!" Liz finished.

Claire came around the desk, carefully moving her black leather boots out of the way as she passed. "Thank you!" She hugged Liz before they turned and stared at the whiteboard next to them. They sighed. Claire slouched against the edge of the desk.

"Lunch before we discuss?" Liz suggested looping her arm through Claire's. Liz's stomach growled loudly.

"I think we'd better!" Claire laughed.

The two women parted. Liz dashed into her apartment for her black wool coat that stopped mid-thigh. A bit of an overkill for San Antonio, but an ugly cold snap a couple of years earlier prompted her to buy it, just in case. She pulled the long strap from her crossbody purse over her head as she walked back to the office.

When Liz returned, Claire was ready and waiting, boots on, a thick warm shawl in various shades of purple draped her shoulders, purse in gloved hands.

"Thanks!" Noticing that her shoes had materialized in front of the couch. Liz finished tucking her hair into her multicolored, granny-square crocheted hat, pulling it down to cover her ears. She slipped on her sneakers and straightened up. "Ready?"

"Let's go!"

Chapter Nine

The pair of friends stepped into the crisp afternoon air, locking up behind them. Linking arms at the bottom of the stairs, Liz and Claire turned right and walked through the long passageway directly beneath Liz's home and office. The brown wrought iron gates hung wide open to allow pedestrians access to the restaurants and businesses within the courtyard of the comically named Kangaroo Court Building. The oddly angled arch overhead was meant to display the familiar Alamo rooftop shape and, to the sharp-eyed passerby, displayed a layout of downtown city streets.

"It feels like the forecast for this afternoon has changed! It sure doesn't feel like spring!" Claire exclaimed as they stepped past the double gates. A strong gust of wind blew down the narrow street, swirling clouds of dust and the occasional litter as it swept by. They picked up the pace, and within minutes, they were strolling through the heavy glass and wooden doors of San Antonio's oldest restaurant, Schilo's.

They stopped inside, next to a long wooden counter, and waited to be seated. The smell of sausage and sauerkraut drifted to their eager noses.

"Ladies!" A deep male voice boomed from across the crowded restaurant.

"Hi, Fritz!" Liz and Claire responded in unison.

A stocky man sporting a thick bushy mustache, crossed the restaurant and greeted each woman with a quick hug and a scratchy kiss.

"How are my favorite customers this fine, chilly morning?" he asked cheerfully.

Although she knew Fritz was born and raised in Texas, Liz could swear she heard a hint of a German accent in his voice.

Not waiting for a response, Fritz straightened his long white apron around his barrel-like torso and grabbed a couple of menus from the worn long wooden counter that ran along the wall next to the door.

"Come!" His voice boomed, and yet nothing was threatening about it. He led the way to a booth by the front windows. "I always sit pretty ladies in the front window. Helps draw in hungry men!"

As if on cue, a man walked through the front door.

"See?" He wiggled his eyebrows wildly as they laughed.

They slid onto the smooth, dark wooden benches, worn from decades of use.

The kindly restauranteur handed each a menu. "What would you like to drink? Water and something warm, I bet. Hot chocolate!"

Before they could respond, he turned and ran off to the kitchen at the back of the restaurant.

Liz shook her head and laughed softly. She took off her warm hat, running her fingers through her soft locks to tidy them. She slipped her arms out of her jacket and mounded everything on the bench next to her. Liz reached for the menu, hesitated, and closed her hands into tight fists. She released her grip before picking up the menu. Nothing. Psychometry was still on vacation. Her shoulders slumped as she stared blankly at the menu in her hands.

Claire smiled at her gloomy friend. "I'm sure it'll come back," she said softly.

"Yeah," Liz replied, not believing the sentiment. She swiped one hand across her face, brushing away the single tear that threatened to fall, and the words on the menu came into focus.

A deep sigh escaped as she decided on what to eat. The restaurant offered a combination of German, American, and Tex-Mex cuisine in a unique blend of deliciousness.

Liz decided on the Papa Fritz sandwich, named for the current Fritz's ancestor, who first opened the restaurant. Claire decided to stick with a classic BLT on wheat toast.

A young server walked toward them, cautiously carrying her tray in both hands. Resting it on the edge of the table, standing next to Liz, she unloaded the tray of drinks. A small amount of water sloshed to the table, but the mugs of hot chocolate, heaped high with whipped cream and sprinkled with chocolate shavings, made the transition from tray to table without a hitch.

"Hi. I'm Susie. I'll be your server," the pretty blonde said, mopping up the water with a clean rag she pulled from her apron. She rested the large brown tray against the bench next to Claire.

Liz and Claire smiled up at the unfamiliar girl. "Hi, Susie," Claire said gently. "When did you start?"

Susie smiled nervously. "Um, three days ago. I decided to get a job after New Year's, while at college. I figure the extra money will help."

Claire nodded. "I'm sure it will. You're doing fine."

Susie's smile turned into a smirk as a snort escaped her. "I broke three dishes yesterday. Fritz is sweet, but he's going to fire me. I'm positive."

Liz grinned and crooked a finger at the young server conspiratorially. "Here's what you do. Ask him to teach you. He's been in this restaurant his entire life. It'll make his day if you ask him."

Susie lit up. "Really? I will. Thanks." She walked off.

Claire and Liz waited patiently, placing their hands on the closed menus.

Susie returned to the table, looking a little sheepish. She offered them a lopsided smile. "Are you ready to order?" She fished in her apron for the order pad and pen.

Liz smiled brightly and patted Susie's hand. A small weight formed in Liz's chest, that time, it felt like a heavy balloon full of fluttering butterflies. "Take a deep breath, Susie."

Susie did as she was told and released it. "I'm good now, thanks." She composed herself.

"I'll have the Papa Fritz with plain chips. And a second order to go."

Susie paused. "Really? That's a lot of food!"

Liz nodded. "I'm sure."

Susie shrugged and wrote down the order.

"Ask Fritz. He'll understand."

Claire placed her order for a BLT with chips and made the same request to double the order.

"I'll be back to check on you shortly." Susie turned too quickly and nearly walked into a passing customer. "Oh, excuse me!"

Claire and Liz giggled softly.

"Do you think she'll last?" Claire asked Liz quietly, setting the menus the nervous employee forgot to collect on the table's edge.

"Maybe. Susie'll last longer if she asks Fritz for help. You know how much he loves that!" Liz grinned.

Claire agreed, using a spoon to eat some of the whipped cream heaped inches above the rim of her mug.

Liz smiled conspiratorially at her friend. "It happened again. Twice." She patted herself on her chest.

Confusion passed over Claire's normally cheery face. "What?" Her gaze dropped to Liz's hand. "Oh, really?"

Liz nodded, her eyes sparkling. "Once when Fritz hugged me. That man is truly as happy as he appears."

"No big surprise there. And the other?" Claire asked quietly, scooting forward on the bench.

"Susie is one giant ball of nervous butterflies!" Liz grinned.

"That's wonderful! Anything else yet?"

Liz shook her head, staring down at her hands.

"But it's a start!" Claire patted her hand gently. "Anything?"

"No, you nut." Claire always hoped that Liz would have a vision of her future husband.

The front door opened, and a chilly breeze invaded the cozy restaurant.

"Detective! Your order is almost ready!" Fritz boomed from the back of the dining room.

"Thanks, Fritz!" A. J. called back, lifting his hand in a wave. He stopped by the counter to wait.

Claire raised her manicured hand, wiggling her fingers in the air. "Detective Hottie is here," she muttered to Liz.

"What?" Liz asked. She turned in the direction Claire was looking and bumped her head into A. J.'s elbow when he appeared at her side. "Ow." She rubbed her temple.

A. J. smiled apologetically at her. "Sorry."

"It's okay." Liz slid over on the bench, shoving her coat and purse onto the wide windowsill, so he had room to sit. "Hi," Liz said shyly.

A. J. lowered himself to the bench next to her, their elbows bumping as they got comfortable. "Hi, Liz. Claire. How are y'all doing today?" he asked in his pleasant manner.

"Good. Better than last night, that's for sure," Liz responded, a little embarrassed that he saw her in such a state the night before.

"I'm glad. I was worried." A. J. fiddled with Liz's cutlery.

A faint flush heated Liz's cheeks. She noticed redness creep up A. J.'s neck from under the collar of his plaid shirt. *Why is he blushing? Could he be reciprocating the feelings I have for him?*

"How is your day going?" Claire scooped up another spoonful of whipped cream and winked at Liz.

A. J. hesitated. "Good, busy. How 'bout you?"

Liz grinned. She knew he never seemed sure how to take Claire Henderson. He first met her as Liz's assistant, only to learn later that she was one of the wealthiest people in San Antonio.

"Great! We have a case!" Claire said cheerily, setting down her spoon and picking up her mug of hot chocolate to take a sip.

"Uh, what case?" A. J. asked, looking back and forth between the two women.

"Um, I was going to call you later and fill you in. I'm investigating Brittany Cabot's murder. Thought you'd want to know."

A. J. nodded. "I'm not surprised. You turned that case down originally, didn't you?"

Liz stared into her hot chocolate, nodding imperceptibly.

"What happened was not your fault. You know that, right?" he asked quietly, moving his head closer to hers.

"I know, it's just, well, you know." Liz responded, knowing that he understood what she was trying to say. As a police officer, he knew from experience that you couldn't save everyone.

A. J. grimaced. "Yeah, I know." He bumped his shoulder against Liz's.

Claire cleared her throat.

They stopped whispering and turned their conversation to lighter topics. Laughter soon drifted from their table.

"Detective! Stop flirting! Your order's ready!" Fritz roared from behind the counter.

The blush creeping up A. J.'s neck colored the rest of his face in a flash. Claire and Liz giggled.

"Hush up, you two," he said, standing. "I'll call you later, Liz. Claire." He reached out lightning-fast and swiped a large dollop of whipped cream from Liz's hot chocolate with his finger.

"Hey!" Her jaw dropped open in pretend shock.

He put it in his mouth and winked before walking away.

Liz and Claire watched as A. J. and Fritz quietly talked at the counter.

Scooping up the bags, A. J. pushed the door open with his back and nodded to Fritz. "They'll *never* find the body, pal."

Fritz roared with laughter as the door swung shut.

Liz and Claire joined in, caught up by Fritz's infectious laughter.

"Well, Detective Hottie certainly lives up to his nickname!" Claire commented, fanning her face with her manicured hand.

Liz rolled her eyes at her friend. "You have to stop calling him that! Someday I'm going to trip up and say it, and he'll never let me live it down!"

Claire giggled, sliding her napkin and cutlery to one side. "Something tells me that he'll forgive you. But I do have to say. I can't wait until you two get past this awkward stage."

Heat rushed to Liz's cheeks. She hid her face by sipping her hot chocolate, but it didn't help.

"Are you still saying nothing happened between you on that last case? Nothing at all?" Claire asked, daintily drinking her water through a straw.

Liz shook her head. "Nothing." She wouldn't tell her friend how it felt when he held her, comforting her in her despair at their failed rescue. She also wouldn't tell her friend that she thought about that single embrace often.

Thankfully, Susie brought their food to the table, interrupting Claire's questions and Liz's train of thought. She held the tray while the ladies helped unload it for her.

"Thank you, Susie." Liz smiled at the frazzled server. "Why don't you leave the checks, and you won't have to worry about us anymore?"

Relief passed over Susie's face. "Really? Thanks!" She pulled the papers from her pad and placed them on the table. "Oh, and the other orders will be ready in about twenty!"

"Perfect."

Susie walked off to check on another table, while Liz and Claire dug into their lunch without further conversation. They enjoyed a companionable silence as they watched people come and go. They saw Susie speaking with Fritz at the back of the dining room, quickly followed by a loud, "Of course!"

The rotund man accompanied Susie as she made her rounds of her tables. They heard a group laugh as he regaled employees and guests alike with the story of the first dish he broke at that very table. Liz and Claire listened in.

"Of course, I was only six at the time. I dropped a glass of water into the lap of none other than James Stewart! Luckily, Mr. Stewart only suffered from the indignity of wet pants, but the glass shattered on the floor. My parents were mortified! They rushed him to our apartment upstairs. My mother draped his pants over a chair to dry in front of the fireplace while Mr. Stewart sat on the couch wearing my father's housecoat. He was wonderful during the whole affair. Beyond our family and the people in the dining room at the time, the story never got out, and he left the restaurant in the same state as he arrived! Such a nice man."

Liz and Claire joined in the brief round of applause at his story. Fritz beamed and gave his audience a quick bow.

Before long, Liz and Claire finished their meals and approached the counter to pay and pick up the extra food. Fritz rushed to the register with his new shadow, each carrying a heavy bag. He rung them up. "I threw in a few extras too." He gave the ladies a conspiratorial wink.

"Thanks, Fritz. You did great, Susie!" They left, loaded down with their bags, each filled with decidedly more than a sandwich and a little something extra.

The ladies turned right to walk toward the crosswalk. Their first stop was at the bus stop near the corner. A waist-high concrete barrier surrounded the benches. An elderly man sat on the ground with a rolled-up sleeping bag in his lap and an overstuffed backpack at his side.

Claire handed him the bag of food. "We thought you might be hungry. And please, take this card for the Henderson Shelters. If you show it to the bus driver, he'll get you to one free of charge. Whichever shelter you go to will give you somewhere warm to stay today and a bed to sleep in tonight."

The elderly man gave her an almost toothless smile. "Thanks, honey. God bless you." He accepted the large bag, his eyes grew big when he looked inside.

The ladies walked to the intersection and crossed to the other side. Another man sat on the bridge. He was only about ten years older than Liz and Claire but still in need.

"Hi, George," Liz greeted him by name.

The man with short silver hair looked up, dressed in a heavy camo jacket, with a sizable military pack next to him. "Hi, Liz. Claire." He nodded to each in turn.

"How are you doing today?" Liz asked, studying his face closely while she waited for his answer.

He shrugged. "Same as yesterday, better than the day before." He didn't look at them for long. His eyes were always on the move, checking everything around them. George flinched when a truck backfired further down the road.

"We thought you might be hungry. Here's a good lunch." Liz handed him the heavy bag. "I don't know what all is in there. I ordered a sandwich, but Fritz added more to the bag."

George accepted the gift with a small smile. "Fritz is a good man. Y'all're good people too. Thank you."

Liz and Claire smiled at him.

"George, please take this card and go to the shelter?" Claire held a card out to the homeless veteran. "Please?"

The man smiled at her. His mouthful of bright, straight teeth alone told passersby that he had not always been on the streets. "I can't sleep indoors, miss, but thanks for the meal." He pulled a bag of wipes out of his pack and cleaned his hands before digging into the sandwich. Even though he lived on the streets, George was in better shape than other homeless people they've encountered. He'd always kept his reasons for living on the streets to himself. Liz suspected that it wasn't money problems that had driven this man to his current situation.

"Bye, George." They left him to eat, knowing he'd eat some of the food and share the rest.

The women walked quickly to the passageway, where the buildings immediately blocked the cold wind. They sighed in relief. The metal stairs were loud under their feet as they made their way up, eager for the warmth of the office.

After they shed their outerwear, they resumed their position next to Claire's desk to study their morning's work.

Chapter Ten

Claire started with a summary of her research for Liz. She looked away from the whiteboard "Do you know how she was killed yet?"

Liz shook her head.

Claire took a quick breath before continuing. "As I said before lunch, her social media is almost entirely shopping related, at least as far back as a few months. I did locate a picture of an ex-boyfriend, Frank, on her social media feed. I don't have a last name for him yet. Maybe Rosemary will be able to tell you." She retrieved the photo from the desk behind them and hung it on the whiteboard.

Liz studied the clipboard in her hand. "That's funny. Rosemary didn't mention a boyfriend or ex-boyfriend on the form this morning. Do you know how long ago they broke up?"

Claire stepped away from the whiteboard. "No, I..."

Liz looked up and gasped.

"What?" Claire asked, looking between Liz and the whiteboard.

"I've seen him before. Last night!" She set the clipboard down and walked closer to the picture Claire had just hung.

"Really? Where?"

"At the crime scene," Liz answered, turning. "He was the man I saw with Rosemary on the other side of the river. They didn't stick around very long. I don't know if they saw what was causing all the fuss."

"Well, that's a little suspicious, that's for sure."

Liz straightened up and bit her lip. "I think that bodes a bit more investigation. Do you have a picture of Rosemary too?"

Claire looked at Liz. "Really? It might be completely innocent."

"And it might not. It's a question, and in a murder investigation, I like to have *all* the answers."

The printer hummed and a picture of their client came out on the tray. Liz hung it on the board, stepped back, and nodded.

"Definitely bears some looking into. Okay, my turn. Financially speaking, Rosemary is correct. Brittany had dismal credit, no credit cards that I could find, and a single bank account in her name with less than a hundred dollars in it."

"Yikes. I can't imagine!" Claire shuddered. Of course, that was less money than Claire walked around with on a daily basis.

Liz continued. "Her background check is pretty clean, other than the occasional parking or speeding ticket, but those were years ago. To my knowledge, she didn't own a car at the time of her death."

"Huh." Claire stared at the information before them. "Not much to go on."

Liz stepped away to the kitchenette. "So far, I'm not seeing a reason why someone would want to kill her. Do you get a feel for who she was as a person yet?" Soft clinks echoed in the sink as Liz washed their mugs from the morning.

Claire shook her head. "Other than appearing to be extremely shallow and obsessed with shopping, no. But I'm only back a couple of months before her death. She seemed to like her boss, Mr. Moore. But that's it."

Liz dried her hands, biting her lip as she thought, grabbing a couple of water bottles from the small fridge next to the counter. "Of course, since she wrote the posts, that's not exactly a reliable source for what she was like in real life. She cleaned rooms in the upper parts of the hotel, so I never met her. I can confirm that there was zero financial activity after December seventh. But that doesn't help, because she didn't use her bank account regularly, and since she didn't have a car, there weren't any recent traffic violations."

Liz handed a bottle to Claire. "Looks like I'm joining you on the social media hunt this afternoon." Liz kicked off her sneakers by the coat rack and padded off to her desk. A bright red light on her desk phone told her she had a message.

She hit the button to activate the speakerphone, punched in the code when prompted, and waited. Mac Murphy's velvety voice filled the air as he asked for an interview. Liz swore under her breath. She felt like she owed him one, since he helped her last night, but he made her nervous.

Liz deleted the message and ended the call. *I'll worry about that later*, she thought.

"Ooh, his voice is lovely!" Claire called out from her desk. A low giggle followed the comment.

"I'll tell him to interview you instead then!" Liz replied, wondering how Mac would handle Claire in an interview.

"Fantastic! I can't wait."

Silence fell over the office as they returned to work. Liz logged into a different social media service using her fake account credentials and navigated her way to Brittany Cabot's feed. Unfortunately, Rosemary didn't know any of her late roommate's passwords, so they were limited to looking at the public side of her accounts and couldn't read any private messages she may have sent or received.

It didn't take long for Liz to see what Claire was complaining about earlier. Brittany was extremely shallow. She didn't have a large circle of friends, virtually speaking, and her obsession with shoes and fashion was off the charts!

One thing Liz did notice that was kind of sad. There were none of the typical "I'll miss you!", "RIP, Brittany!", "Where are you, Brittany?" posts, neither for when she disappeared nor now that her body had been discovered. That alone gave Liz a tiny peek into Brittany's world, and it must have been lonely.

Liz clicked on the "followers" list, and there were only a handful of people. No one appeared to be local, if their social media account details were accurate. As for the people the victim followed, those were all high-end fashion houses and stores.

She walked out to the whiteboard and updated the list of information they'd gathered about Brittany. Below notes of "shopaholic" and "expensive tastes," Liz added, "Not many friends on social media."

On a whim, Liz checked the prices of some of the items Brittany had been obsessed with. Her eyes grew large when she saw the cost of a single pair of shoes. A purse she posted about was valued in the thousands.

"Woah! How could she afford these?" Liz made a note to ask Rosemary if Brittany ever actually bought the items she was obsessed with.

An idea dawned, and Liz jumped up from her desk. "Claire! I want to change your direction!" she called out as she walked around the wall. "What are you doing now?"

"Just reading inane post after inane post. No one is making a movie out of this woman's life anytime soon!" Claire's jaw dropped, and her eyes opened wide as a look of absolute mortification passed over her face. "That was awful! I can't believe I just said that!" She clapped her hands over her mouth.

"It's okay. I can't say that I wasn't thinking the same thing. But, since you said it first, wow! You are a monster!"

Claire crossed her eyes at Liz.

Liz knew she did this because her friend knew it bugged her, because she couldn't do it. She stuck out her tongue in a childish response.

Their moment of juvenile behavior passed. Claire looked up at Liz, clasped her hands under her chin, and batted her long mascara'd eyelashes at her. "What do you want me to do? Please, anything but this social media feed. I can't take anymore!"

Liz grimaced. "Well—"

Claire's shoulders dropped. "Oh no! Come on!" She rolled back from her desk, crossing her arms in defiance and shaking her head.

Liz giggled. "Yeah, yeah, I know. I want you to crawl back through her account, but this time I want you to make a shopping list."

"Huh?" Confusion altered Claire's voice. One side of her mouth turned up, and her brow wrinkled.

"Make a list of the items she got fixated on. I want pictures and costs. Stores here in town where she'd most likely buy them. I wonder if Rosemary still has any of Brittany's belongings?"

Claire's look of confusion changed as understanding dawned. "We want to know how Brittany could afford to buy these things! I know one pair of shoes I saw is worth at least fifteen hundred dollars!"

"Exactly!" Liz pointed at Claire. "That's what I'm looking for. We need to find out if she managed to buy this stuff, or if it was just a pipe dream. If she did buy any of it, we follow the money."

Claire rolled back to her desk, rubbing her hands together gleefully, perking up. "This might be fun!" She took a sip of water and returned to the social media feed with renewed vigor.

Liz returned to her desk and continued scrolling backward in social media time. After several months of posts about shoes, purses, and clothes, she noticed a shift. More posts were complaining about work, specifically about her boss, Mr. Moore. Lots of complaints, multiple times a day at one point. Wow! How did someone go from despising her boss this much to liking them? If it wasn't for the murder, this case could be the basis of a romantic comedy.

After reading through weeks of posts complaining about her employer, Liz decided to add him to the suspect list. She visited the hotel's website and found a picture of the older man. His graying hair was neat and slicked back. Even in the photo she could tell he had perfect posture. Her gut reaction was that he looked like a butler.

As she stood, she noticed the time. It was almost five-thirty!

When Liz came around and retrieved the picture from the printer, she noticed that Claire was all smiles at her desk.

"This may be my favorite assignment yet!" she announced. "I'm going shopping this evening. Do you want to come?"

Liz was happy to see Claire's mood had improved. She grinned and shook her head. "No, it's family night. Thanks, though."

Claire nodded, understanding. "That's nice. My parents are in France this month. They'll be back in February."

"Our lives are so different!" Liz exclaimed. While Claire's childhood was filled with mansions, servants, and world travel, Liz's was filled with family barbecues, game nights, and dealing with psychic visions.

"Ah, but we have one thing in common." Claire lifted a finger into the air. "Awesome parents."

Liz agreed and nodded. For all their wealth and prosperity, Claire's parents were down-to-earth and warm.

"By the way, it's after five. We're done for the day!" She flipped through the small stack of pictures on Claire's desk. They showed a variety of expensive items. "Wow!"

"I know, right?" Claire commented. "She had great taste, that's for sure."

Liz retrieved a paper from the printer, crossed to the whiteboard and added the picture in her hand to the board.

"Who's that?" Claire asked.

"Mr. Moore," Liz replied, turning, and leaning against the wall.

"Her boss? I thought she liked him!"

"That was during the months before she disappeared. Before that, wow, it was bad."

"Really?" Claire sat back in her seat, staring at his photo, stretching her arms before interlacing her fingers behind her head.

Liz crossed to the couch and sat down, propping her feet on the edge of the low table.

"Oh yeah, loads of complaints. I finally broke down and decided to add him to the list."

Right then, multiple notifications sounded from Claire's cell phone.

Liz heard muffled *dings* from her own phone from its spot on her desk.

Claire reached for her device. "Um, Liz, it's from the news apps. Turn on the television to any of the local news channels."

"Okay. What happened?" Liz asked, picking up the remote for the small television mounted to the wall of their waiting area. She sat on the couch to watch.

Her question was answered within seconds. A photo of Brittany Cabot was on the screen next to the news anchor's head, the same photo that was gracing the center of their whiteboard.

The anchor's voice filled their office. "...river. Police have brought in a suspect for questioning in the Brittany Cabot murder. They have yet to release the name of the suspect. After the gruesome discovery by a pair of unnamed women last night..."

Pictures started to appear on the screen. Liz looked away and tuned out the news anchor's voice. She knew what the crime scene looked like firsthand. If she felt the need to refresh her memory, she'd watch it later on her computer.

Claire watched intently.

A collection of amateur photos sent in by curiosity-seekers at the crime scene filled the screen. At last, Liz looked, even though she didn't want to. She studied the pictures in case there was anything that might be a clue she missed last night.

The news broadcast ended, and a commercial for a local museum began to play.

"Wow! That is, wow!" Claire joined Liz on the couch. "You okay?"

Liz stared down at her hands before looking up at her friend, smiling weakly. "I'm fine. That makes me want to find out who did this even more. I wonder who the police brought in for questioning?"

Chapter Eleven

The evening with her parents went as expected. They weren't thrilled to learn that Liz and Pam had been the ones to discover the body in the river. But they were happy to hear that her abilities were returning after their extended rest. Even though she felt a little sad from the uncertainty in her life, she was smiling. Her parents were good medicine.

Now that Liz was back at her apartment, she dropped her purse on the kitchen counter and grabbed a beer from the fridge. She headed back to the balcony to watch the River Walk get busier with a combination of locals and tourists.

I guess the absence of water isn't affecting business, she thought, watching more people gather on the outside patio of the No Name Bar below her. Tonight was Nineties Country Night, so there was a sea of cowboy hats, and a mix of the biggest names in country music poured out of the speakers placed around the patio.

Liz took another sip of beer, leaned on the railing, and let her mind drift. She sang along with the music under her breath and tapped her foot. There was something about the country music from that decade that you couldn't help but sing along with. She lost track of time until someone calling her name snapped her from her reverie.

"Liz!" a male voice called out.

Liz looked over at the crowd of young men partying on the patio below, but they were focused on the young women among them.

"Liz! Down here!" the voice called out again.

At the bottom of her staircase stood A. J., handsome in worn jeans, scuffed cowboy boots, and his favorite dark brown leather jacket. Her gaze took in his rugged square jaw and his short messy brown hair.

"Hey, A. J., wanna come up?" Liz called down to him.

"Yeah!"

Liz raised her hand so he'd wait and slipped into the office to press the release button for the gate. A. J. was halfway up when she came back outside.

"Hi," Liz said. The detective got more handsome the closer he got.

"Hi," A. J. replied. A friendly smile lit up his face. "I hope you don't mind. I was out walking, mulling over the case, when I saw you up here." His warm brown eyes passed over her face.

"Not at all. But be careful. I was walking and mulling Sunday night when I found her body. Do you want a beer? I can get you one," Liz offered, already moving for the door.

A. J. shook his head. "This'll do." He took the bottle from her hand, took a quick sip, and gave it back. He winked at Liz's slack-jawed expression.

They leaned against the railing, side-by-side, shoulders touching. Not talking at first, the atmosphere around them was far from quiet. The crowd of patrons at the bar below slowly got bigger and louder.

"Wow, that racket must get to you after a while," A. J. commented as music poured out of the outdoor speakers.

Liz waved her hand dismissively. "This is nothing. The weekends are far worse."

"How do you stand it?"

Liz grinned and leaned toward him. "Soundproofing on the walls and floor of my apartment." She took another sip of the beer in her hand. "I made a deal with the landlord after I helped him out with his...well, family problem."

"Cool." A. J. took the bottle. "Sorry I didn't call you this afternoon. Things got busy with the case. Are you better now? Really?" A. J. asked, staring out at the busy River Walk. He took a quick sip and handed the bottle back.

Liz nodded, rubbing her jaw with a knuckle. "My jaw is tender with all the yawning I did on the walk home. Thanks for asking Mac to walk us." Liz took another sip before handing the bottle to A. J. "I wonder why shock makes me so sleepy."

He shrugged, his shoulder rubbing hers. "It's my experience that shock hits everyone differently. I've seen grown men slip into a near-catatonic state for hours and watched children shrug it off in minutes." He gestured to Liz with his head. "You shake for a few minutes, get cold and tired. Although I have to say, you crumpling the way you did caught me off guard." He sipped and gave the bottle back.

"What happens to you?" Liz asked, her fingers brushing his as she accepted it. She felt a weight form in her chest, but it disappeared before she could identify an emotion.

"Don't know," A. J. replied, shrugging again. "It hasn't happened to me yet."

"Hey, y'all!" a patron yelled to them from the bar's patio, his words slurring.

The pair looked down to see an intoxicated young man waving his cowboy hat.

Liz simply lifted her beer to him and smiled. She whispered to A. J., "It's best not to engage them in conversation. I made that mistake when I first moved here."

The tipsy cowboy-wannabe turned away. "Hey, y'all!" They heard him say too loudly to a couple of young women at a table. Giggles floated on the air in response.

A. J. turned to face her. "There is *so* much more to that story!"

Liz shook her head, refusing to look at him, but couldn't stop the smile that formed when she knew he was looking at her. "No way. Let's just say the guy was an octopus, and he got a quick lesson in boxing."

A brilliant smile lit up A. J.'s tanned face. "Good job! And, boxing, really?"

Liz tried to smile as she sipped. She wiped a drop of beer from her chin, blushing slightly.

A. J.'s lips twitched as he smothered a grin.

"Yes. I have a dual-bag set up inside, and I normally go to the gym to spar, or take a class, once or twice a week." Her eyes dropped sadly. "I haven't been in a while."

"Why? Oh." His gaze fell to the beer bottle she was handing to him. "Are you doing okay after the Masterson case?" He kept his voice low.

This time it was Liz's turn to shrug. She couldn't tell him how deeply that failure affected her, because he didn't know about her extrasensory perception. Or how her abilities had vanished in the days following that gruesome discovery in December. Silence fell as they passed the bottle.

"You okay?" Liz glanced at him from the corner of her eye.

"Yeah. I'm angry we didn't arrest the perp, but I'm okay. I've been more worried about you, since that was your first homicide. Then with last night's discovery. Um, I've been meaning to ask. When Murphy walked you home last night, did you, did he?" A. J. faltered.

"Did he what?" Liz asked, oblivious to what A. J. was implying. What did he think could have happened with Mac? "Oh," she responded suddenly, and then what she thought was his meaning hit her. Her eyes opened wide. "Oh! No, he and I, *no*!" she said a little too firmly.

"No, nothing like that!" A. J.'s neck flushed. "Did he ask you any questions about the body?" His words came out in a rush.

Liz grinned, relaxing, not fully believing that was what he had meant. "Oh, sure. He asked one or two, but I refused to answer. He was a perfect gentleman." She raised a finger. "Wait. There was one thing he got out of me: the body was female. That's it."

A smile crossed A. J.'s face. "Well, that's okay. With the number of gawkers who were taking pictures and videos, that much was bound to get out pretty quickly. I wish I could have confiscated every single one of their phones. Disgusting!" A snarl passed over his face and left just as quickly.

Liz nodded. "I know. I couldn't believe how many phones I saw out last night. I've never, well, I have, but it was for work." She stopped and shook her head. "I still find it hard to believe that anyone could stop and take pictures like that of a person's absolute worst moment."

The bottle dangled, forgotten, in A. J.'s hand as he shook his head.

"On a different note," Liz started, taking the bottle for another sip before handing it back. "I didn't tell you earlier. The person who hired me was Brittany's roommate, Rosemary Travers."

"I'm not surprised. When I looked at the reports, I saw that she came in twice to report Brittany's disappearance." A. J. turned to face her. "Normally, the idea of a PI working on a homicide case isn't ideal, but neither is a crime scene that's over a month old and had thousands of people trekking through it during that time. I'll appreciate the help."

Liz met his steady gaze. "It's your case?"

A. J. nodded, sipping again. "The captain assigned it to me officially this afternoon."

That fact made Liz happier than she expected. "I saw on the evening news that you already brought someone in for questioning. Is the case over? Did they do it?"

"I don't know. The weights used to sink the body came from the suspect's gym, but that's all we have to tie him to the scene so far. It's all circumstantial. We had to release him, but I'll keep a close eye on him. He wasn't exactly forthcoming."

Liz's eyebrows shot up. "Jim Stephens, the hotel's personal trainer? Really?" She remembered the first picture she and Claire added to their list of suspects.

"How did you know his name?" A. J. asked, his eyebrows raised.

Liz flashed him a crooked smile. "The weights. We figured out that the murderer was connected with the hotel, either among the staff or a guest. I really hope it's not a guest." Liz rolled her eyes skyward.

"That's where we started, too, because of her uniform. What makes you so certain her death is connected with the hotel?" A. J. set the empty bottle on the floor by the door, all work now. They faced each other, leaning against the balcony's iron railing.

"Her roommate helped me with that one. When we spoke this morning, she mentioned that Brittany *always* changed before leaving the hotel. Since she was wearing her uniform when her body was dropped into the river..."

"She was still working at the hotel when she was murdered!" A. J. finished for her.

"Exactly."

"That's really helpful!" Silence fell over the pair as music boomed from the speakers below. The air between them started to come alive, but the moment broke when A. J. smiled and straightened up. "Well, uh, I should get out of your hair. I just wanted to check in and make sure you are good. Keep me in the loop about the case?"

Liz smirked, cocking one eyebrow. "Will *you* keep *me* in the loop?"

A. J. grinned knowingly. "How about if something big comes up?" He held out his hand.

"Deal." Liz shook his hand, and just like that, the weight formed in her chest again. She couldn't easily describe what she was feeling or, more accurately, what he was feeling.

He gave her hand a light squeeze and released it. "You better get inside now, before our overly friendly cowboy notices you're up here by yourself."

"I will. Y'all come back now, ya hear?" Liz quipped as he started down the steps.

He lifted his hand in a backward wave. Liz walked inside and pressed the button to release the gate. She waved from the door.

"Night!" he called out.

A. J. flipped the collar up on his jacket as he disappeared under her balcony and into the passageway below.

Chapter Twelve

After a quick run the next morning, grateful after a dreamless night's sleep, Liz rushed through a shower and pulled her shirt on as she headed down the stairs, her stomach growling. Her still-damp hair wet the shoulders of her thin tshirt. Liz grabbed a breakfast burrito from the small stash in her fridge—courtesy of her mother. She put it in the microwave and pulled on a fresh pair of sneakers while her breakfast heated up.

Wrapping the hot burrito in a paper towel, she began the short commute to work. When she reached her fitness studio, she paused. *I wonder. I slept pretty good last night, maybe...*

On a whim, she set her burrito on the low table. Drops of wax coated the middle of the surface, a reminder of candles thrown out in a fit of anger last month. Ignoring the waxy residue, Liz settled onto the soft, but firm, purple cushion on the meditation chair.

Crossing her legs and placing a hand on each knee, Liz took several deep, calming breaths to center herself. Changing to long, slow breaths, she closed her eyes.

At first, she felt calm flow over her as she focused only on her breathing. Then it started. The flicker of a candle appeared in the darkness behind her eyelids, followed by another and another. She felt her chest tighten as fear took hold.

Faster and faster, lit candles appeared until the barn's interior from her memory and nightmares was fully aglow in candlelight. Cold spread through her limbs, making them feel too heavy to move.

It was becoming harder to catch a full breath. Something was different this time. Regina Masterson wasn't lying dead, tied to a chair on the floor in the center of the room.

Liz approached the body slowly. It was Brittany Cabot, soaking wet, the heavy weights secured to her waist with a dirty white cord. The logo on her uniform glowed like the neon sign on the side of the hotel.

Liz forced her gaze to the dead woman's face when Brittany's eyes flew open!

She screamed as she tipped sideways out of the low chair, landing on a soft pillow.

Liz just lied there. She gasped for breath as tears of frustration rolled back from her eyes and into her damp hair. Wiping them away with a slash of her hands, she got up, grabbed her burrito, and stomped across to her office door. She slapped off the light switch as she passed.

Liz banged around the office, preparing for the day ahead by taking her frustrations out on everything. She dropped her burrito on her desk, in no mood to eat now. She checked her phone for messages. Just one. She punched in the code to listen to it. She slammed the receiver onto the phone's cradle when she heard Mac's recorded voice. She'd listen to it later.

She pounded the floor to the small kitchenette, where she managed to slam the two cupboard doors at least three times each while she prepared the coffee maker.

By the time Claire breezed in, humming and smelling of flowers, Liz was sitting on the couch, feet on the coffee table, holding a floral decorative pillow with the words *Buzz off* stitched on it over her face.

"Good morning!" Claire called out cheerily as she passed.

Liz grumbled beneath the pillow.

Claire sat next to her friend and waited quietly. At first.

After a few minutes of silence, Claire started talking without prompting or interruption. "Good morning, Claire. How are you? I'm wonderful, thanks for asking. How are you, Liz?" Claire lifted the edge of the pillow and peeked at her friend's face. "Well done, from the looks of it. What's wrong?"

Claire moved the pillow to Liz's lap and stood. Her skirt flowed around her legs as she paced, continuing her monologue.

"What's wrong?" She raised her voice and pointed into the air. "I'll tell you what's wrong! *The Glades* was canceled on a cliffhanger! Can you believe it?" Claire glanced at her friend.

Liz watched her blankly.

"Okay, so this isn't about a television show that ended in 2013. Coffee maybe? The entire state of Texas ran out of coffee, which I'm pretty sure is against some kind of state law. Someone's going to hang!" As if on cue, the coffee maker gurgled and beeped. Claire giggled. "Nope, that's not it either. Let me see. You've watched every cat video on the internet, and you must have just one more?"

Claire's lips pursed to one side of her face. "You dropped a pen, and gravity is irritating you?"

At last, a giggle escaped from Liz's tight lips.

Claire smirked and stopped pacing long enough to pour coffee. She rejoined Liz on the couch, nudging her elbow with the yellow dragonfly mug.

Liz moved the pillow from her lap to the arm of the couch. "Thanks," she muttered, accepting the mug from her friend.

"Do you want to talk about it?" Claire asked before taking a sip.

Liz responded with a mumble, but she was half smiling as she grumbled. She took too big of a gulp of the hot drink, swore, and set the mug down.

"That's some serious stuff there. I can see why it's so aggravating," Claire teased gently. She sipped her coffee and waited patiently.

Liz picked up her mug again. "Fine. I was in a great mood at first. I slept pretty good last night and got in a run. Then, on a whim, I decided to try meditating."

Claire groaned. "I know that's been difficult for you lately. I'm guessing it didn't go well?"

Liz set her cup on the table a little too hard, and coffee sloshed over the edge, spilling onto the surface. She smothered another curse, reaching for a tissue to wipe up the mess. "Not only did it not go well, but it scared the crap out of me, and then I fell out of my chair!"

A snort escaped Claire. She immediately apologized. "I'm sorry, but isn't that chair only four inches off the ground?"

Liz made a face. "You can stop any time, you know."

Another snicker escaped Claire. "So, you *can* say gravity is irritating you today?"

"Really?" A smile forced its way to Liz's snarling lips. The pillow next to her fell to the floor. "Son of a—"

Claire laughed outright, setting her coffee on the table as her whole body shook with mirth.

A giggle escaped Liz. "Stupid gravity." She picked up the small square pillow, hit her friend with it, and stuffed it between them.

"So." She reclaimed her mug, propping her feet on the table again as she sat back. "I found out who the police brought in for questioning yesterday. Our first suspect, Jim Stephens."

Claire lit up. "Really? Well, look at us! Wait a minute." She touched Liz's arm. "How did you find out?"

Heat crept slowly over Liz's cheeks. Suddenly, she was very intent on drinking her coffee. She gulped the hot liquid, swallowed, and muttered another curse as her already tender mouth tingled from the heat. "A. J. came by last night," she replied after composing herself.

"What? Detective Hottie was here last night! Are you two...?" Claire wiggled her eyebrows at Liz.

In her agitated state, it took Liz a moment to register what her friend was asking. Her eyes opened wide as realization dawned. "What? No! He...He didn't," Liz stammered. "We didn't!" She felt her face get hotter by the second. She tried to hide it by sipping her coffee again but failed as a smile passed unbidden across her lips. Straightening up, Liz set her mug on the table while her friend giggled gleefully next to her.

Suddenly, each moment with A. J. came back to her in a flood. Their shoulders touching, their fingers brushing. The intimacy she felt as they shared a beer, how she felt when his eyes bored into hers. None of this helped to ease her blushing. She hid her face behind her hands.

"Wow," Claire teased, "with all this blushing, that must have been some visit!"

"On that note." Liz stood, busying herself around the office, tidying things, retrieving her now cold burrito.

Refusing to look at her delighted coworker, Liz reheated her breakfast in the microwave. Ignoring her heated face, she ran through her plans for the day. "I'm going to interview Jim Stephens this morning," she called out as she rounded the wall by her desk. "I don't expect to find him at work, but..."

Liz ran Jim's name through the databases on her computer. Luckily, there was only one result in San Antonio, and the accompanying picture showed a non-smiling man, definitely the same person from their whiteboard. She jotted his information down in her notebook. "I've got his home address if I need it." Liz felt her cheeks begin to cool as the blushing subsided. "Could you review Jim's social media accounts while I'm gone?" Liz came around the wall, pulling on her jacket. The microwave beeped. "And call me if anything big stands out that I can use in my interview?"

Claire carried her mug to her desk and settled in, all business now. "Will do, boss. Do you want me to do the same with our other suspects?"

Liz nodded, swearing under her breath when she burned her fingers, retrieving her breakfast from the microwave. "That will be great. Thanks." Leaving the burrito on the counter, she grabbed her purse from the coat rack where she had left it the night before. Dropping the long strap over her head, her small brown leather purse settled against her hip. She hesitated as she reached for her hat. "What season is it today?" Fifty-degree temperature swings in a single day were not uncommon. It made dressing for Texas winters challenging. "It felt like fall when I went for my run this morning."

"Spring. Definitely. It was beautiful when I arrived. I even left my coat in the car."

Opting to leave the hat, she shoved her black gloves into her coat pockets, just in case. "I'm walking to the hotel. See you in a bit!" She scooped up the burrito and headed out the door.

"Have fun!" Claire waved from behind her desk. "And maybe you can tell me all about your night with A. J. at lunch!"

Liz closed the door as those last words reached her ears. She pointed at Claire through the tall window and grinned as Claire giggled uncontrollably.

Liz took the first bite of her breakfast as the gate latched behind her. *Wow, it is like spring*, she thought, unzipping her jacket.

Taking the River Walk to the hotel allowed Liz to avoid traffic and busy crosswalks while eating her breakfast. She heard workmen greet each other down in the concrete riverbed as they arrived for their day of cleaning and inspecting the man-made river for potential repairs. Their voices echoed off the walls around them.

Liz's thoughts drifted as she ate and walked. Before long, the hotel loomed above her as she finished her breakfast. She stopped by the bridge closest to the hotel, which happened to be next to where she found Brittany's body. The police tape no longer closed off that area of sidewalk. A chill ran down Liz's spine as she stood there, keeping the riverbed behind her as she looked up at the building where Brittany was most likely murdered.

Will I ever feel comfortable walking through this spot again? she mused. Determination filled her entire being as she took the stairs to the street level so she could enter the hotel through the main entrance.

The traffic on the roads had increased considerably since her run earlier. The broad, circular driveway at the front of the hotel was filled with cars. Staff members pushed tall brass luggage carts stuffed with suitcases. Their uniforms were different from those worn by the wait and housekeeping staff. They all wore the same white button-down shirt covered by a black vest emblazoned with the hotel logo on the left side of the chest. Black slacks and black rubber-soled shoes completed the uniform. Staff and guests bustled around Liz as she wound her way toward the tall automatic doors. A family of three walked out, accompanied by a smiling employee pushing an overstuffed luggage cart. Liz slipped past them to arrive in the lobby.

She joined the line at the front counter, prepared to do the most common aspect of her job: wait. Liz took off her jacket and draped it over her arm. A variety of people formed the line ahead of her. Liz stood behind a tall man holding a magazine in one hand and a cup of coffee in the other. The smell of coffee and vanilla drifted to her nose.

"Hmmm! Excuse me. Where did you get your coffee?" Liz asked the guest in front of her. "It smells wonderful!"

The tall man turned to her, a broad smile crossing his face. "So, this is what it takes to get you to speak with me!"

"Mac? What are you doing here?" Liz asked, failing to hide her surprise.

Instead of answering, Mac took a sip of his coffee. His eyes drifted closed while she watched.

Liz tapped her foot, glaring at Mac. Another sip. And waited. She crossed her arms. And waited. Her lips pressed into a straight line.

"Wow, this is really good," he said before taking another sip. He glanced over his shoulder to see if the line had moved. Taking a short step backward to maintain his place, he offered the cup to Liz. "Sorry, I'm being rude. Do you want a sip?"

Liz shook her head. "I'll get my own, thanks." Annoyance spread to every inch of her being. She crossed her arms over her chest, glaring at the reporter.

At last, he drained the cup. "Sorry, I wanted to drink it while it was still hot." The line moved a bit more. Mac turned and moved ahead but stopped short, causing Liz to bump into his back.

Mac maintained his good humor as he turned to face her again. "Hey, Liz?" he asked, slouching so he could look straight into her eyes.

"What?" She gritted her teeth, locking eyes with him.

"Isn't it annoying when someone is asked a question, say, for example—" he gestured to himself with the empty cup, "—'Can I interview you for my article?', and the person—" he gestured to Liz with the cup, "—doesn't answer?" His lips twitched.

Liz opened her mouth to offer a sharp retort but knew she didn't have a leg to stand on. Her irritation with the reporter dissipated like air being released from a balloon. "Sorry," she muttered.

Mac stepped to the side and leaned closer, holding the empty cup behind his ear. "What was that?"

Liz fought the urge to flick his ear. "I'm sorry," she said clearly. "I should have returned your call. You did me a big favor Sunday night and—"

"*Calls.* You should have returned my calls, plural. But, please, continue." His blue eyes sparkled through his glasses.

"Calls. I shouldn't have been rude by ignoring your calls," Liz corrected, feeling chastised. She did feel guilty. It was difficult when he was so damned annoying and in the right to boot.

"Excuse me, sir?" an employee asked, as the large family behind Mac moved away from the counter.

Mac turned, smiling brightly at the twenty-something female employee. "Sorry—" he paused to read her nametag, "—Laurie."

A blush crept across employee's face. "That's all right. How can I help you?" She typed rapidly on the keyboard in front of her.

"First, you can answer my friend's question." Mac reached out, placing a hand on Liz's back, bringing her to stand at the counter next to him.

Liz fought the urge to shrug off his hand. The thin tshirt didn't offer much protection against her weak empathic abilities. She could already feel the weight begin to form in her chest, and she was too irritated with him to want to know what he was feeling right then. Thankfully, Mac removed his hand before Liz learned anything.

"Thanks, Mac," she said. She smiled politely at the young lady behind the counter. "Hi, Laurie. Just a sec. Are you sure?" she glanced up at Mac. She wished he would just go away so she could ask her question out of reach of his prying ears.

"I insist. Go ahead. I'm positive Laurie can answer any question you might have." Mac's compliments triggered another blush from the hotel employee.

Liz pressed her lips together, wishing she didn't have to ask for Jim in front of Mac. "Where can I find Jim Stephens?" The question came out through gritted teeth.

"He's in the hotel's fitness center," Laurie responded automatically, reaching for a paper map from the stack next to her. She drew a path to the gym with a blue marker. "But, you must be a guest of the hotel to use the facilities."

Liz opened her mouth to respond, but Mac cut her off. "That's okay. She's with me." He dangled a keycard in front of Laurie and Liz.

Liz turned to face him, her mouth agape. "You're a guest here?"

Mac smiled broadly at her reaction.

Liz bit her lip to hold back a variety of retorts that came to mind for no reason other than he was annoying her with his foresight. She stepped to the side to wait for him while Mac charmed the blushing female employee a bit more.

"I had a message on my phone, Laurie. It stated that I have a package to pick up."

"Which room are you in?" Laurie asked.

"Twelve-nineteen," Mac responded, leaning on the counter. He turned to Liz. "Can you hold this, please?" he asked, holding out his empty disposable cup to her.

She took the cardboard cup from his hand, biting her lip to hold back her ideas of what he could do with the cup.

Laurie handed a large, thick manila envelope to the reporter.

He winked at the young lady behind the counter. "Thanks, Laurie." Mac led Liz away. "So," he started, dropping his keycard into a pocket of his cargo pants. "Who's Jim Stephens? And why are you looking for him?"

"Client privilege," Liz spouted automatically. In all honesty, no code or rule prevented Liz from answering Mac's questions. She just really didn't want to.

"Really? Curiouser and curiouser," Mac responded to her non-answer. They wove their way past crowds of people before they reached the ornate circular staircase. A sign pointed the way to the gym on the second floor. They walked up the stairs side by side.

Liz staggered when her foot hit the top step and bumped into Mac. "Excuse me," she said, flustered.

Mac reflexively grabbed her arm.

"You good?" he asked.

"Thanks," she mumbled, ignoring her twinge of guilt.

They stepped onto the landing. Another sign pointed the way to the hotel's fitness center down a deserted hallway. As they approached the door on the right, Liz took a couple of steps ahead of Mac. She swiped the keycard concealed in her grip and opened the door while Mac was still rooting through half a dozen pockets in his shirt, pants, and leather messenger bag.

"What...?" He looked up as the door closed in his face.

Liz smiled gleefully from the other side of the door. She tapped his keycard on the glass. "Thanks, Mac. I'll get this back to you!"

The reporter pointed at her. "I will get you back for this. You know that, right?"

Liz grinned and nodded. "But not today!" She wiggled her fingers at him in a childlike wave and turned away. Happy in the knowledge that she could question Jim without Mac hanging on every word.

Chapter Thirteen

Liz turned away from the door, a grin spreading across her face. She felt Mac's eyes boring into the back of her head through the glass. *I'll pay for that later*, she thought.

"Worth it!" she said aloud.

The gym was deserted. Treadmills, stationary bikes, and ellipticals lined the walls facing flat-screen televisions mounted high near the ceiling. Mats covered the furthest half of the room, surrounded by fitness balls, yoga mats, and free weights. A shiver ran through Liz at the sight of the pair of fifty-pound weights on the rack. The only sound in the room came from the televisions, tuned to the local public station.

"Hello?" Liz called out, sliding the keycard into her back pocket as she stepped further into the room. Her sneakers didn't make a sound on the light-colored tiled floor.

A tall, muscular man stepped through a door near the far window. He wore black sweat pants, sneakers, and a white polo shirt with the hotel logo stitched on the chest. While his mouth was smiling, his eyes were wary. "Can I help you?" he asked, not leaving the doorway.

Liz walked toward him, pulling her private investigator credentials from her purse. "My name is Liz Pond. Can I ask you some questions?" She held her hand out to the trainer, and he accepted it with a firm handshake. The familiar weight formed in her chest but disappeared when Jim released his grip on her hand.

"Um, I don't think the police want me talking to anyone." His gaze darted quickly around the room. "I didn't hurt Brittany," he said defensively, taking a step back from Liz.

"It's okay." Liz raised her hand in front of her, the leather folder with her identification gripped in her left hand. "I've been hired to look into Brittany's murder. The police, Detective Sowell, knows I'm speaking with you."

Jim relaxed slightly. "Really?"

"Really. Do you mind if I record our chat?" Liz asked, pulling her phone out of her purse.

Jim shook his head. He led her to a small table and chairs set near the windows. A balcony outside offered an elevated view of the River Walk.

Liz launched the app and laid the phone on the table. She announced the date and Jim's name for the recording. "Okay. So, Jim, how well did you know Brittany Cabot?" She kept her pen and notepad nearby if she needed to take additional notes.

Jim rubbed the back of his neck, the sleeve of his shirt strained at his bicep as he moved. "Um, not very well. She didn't come in much after the first week of working here." He looked at the table. He shrugged one shoulder.

Liz raised her eyebrows. "So the employees have use of the facilities?"

Jim nodded. "It's one of the benefits of working here. As you can see—" he gestured, holding his arms wide to the room devoid of people, "—they don't take advantage of that. Typically, any new employee comes here regularly at first and then not at all. There are a few exceptions, but not many."

Liz agreed. "It's hard work to stick to an exercise regimen."

Jim brightened suddenly and snapped his fingers. He pointed at her. "That's where I know you from. You jog past here almost every day. Great form and impressive discipline," he complimented her.

She offered him a lopsided grin. "Thanks. I try, at least. So, which employees are good about coming to the gym?"

Jim ran down a list of names. It was a short list, but one name stood out. "Rosemary Travers comes in here?" Liz asked, her eyebrows shooting up her forehead.

"Yes. Rosie's always on her feet, but she comes here a few times a week to stretch and do time on the stationary bicycles. Then she goes for a swim downstairs."

"Has she been doing that long, or is it a recent habit? Since New Year's just passed and all."

Jim grinned brightly, his shoulders relaxing the longer they spoke. "Yes, that typically causes a surge for at least a month. Of course, the hotel has been busy with weddings and receptions, so I haven't seen any increase. But, no, it's not a new habit. Rosie's been doing that for years."

"Have you two ever gone out?" Liz asked, cocking an eyebrow.

Jim rubbed his neck again. "Me and Rosie? No, never. I think she has a boyfriend, though." He shrugged a shoulder.

"Brittany was a pretty girl," she said, switching tactics, trying to steer the conversation.

"Yeah, I guess." Jim rubbed his neck again.

"You don't think so?" Liz asked, a little surprised. Judging by the photo on her phone, there was no question. Brittany Cabot had been a beautiful young lady.

Jim shifted in his seat. "Well, yeah, when I first met her, I thought so, too. We even went out once." He ran his thumb distractedly along the edge of the table, not meeting Liz's gaze.

"Really? Just once?" She considered Jim briefly. They would have made a good-looking couple.

He shrugged a muscular shoulder again. "Yeah, well, I, um, don't..." He stared at the table.

Liz opted to wait him out. She sat quietly, her hands folded in her lap.

Suddenly, Jim pushed himself to his feet, the table shifting with a loud screech. Liz jerked back, surprised at the suddenness of his movement. From her seated position, she was reminded of just how big the man she was questioning was. She glanced toward the door. The path was clear. She wondered if she'd need the card to get out. *Is Mac still hanging around out there? Maybe ditching him hadn't been the best idea.* Thoughts tumbled through her mind as her anxiety rose.

Jim paced along the windows. He stopped, opened his mouth to speak, closed it again, and resumed pacing. He cracked his knuckles.

Liz's hand gripped the strap of her purse that crossed her body. The bonus of a bag with a long strap was that it made for a great weapon if needed. Her heart raced, and her pulse pounded in her ears; her fight or flight instinct was in full swing. She felt beads of sweat start to form at the back of her neck.

Finally, he stopped pacing and dropped back into the seat opposite Liz. "I've never told anyone how our date went that night." His gaze stayed on the table between them.

"Okay. Will you tell me?" Liz's guard was still up, but she was grateful he was sitting down again.

"Things didn't go as planned, that's for sure."

Liz laid her pen down, keeping her attention entirely on Jim. "And what did you have planned?"

Another shrug. "Dinner. A movie. Maybe a walk along the River Walk."

"That sounds nice," Liz commented quietly, keeping a wary eye on him for any more sudden movements.

"I thought so. But dinner didn't go so well. I took Brittany to a small Italian restaurant that has great pasta. Good for carb-loading, you know. She was, um, disappointed."

Liz crinkled her eyebrows. "Why?"

"I don't know!" Jim snapped. "She kept turning her nose up at everything. The red-and-white checkered tablecloths, the wine selection, even the bread! And..." Jim hesitated. "She was so rude! To everyone!" he blurted out finally.

Liz fought back a smile. That was not what she had expected him to say. "Why was she rude?" Liz asked, relaxing slightly.

Jim looked up, his eyes wide. "No idea. I worked at that restaurant all through high school as a busboy. They're the nicest people. The server was young and new, but she was learning, ya know? I overheard her crying in the kitchen when I went to the restroom." Jim shook his head.

Liz smiled gently, releasing her grip on her purse strap, suddenly aware of how tight she had been clenching it in her fist. "And what happened next?"

"I paid the check, left a big tip, and took Brittany back to her place."

"And that's it?" She was taken aback.

"That's it."

"What about the rest of the date, the movie, the walk?"

"No way."

"Wow," Liz commented. "Not many men would have canceled a date with a pretty girl midway through, no matter how badly she behaved."

"I wasn't going to subject the people at the Bijou to her too." The Bijou was an upscale movie theater on the north side of the city. "I thought dessert and a glass of wine while watching a movie might be fun." Jim shook his head. "It was hard enough to go back to the restaurant the next day to apologize for her bad behavior."

Liz's jaw dropped. "You went back to apologize? What else happened?"

"Nothing. That was the last time we spoke. Brittany was angry about being taken home early, I can tell you. So, to answer your earlier question. No, I don't think she was pretty at all."

"Wow, a man with standards. You're a rare breed, Jim Stephens!" Liz smiled kindly at his discomfort after relaying what sounded like an awful evening. "Do you know if she ever had a boyfriend after that?"

Jim nodded. "I think so, only from what I heard on the hotel grapevine. Rosie can tell you more, I'm sure. You should check with her."

"I will, thanks. I'm sure the police already asked you this, but what were you doing on the night of December seventh?"

Jim's discomfort returned in a flash. His hand stopped mid-movement as he reached for the back of his glowing neck for the umpteenth time. "Uh, watching a fight on pay-per-view at a sports bar. It was pretty crowded."

"Really?" Liz had developed a sense of the man opposite her and that didn't fit. She let it slide for now, even though everything about that statement made her think he was lying. "Who was fighting?"

Jim's face flushed. "Um, I don't remember."

"Really? Which sports bar were you at?" Liz asked, leading Jim through his suspiciously fabricated story.

He stammered, his gaze flitting to the windows. "It's... It's on the north side of town."

Liz studied the profile of his face, his jaw working from side to side. "You can't tell me which one?"

Jim's lips tightened into a straight line when he finally turned to face her, his gaze drifted to the table. "No. It was my day off. I stopped for a late lunch and decided to stay for the match." He forced his eyes to meet hers at last. "If I'd known I was going to need an alibi, I would have paid better attention to the details," he responded. Each syllable was clipped as it came out of his tight lips.

Liz decided to abandon that line of questioning. For now. He was so obviously lying about what he had been doing and would continue. "So, is there anything else you can tell me? Do you know how someone got the weights that were—you know?" She chose not to finish the question. The memory of finding Brittany at the bottom of the river, the weights tied to her waist flashed through her mind. A shiver ran down her spine.

Jim shook his head. "No. The police asked me that same question. Since guests and staff can access this area night and day using a keycard, they could have been taken at any time. It's not unusual. I've had to order replacement equipment before—yoga mats, free weights, that kind of thing, which reminds me. How did you get in here?"

Liz leaned forward. "I stole an access card." She winked conspiratorially. She could tell that he assumed she was joking based on his smile. "Did you tell the hotel manager, Mr. Moore, that they were missing? Or did you show him that they were gone? How does that work?" She watched Jim as his jaw softened, his gaze met hers directly, and his shoulders relaxed.

Jim shook his head. "Show him, no. He never comes down here. I would have gone to his office to get approval to order replacements. That's how we typically do it. He's never denied purchases like that, but he prefers to be consulted. The weights that were, um, used, are expensive. A couple of hundred dollars for the pair, at least."

Liz's eyes grew big, and her eyebrows shot up. "Wow! That much? That makes me glad I didn't get into weight lifting."

"Well, a light weights regimen is a good addition to any fitness routine," he advised. He returned to their discussion at hand. "Part of the cost is that each weight is stamped with the hotel's logo."

"So, there's no doubt that the weights came from this gym at this hotel." Liz indicated the rack of free weights with a jerk of her thumb.

"None whatsoever. The police showed them to me. The stamp was still visible." Jim gulped.

Liz nodded. Discussing murder made anyone uptight, but there he was offering her fitness tips mid-questioning. And yet he was lying about what he had been doing the night of the murder. Such a dichotomy. "Is it normally this quiet in here?" Glancing around the empty gym, Liz shook her head sadly. Such a shame his skill was not being truly appreciated.

Jim took in a deep breath before nodding. "Unfortunately. Other than an occasional special request from a guest, I spend the majority of my time in here, alone."

"Too bad. It sounds like you know your stuff when it comes to health and fitness."

He shrugged. "They say do what you love." His voice dropped as he gestured to the empty room with his muscular, toned arms. "Which is why this is so disappointing."

She stopped the recording on her phone and stood. "Well, that's all I've got for now. Thank you for your time, Jim." Liz extended her hand to him.

They shook hands briefly, interrupted by the door opening. The interruption meant Liz didn't have time to pick up any feelings from their fleeting contact.

"Anytime. And if you decide you want to add light weights to your fitness routine, just ask. I'll be happy to give you some tips." Jim excused himself, crossing the room to greet the hotel guest by name.

Liz didn't need her empathic abilities to know that her first suspect was far more relaxed now than when she first arrived. She just wished he wasn't lying about his alibi.

Chapter Fourteen

There was no sign of Mac when Liz came out of the fitness room, so she found her way down to the lobby when she spied someone else from the suspect wall in her office. Mr. William Moore, manager of the hotel. He was standing with perfect posture just inside the entryway to the busy dining room. He looked like a butler, standing in his black suit, hands clasped behind his back, his salt-and-pepper hair neatly combed. The flashiest thing about him was his red tie, which matched the color of the thread used to stitch the hotel's logo on all the uniforms.

"Excuse me, Mr. Moore?" Liz cleared her throat when she stopped next to him.

"Yes, can I help you?" He turned away from the busy dining room to face her.

"Yes, my name is Liz, uh, Elizabeth Pond. I'm a private investigator. I've been hired to look into the murder of Brittany Cabot." She kept her voice low so as not to draw attention.

Instead of answering, Mr. Moore turned on his heel and took several long strides away from the crowded dining room. He stopped in the second dining room, behind a sign stating that room would open at dinner time. He turned to face her—waiting.

Liz was caught off guard. At first, she had the strangest feeling that he was trying to flee. But then she realized that he simply wanted to speak away from the watchful eyes of both guests and employees. "Oh!" Liz hurried to join him.

His voice was low when he stated, in clipped words, "Please, Ms. Pond, keep your voice down! We do *not* want to alarm the guests, do we." It was not a question.

Suddenly, Liz felt like she was being chastised by her high school principal for talking in class. "Sorry, Mr. Moore. I didn't think—"

William Moore cut her off with a quick wave of his hand. "No, Ms. Pond, you did not. I understand there will be questions while the police determine the manner of Ms. Cabot's unfortunate demise. However..." He paused and looked down at her, his manner turned colder, if that was even possible. "Wait a minute. A private investigator?"

Liz nodded. She was used to this part. The surprise people expressed when they learned what she did for a living. This was the first time she'd ever felt like she'd done something wrong by her career choice though. She straightened up, reached into her purse, and retrieved her identification. She showed it to him. "Yes, sir."

He ignored the credentials she held up for his inspection. "You are *not* with the police then?"

"No, sir, I'm not, but—"

He cut her off again. "I am sorry, Ms. Pond, but the police have asked that I not speak with anyone about this matter. My employers have made the same request. Please excuse me." He brushed past her.

Liz scrambled to stop him. "I'm sure they did, sir, but the police, Detective Sowell, knows I'm here."

He turned to face her again. "Really?"

"Yes, you see, A. J.—sorry, Detective Sowell—and I have worked together before." The longer she spoke with the hotel manager, the more she felt like *she* had done something wrong. She'd never had a reaction like this to a suspect before. "Mr. Moore, I assure you, this is completely above board. You can call Detective Sowell if you'd like, but I only want to ask you a few questions."

"Oh, I will, believe me." His lips pressed into a straight line before, at last, he agreed with an almost imperceptible nod. "Am I a suspect now?" he asked sharply.

"No. Not yet anyway," Liz teased but stopped mid-laugh in response to his glare. She gulped. "Sorry." She pulled out her notepad and pen, instinctively feeling that he'd prefer this to a recording of their conversation. "Can you tell me anything about the night Bri- Ms. Cabot disappeared?"

Mr. Moore let his breath out in a slight huff. "Ms. Pond. I oversee well over one hundred staff members in this hotel. I do not see them regularly if they are doing their jobs correctly. If I go for a time without seeing a housekeeping staff member, I am not in the habit of assuming they are missing nor, heaven forbid, murdered!"

"That's a good point," Liz conceded, "but does anything stand out to you about that day? Or maybe from the last time you remember seeing her?"

Mr. Moore straightened his single-breasted blazer with a quick tug at the lapels and bottom hem before clasping his hands behind his back again. "When did she go missing again?" He looked past her and nodded curtly.

Liz looked over her shoulder and saw an employee leading a large family into the other dining room.

"December seventh," she replied, turning back to face him.

"I will have to check my calendar to know for sure, but I honestly cannot say. Oh..." The manager paused, his eyes widened.

"Yes?" Liz asked, her pen poised on her pad.

"I cannot be positive of the date, but there was that disgraceful scene in the kitchen." He looked up at the ceiling. "It was early December, of that I am certain."

Liz fought the urge to rush him. Guilty or innocent, people were often more willing to talk if you let them do exactly that. Talk. At their own speed and in their own way. She waited.

"Yes. Just horrible." Mr. Moore shook his head. "So improper!"

"What happened?" Liz asked, eager to know what happened to upset him still more than a month later.

"Ms. Cabot and her roommate, Ms. Travers. I did not even know they were roommates until that day."

Liz let a breath out slowly, mentally counting to ten. "Yes, they were roommates," she confirmed.

"They caused an awful scene in the kitchen. I am only grateful there were no guests nearby to witness it. I made a note of it in their employee files."

"What happened? Why were they arguing?" Liz tapped her pen on the notepad.

"I do not involve myself in the private lives of my employees, Ms. Pond." He looked down his nose at her, literally and figuratively, disdain dripped from every word. "All I do know is how it ended. In the most vulgar language, Ms. Travers told Ms. Cabot to move out."

"Really?" Liz asked, surprised. That was an intriguing detail to be omitted by her client. What else had Rosemary not told her?

"Yes. Is there anything else?" The hotel manager looked past Liz.

"No, well, yes. I'm sure you know that Jim Stephens was brought in for questioning."

Mr. Moore interrupted her again, waving her words aside. "Absolutely not. He is a good employee, extremely reliable, but smart enough to pull off a murder?" He answered his own question with a shake of his head.

Is there anyone this man doesn't look down on? Liz wondered. "Well, the weights used to—"

The manager raised a hand to stop her. "Please. I will not discuss the matter further." He closed his eyes. "This is not appropriate conversation."

A little taken aback, Liz decided to save further questions for another time. "Okay. Well, thank you. Here's my card. If you think of anything, please don't hesitate to call. If you wouldn't mind confirming the date of that argument for me, I'd appreciate it." Liz smiled up at the stern man. "You'll probably see me around the hotel."

He gave her a sharp look. "You will *not* be harassing the guests."

Liz smiled. "I can't promise that, but I'll do my best to stay out of the way."

"Fine." He accepted her business card between two fingers, holding it as though he'd just picked up a stranger's dirty tissue. He dropped it into his jacket pocket before resuming his extremely erect posture.

Liz held out her hand. "Thank you for your time."

"You are welcome. Please, if you will excuse me." He breezed past her, ignoring her proffered hand. He returned to his earlier position, overseeing the busy dining room.

So much for checking to see if her empathy would pick up anything from that suspect. Liz slipped away from the dining room without another word.

Liz heard her name above the din when she entered the busy lobby. She looked around and saw Mac wading through a crowd of people.

"Hey, Mac. Thanks for the help!" Liz called out.

"I want my keycard," he yelled over the heads of the people around him.

People from all walks of life looked back and forth between the two individuals. Whispers floated around the lobby.

"Sure." She waved, keeping people between them. "I'll get it back to you. Thanks!" Liz mixed into a crowd of tourists as they moved outside en masse.

"Liz!" Mac called out to her again, his frustration followed her as he glared at her, trapped behind a train of baggage carts that rolled in front of him.

"Wow, he sounds upset!" Liz commented to the elderly lady next to her, her eyes twinkling.

"Keep 'em on their toes, honey." The small woman giggled, straightening her violet-purple knitted hat before patting Liz on the arm.

"Oh, we're not—" Liz replied, shaking her head. *Why do people keep thinking we are together?*

"Sure." The lady nodded knowingly. "That's what I used to say about hubby number three. God rest his soul."

"You vixen!" Liz grinned at her, offering the woman her arm as they stepped off the curb. An extra-large, colorful tour bus waited a few feet away. The engine rumbled loudly, and a waft of diesel exhaust fumes drifted toward them.

While they walked arm-in-arm, Liz felt the weight form in her chest. Love, sadness, anticipation. This was the most powerful empathic experience she'd had yet!

"Love, honey, it keeps you young! Do you need me to smuggle you onto the bus?" The lady's eyes sparkled mischievously.

Liz was tempted because she was curious to see what the lady would do to make it happen, but instead, she patted the kind woman on the arm. "I'm good, but thanks. Have fun today, okay?"

"I always do, honey. I always do." She winked at Liz, a small chuckle escaping her bright red lips.

Liz hugged the sweet older woman impulsively before helping her climb into the high bus. The woman gave her hand a quick squeeze before letting go.

Liz jogged down the busy sidewalks, and she was back at her building in no time, jumping victoriously on the Texas star in the concrete. Endorphins coursed through her body due to the run, teasing Mac, and that wonderful little old lady. *I hope I'm nearly that much fun when I'm her age.*

Chapter Fifteen

"Welcome to... Oh, hi, Liz!" Claire corrected herself when Liz walked into the office.

Liz dramatically plastered her back against the door, a big grin on her face. She slid to one side and peeked out the side window.

"What's going on?" Claire leaned conspiratorially across the desk. "Are you being followed?"

Liz straightened up and laughed out loud. "Nah, I'm just messing with you. But, then again..." She grimaced and turned back to the window to look, expecting to see Mac stomping up the stairs. "Maybe. Probably not." She giggled and pulled the hotel keycard out of her back pocket. "Can you put this in lost and found, please?" She handed the card to Claire.

"Sure. Um, we don't exactly have a lost and found, so..." Claire looked around before opening the top drawer of her desk and dropping it in unceremoniously. "Who does it belong to?"

Shrugging out of her coat, she dropped it in a heap on the chair. Liz collapsed to the couch, kicking her shoes off under the table. "Mac." She grinned. "He may come looking for me, and he'll probably be angry."

"Hemingway? Why?"

"Hemingway? Oh, you mean Mac." Liz shook her head at her friend's nicknames. "He got a room at the hotel, can you believe it?"

"No, how dare he?" Claire placed one hand on her chest, and the other arm draped dramatically across her forehead. "The nerve." And then it hit her. "Wait." She straightened up. "What hotel? Not..." Her eyes opened wide, and she jerked a thumb at the whiteboard.

Liz smiled at her friend's antics and stretched out on the soft, brown couch, dropping her head on the colorful *Buzz Off* pillow. "I'm pretty sure he thought it would give him better insight into the story he's trying to write."

"So, why did he give you a keycard?" Claire's eyes grew big. "Oh. Are you and he?" Claire wiggled her eyebrows suggestively.

Liz shook her head and laughed some more. "No. Not at all. Why is everyone saying that lately?" Her arms dropped out to the sides, and her right hand hit the table's edge. Muffling a curse, Liz sat up, cradling her hand. "I picked his pocket!" she announced proudly.

Claire looked impressed, sitting back in her chair. "Really?"

"Yes. I wish you could have been there. The look on Mac's face! Priceless!" Liz giggled some more before standing. "So, he *may* be slightly upset with me when he comes to get that card."

"That's okay." Claire waved Liz's concerns aside. "I'll handle him. So, how did it go with Schwarzenegger?" Claire asked, straightening her tidy desk.

Liz crinkled her eyebrows and tilted her head. "Huh? Oh, you mean Jim Stephens. You and your nicknames!" Liz walked over to sit on the edge of Claire's desk, studying the whiteboard. "He's lying about what he was doing the night Brittany was murdered, so he's not off the hook yet. It's strange. He was being honest up to that point, I'm positive." Liz stared at Jim's picture thoughtfully. "I wonder what he was doing?"

"Do you think he did it?" Claire asked, rolling her chair around the desk to join Liz in front of the whiteboard.

Liz rocked her open hand back and forth in the air while pinching her lips to one side of her face. "Maybe. Maybe not. I don't know. He had access to her at the hotel, and the weights used to weigh her down."

Claire shuddered.

Liz continued, "He didn't like her. That much is clear. But I don't *think* he'd murder someone just for being rude!"

"I should hope not!" Claire exclaimed. "If rudeness becomes a motive for murder, we'd *all* be killed! Can you imagine?"

"I just wish I knew why he was lying about what he was doing on the night of the murder, but telling the truth about everything else." Liz pushed away from Claire's desk. "Well, we're not going to figure that out right now. So, how were things here this morning?"

"Good. I reviewed everyone's social media accounts. When I finished with the suspects, I went further back on Brittany's account. Last summer, she was still obsessed with fashion, but there was a definite line where it changed from reasonably priced items to high-end couture. The change happened around the same time as the shift in her attitude toward her boss. But, I can't see any explanation for the sudden change." Claire flipped through her notes after rolling her chair back to her desk. She skimmed her finger down the page. "The hotel manager has no social media presence, no big surprise there. Jim Stephens has accounts but very rarely posts anything."

Liz brightened up. "Anything for the night of Brittany's murder?"

Claire pressed her bright red lips together. "No, in fact, he hasn't posted anything since early last summer! Which is odd in its own right." Claire flipped the page, "Rosemary seems to have a boyfriend, but I don't know his name and I don't see any pictures. Just occasional references to dates they've gone on. Never mentions his name."

"Sounds like we have even more questions for Rosemary." Liz bit her lip. "Well, we've probably done all we can using social media."

Claire shook her head sadly. "I think so too. From what I can tell, when Brittany wasn't obsessing over things she wanted to buy, she was something of a troll online."

Liz crossed the room. "Yikes."

"So, what's next?" Claire asked, pen poised.

Liz dropped onto the couch, crossing her ankles on the table. "Well, I want to meet with Rosemary Travers next. I want it to be at her apartment, and I want *you* to be there!" Liz pointed at Claire.

"Me? Why me?" Claire asked, dropping her pen. She shuffled papers, tidying away office supplies.

Liz grinned at her nervous habit. "There is no way I'll be able to tell if she managed to buy any of the things she posted about. Like the items you researched and probably bought yesterday."

Claire blushed, reached into the big drawer in her desk and plopped a new purse on the surface. "Isn't it gorgeous?"

Liz bit back the urge to say, *It's a purse.* Instead, she grinned at her friend's enthusiasm. "Um, yeah, I guess?"

"I guess?" Claire exclaimed. She waved Liz over to her desk. "Check out this hand-stitching. The gold hardware.

I spent an obscene amount of mad money on this last night!"

"How obscene? And what is 'mad money'?"

Claire gave a dollar amount and Liz whistled. "Mad money is money set aside for fun stuff or beautiful pieces of art like this right here!" She caressed the hardware, and dragged a finger along the neat lines of stitches.

"I wish I had some mad money." Liz grinned at her wealthy coworker. She straightened up. "So if Brittany could buy this bag or any of the other items she's been obsessing over, why did she and Rosemary fight over money?"

"Really? That isn't on the forms Rosemary filled out." Claire grabbed the clipboard from the corner of her desk.

Liz agreed. "It isn't. Neither is the fact that she and Brittany had a big fight at work during which she kicked Brittany out of their apartment!"

Claire's eyes grew large. "Oh. That doesn't look good."

"No, it doesn't. But..." Liz paused, staring at the purse. "She had the same access to the gym equipment. Why would she hire me to find out what happened if she was the one who killed Brittany?"

Claire shrugged. "Guilt, maybe? A desire to be caught so she can confess?"

"Maybe." Liz drifted off, lost in thought. "I'm going to call Rosemary. I want to set up a visit for tomorrow."

Liz slipped around the dividing wall and called her client from her desk phone.

Music from what sounded like a mariachi band could be heard in the background when Rosemary answered the phone. "Hello?"

"Hi, Rosemary! It's Liz." Liz smiled, it's hard to go out in San Antonio and *not* encounter a mariachi band.

"Oh, hi, Liz. How's the case coming?"

"We're making some headway. That's what I'm calling you about. I want to speak with you at your apartment. Do you still have Brittany's belongings?"

"Yes, it's all still in her room. I'm going to ask her family what they want to do with it," Rosemary replied, the background music lessening.

"Please wait on that call. I want to bring my resident expert over to take a look first, if that's okay with you?" Liz asked, crossing her fingers. Claire's face popped around the edge of the wall, and she pointed a finger at herself and mouthed, "Me? Expert? Wow!" She looked thrilled with her new title.

"Sure, I guess. What expert?" Rosemary asked. "When do you want to come over? I'm, um, busy at the moment."

"My coworker knows all about high couture, way more than me so I want to bring her to look at Brittany's belongings. How about tomorrow?"

"That works. I'm off all day, so I'll be home. In the morning?"

Liz accepted. "Perfect." They decided on a time and hung up. "Nine in the morning," Liz announced, then groaned. "That means I don't get to sleep in tomorrow."

Claire waved her concerns aside. "I'm more curious whether a raise goes along with my new title!" Her eyes sparkled with suppressed mirth.

"What difference does it make? You don't let me pay you anyway!" Liz stood up and stretched. "Since I'm on call for my locksmithing job tonight, and I'm starting earlier than usual tomorrow, I'm going to call it for today. Can you handle the office?"

"Pshaw!" Claire responded, grinning, waving the question aside. "It practically runs itself. Go. I'm fine. I'll do more research on the items from Brittany's wish list, so I have a solid idea of what I'm looking for."

"Perfect."

Chapter Sixteen

Liz collected her things and bid her coworker good night. She opened the hidden door by Claire's desk and entered her yoga studio. Closing it quietly behind her, Liz began the conscious effort to leave her work at the door.

She passed through her long apartment, the lines from the golden hickory-colored wood-laminate flooring she had installed throughout made the space appear even longer. As she walked, she focused on changing her mindset from murder to house chores and locksmith duties.

Twice a week, Liz worked as an on call technician for a local locksmith company to bring in some extra money. It was the same locksmith she worked for while attending college. She'd kept up the relationship to maintain her locksmith license and improve her skill set. It was important for her to maintain that license because she planned to add safe work to her resumé. Safe opening and changing lock combinations would prove helpful in her private investigator duties, if she continued doing it, and expand her locksmith work. The course she wanted to take required that students maintain a certain number of hours working with a certified locksmith company—their way of keeping out any potential students wishing to learn the skill for nefarious purposes.

Liz gathered dirty clothes from her bedroom and bathroom floors. She bumped her head on the bed, reaching for dirty socks that had somehow managed to crawl underneath. Swallowing a curse, Liz threw the offending socks into the white plastic laundry basket while rubbing the back of her head. Lugging the basket downstairs, she started a load in the small laundry room next to her kitchen, usually separated from the rest of the room by large, white, folding doors. Grabbing the basket of cleaning supplies from the shelf above the dryer, she headed to her yoga studio.

Pausing at the entertainment unit in the living room, Liz started her favorite music using a digital streaming service. Before long, eighties music flowed out of the in-wall speakers spread throughout her apartment. It was impossible not to be motivated when listening to music from that period.

Singing along, she walked to the next room. She set the basket down and returned to the laundry room for her vacuum and floor steamer.

Her tidy home fitness studio only ever needed a quick dusting, so she usually started there. She slid the faux palms from around her meditation corner, giving them a quick dusting as she did so. With an apartment with little access to natural light, and Liz's deadly touch when it came to gardening, plastic plants were the only way to go. Luckily, these days, they looked nearly like the real thing. Next, she took the time to scrape the remnants of wax from the tabletop with her fingernail. After this morning's episode, she didn't need any more candle-related triggers. The square room, with its marbled green walls, bare laminate-wood floors, and high ceiling usually was one of her favorite rooms. When she moved her low meditation chair to vacuum under it, Liz realized she missed meditating. What had been a peaceful, relaxing time had become a struggle and sometimes, like that morning, unsettling.

Not long after Liz and her parents recognized her gifts when she was a child of nine, her mother started researching ways to help her young daughter deal with them. The most popular method was meditation, something Audrey Pond knew all about, thanks to her yoga practice.

Audrey began teaching her daughter how to meditate, which was initially a struggle. Liz was only nine, after all. They stuck with it, and before long, Liz went from fighting her mom when it was meditation time to relishing it. Meditation went even better when Susan and Pam Whitlow joined them. Pam took to meditation quickly, even faster than Liz. Eventually, with Pam's help, Liz got better at it. Before long, Liz came to value those meditation periods with her mother and their friends.

As an adult, it was a favorite part of her daily activities that she hoped to regain someday. *Maybe I should attend some of Mom's classes and get a refresher like Pam suggested*, Liz thought as she steamed the floor, backing her way through the open divider wall, dragging her supplies along with her as she worked.

Liz turned her attention to the living room. By Liz's standards, it was mostly tidy. Except for the shoes under the table, the magazine under a pillow on the couch, and a stray coffee mug on the floor next to the dual stand that supported a speedbag on one side, a heavy bag on the other.

How did the remote end up between two books? Liz wondered as she dusted the pair of tall, double-wide, oak bookshelves that ran along the wall between the yoga studio and the stairs leading to the loft.

When Liz finished cleaning her living room, an alarm sounded on her phone. Five o'clock. Time to check in for her locksmithing shift.

Pausing the music, she grabbed her cell phone and called the shift supervisor. Liz was one of several on call locksmiths to answer emergency calls at night. That allowed the locally owned company to offer an around-the-clock emergency service and compete with the bigger chains. It also worked perfectly with Liz's PI schedule. Liz took two shifts a week, on Tuesday and Saturday nights. She earned a small hourly wage and a bonus for each call she took overnight—it helped her maintain her independent lifestyle.

Liz grabbed her locksmith tool bag and set it on the clean, dry floor next to the bookshelves so it was readily available if she got a call.

***

After starting the dishwasher, a ringing doorbell grabbed Liz's attention as she removed warm, fresh-smelling clothes from the dryer.

"Who can that be?" She dropped the armload of clean laundry into the empty basket on the floor. Liz fairly sprinted through her clean apartment.

"Surprise!" Pam and Claire yelled when Liz opened the door.

She jumped, her hand on her chest. "What are you doing here?" Liz's friends pushed past her.

"Wow! What a warm greeting!" Pam teased, carrying a large brown paper bag in her arms. Claire held an equally large bag.

The scent of fried food and spices reached Liz's nose. She closed the door and followed her friends willingly, despite her protests. "I'm sorry. You know what I mean. I'm on call tonight, remember? That smells delicious! What is it?" Her stomach growled.

"Didn't I say food would get us through the door?" Pam commented to Claire as they entered the kitchen. They ignored Liz's protests and set the two bags on Liz's clean oak kitchen table.

Liz recognized the logo of the bar next door emblazoned on the brown paper bags. Her mouth began to water.

"Just because you're on call doesn't mean we can't have—girls' night!" Pam and Claire yelled the last two words in unison as Claire pulled a large bottle of non-alcoholic margarita mix from a third smaller bag Liz hadn't noticed. The ladies laughed together.

"Well, I am getting a little hungry," Liz admitted, peeking into the paper bags. "What did you bring?" Now that she was closer, she could identify the smell of melted cheese and jalapeños.

"Appetizers! Grab plates!" Claire announced, unloading the first bag onto the table.

"Yum!" Liz retrieved plain white dinner plates from the cupboard for everyone. She returned to the table, spreading the dishware out among the boxes of aromatic food.

Pam grabbed three margarita glasses from another cupboard and prepared the oversized drinks. "Even though this is non-alcoholic doesn't mean it can't look like the real thing!" Pam dug through Liz's fridge. "Do you have lemons hiding among all these takeout bags and boxes? Ooh, Audrey's breakfast burritos." Pam's voice echoed from within the confines of the fridge. "I usually throw half in the freezer. She always makes too many. But so delicious! Eureka!" Pam straightened up, holding a single lemon in her hand. "Girl, you have got to go through that fridge!" She teased Liz, waving a hand in front of her wrinkled nose.

She returned to the counter, grabbing a paring knife from a drawer without looking as she passed.

"That's what I was about to do before you two barged in," Liz jibed back, popping a small steaming onion ring into her mouth. Her eyes drifted closed as she bit into the crunchy fried breading and the taste of sweet onion reached her taste buds. "I forgive you, though," she mumbled. "Mmmmm!"

Her words were lost with the racket of the ice maker in the fridge door crushing ice as it fell into the pitcher in Pam's hands.

The ladies thought of everything. Small packages of dips of various types and flavors were lined up in the center of the table, bordered by overflowing boxes of steaming appetizers: jalapeño poppers, onion rings, cheesy fries, mozzarella sticks, and overstuffed potato skins.

"Okay, come and get it!" Claire called out, turning away from the spread on the long kitchen table.

Liz folded the empty paper bags and tucked them onto a shelf above the dryer. She moved the laundry basket from the floor to sit on top of the washing machine. She closed the white doors behind her.

Quilted purple placemats under the white plates added a splash of color to the spread on the long kitchen table.

Pam grinned from behind three margaritas on the counter. Light green liquid, filled with crushed ice, rimmed with salt, and a small umbrella added the finishing touch. "Pam's Bar is open for business, y'all!" she said brightly.

Liz and Claire giggled and walked to the kitchen counter, only a few steps away from the table. The kitchen was an open design, opened on both ends, bordered by a row of golden hued maple-stained cupboards along the wall above a counter incorporating the sink and range. The stainless-steel fridge stood at the far end of the space. A long double-height counter separated the kitchen from the rest of the open area next to the table. Tall light oak barstools allowed people to sit comfortably and visit while anyone prepared food. Small hanging lights dangled from the ceiling above the counter. Liz might not know how to cook, but she made sure she had plenty of space for her friends and family to come over for a meal. Of course, if she was cooking, that meant ordering takeout.

"Cheers!" The three friends clinked their glasses together over the tan laminate-covered countertop.

"Huh, not too bad," Claire commented after a quick sip before leading the way to the table.

Liz set her cell phone next to her plate. "Thank you, ladies. I've been needing this." Liz smiled at her friends across the table.

"We know," Claire responded, winking at Pam.

Liz reached for the potato skins, her personal favorite. She jumped up from the table and dug a container of sour cream out of the cluttered fridge, checking the date to make sure it was still good. "It feels good to be working again," Liz said, stopping to grab a spoon from a drawer as she returned to the table.

"How's the case going?" Pam asked before taking a bite out of a ranch dressing-covered jalapeño popper, sighing happily at the indulgence.

"Good. I think anyway." Claire looked to Liz for agreement as she resumed her seat.

Liz agreed. "I always think it's a good sign when we're on the same page as the police. At least to start with anyway." She winked at Claire.

"Especially when that page includes A. J. Sowell!" Pam raised her eyes, hands together in prayer, and mouthed thank you to the heavens. She giggled at Liz's blush.

Claire's tinkling laugh filled the room. "I know!" She and Pam high-fived. Claire leaned toward Pam. "Did you know he was here last night?"

"No!" Pam exclaimed, her eyes wide.

"Yes!" Claire responded in kind.

Liz rolled her eyes despite her blush. "It wasn't anything like that. We just shared a beer and talked about the case. He was worried about me. It was nice," she finished, taking a bite of a potato skin covered with melted cheese, green onion, and bacon, slathered with rich sour cream.

"Shared a beer?" Pam pretended to swoon against Claire's shoulder before straightening up, giggling at her antics.

"He was worried about you?" Claire asked.

The two ladies clasped their hands under their chins, "Awww!"

Liz couldn't stop her face from flushing. "He is cute," she finally admitted.

"So," Claire prodded, "Since Detective Hottie was here Monday night—"

"Evening. For less than an hour, outside—" Liz pointed a mozzarella stick at Claire. "You!"

Claire's eyes twinkled. "Yeah, yeah. Detective Hottie was here Monday night and Hemingway has been calling every day this week. Not to mention you returning to the office carrying *his* hotel key card. Liz, are you courting two suitors?"

"Hemingway?" Pam asked, looking between Liz and Claire, her ponytail swinging wildly. "And hotel? You were in a hotel with someone named Hemingway?" Her eyes opened wider on her narrow face.

"Claire, this is how rumors get started! Mac Murphy is the reporter who walked us home Sunday night. Claire has decided to call him Hemingway," Liz explained, throwing a balled-up napkin at Claire, bouncing it neatly off her wavy red hair. "You and your nicknames!"

"Ooh, he's cute!" Pam sipped her drink. "Why's he calling? And why were you in his hotel room?"

"He wants to interview me about Sunday night—" Liz groaned as she reached for another onion ring, "—and I wasn't in his hotel room!"

"Liz stole his hotel room key!" Claire chimed in helpfully.

Pam sat up, ignoring Liz's lame response for Claire's *much* more interesting one. "She what? What hotel?" Pam's eyes were the size of saucers. "Wait? *The* hotel where that poor woman worked? Okay, why were you in a hotel with, what did you call him?" She pointed a cheese stick at Claire. "Hemingway?" Pam took a small bite out of the appetizer in her hand, a cloud of steam drifted out of the end.

Liz took a big bite out of a hot mozzarella stick to avoid responding. "Ow, ow...!" Muffled swears escaped her as she took a drink to cool her burning mouth.

"Wow, *that* was graceful!" Pam and Claire laughed loudly at their friend's discomfort while she struggled to regain her composure.

A deep sigh escaped Liz as her mouth cooled. She chewed the cooler, now lime-flavored cheese stick. "Why do I always forget how hot those things get? Ouch!" She swallowed.

Undeterred, Pam moved the cheese sticks out of Liz's reach. "So, why was Detective Hottie..." Pam looked to Claire for confirmation on the nickname.

Claire nodded.

Pam continued. "Why was he here Monday night? Really?"

Liz's mouth was still tender after the cheese stick debacle, so she continued to sip her drink. She could feel her cheeks begin to warm in response to the question. Setting down her glass, she shrugged. "He was just letting me know that he is the lead on the case."

"Really? Couldn't he call or text that tidbit of information?" Pam turned to Claire as they acted out a mock conversation that was almost robot-like. "Hi, Ms. Pond. I'm the lead on the Cabot case."

"Thank you, Detective Hottie. I am also on the case," Claire responded, giggling.

Liz threw more wadded-up napkins at each of her friends as they leaned against each other, laughing.

"Now, how about Hemingway?" Pam asked.

Liz waved the question aside. "Again, he wants to interview me for his article. And now he's upset because I stole his keycard to access the hotel gym." She pointed at each friend in turn. "Only so I could interview Jim Stephens without Mac listening to every word." She reached for the mozzarella sticks again, tearing one in half to allow the trapped steam to escape before taking a tentative bite.

Pam stuck out her bottom lip. "I was there on Sunday night too. *I'm* not getting phone calls for interviews or late-night visits over beer from anyone."

Liz pointed at her friend with her straw as she finished her drink. "That's because *you* didn't see anything on Sunday. Be grateful you didn't." A shiver ran through her body as she fought off the memory.

"Good point. Thank you for that." Pam reached for another cheesy jalapeño popper.

"Trust me, I'd rather I wasn't getting calls from reporters."

"Interesting." Pam sat back in her chair, her arms and legs crossed. "Very interesting." She studied her friend's face.

"What's interesting?" Claire asked, looking back and forth between the pair of lifelong friends.

Pam indicated to Liz with a jerk of her chin. "She said she wished she wasn't getting calls from reporters. Nothing about visits from a certain police detective."

Claire's brow crinkled.

"Pay attention. Liz, Claire told me that Mac Murphy called this afternoon."

"Again?" Liz rolled her eyes, reaching for an onion ring while the cheese stick on her plate cooled.

"A. J. Sowell also called after you left," Claire added.

"Really?" Liz felt the warmth creep up her neck.

"There it is!" Again, Pam and Claire high-fived, hands meeting high over their heads.

"There what is?" Liz looked back and forth between her two friends, wrinkling her eyebrows.

"Confirmation," Pam stated, uncrossing her legs and reaching for her drink.

"Confirmation of what?" Liz asked.

"You like A. J. Sowell!" Claire announced, her eyes sparkling.

"What? No? Really?" Liz responded weakly, setting down her drink as the flush continued up her face.

"Really," Pam answered. She looked at Claire. "Ever since we were kids, this one could never control blushing over someone she likes. Not since Kevin Garcia!" She said and looked pointedly at Liz.

Liz giggled at the name of her first crush. "We were ten years old!"

Pam grinned as she turned back to Claire. "She can see the future, the past, and sense emotions." She held up a finger, looking pointedly at Liz. "Normally!" she added. "But she can never tell when she likes a guy. I bet A. J. likes her too."

Claire nodded emphatically. "I think so too. Did you see any of the videos from the crime scene?"

"What? Oh, come on, I was there. What did I miss?" Exasperation radiated from Pam.

Claire patted Pam's hand. "I watched some of the videos people put online while I was researching our victim and suspects today." She sighed dramatically. "A. J. was *so* sweet with her. And when he caressed her cheek!" Claire swooned.

Pam's eyes grew big. "Really? How did I not see that? I've got to see this for myself!"

"Oh, come on!" Liz protested again. "He was just being nice. I had a weak moment, and he was taking care of me!" She stopped protesting when she saw that her friends had stopped listening to her.

The pair walked away from the table. Pam turned on the TV, while Claire searched for the video on her phone. She cast it to the television so they could all watch it.

Reluctantly, Liz joined them, munching on a greasy French fry, covered in melted cheese and crunchy bacon bits.

The muffled din of voices on the amateur video silenced the trio. Pam muted the television to focus on Liz and A. J. in the background.

The ladies watched Liz slowly descend to the ground, A. J. reaching for her arms to catch her. He lowered her gently, crouching in front of her, keeping his hands on her arms. The camera moved up to the bridge and they saw Pam next to a tall black officer. The ladies watched as A. J. looked up and stood. The pair dropped a heavy blanket into A. J.'s waiting hands.

"That's Officer Sanders." Liz gestured to the screen.

"He was so sweet when he swooped in to help me get the blanket," Pam commented. "Officer Hottie and Detective Hottie on the same screen." Pam sighed.

"Shhh!" Claire pulled Liz's arm, so she fell onto the couch next to them.

The trio watched as A. J. settled the blanket around her shoulders. He rubbed one shoulder and took her hand gently. The amateur videographer was at the right angle as the video zoomed in so they could see his thumb rub gently over the back of her hand. His head never once turned from her face. They could even see the set of his jaw. For a brief moment, his hand left her shoulder as he caressed her cheek, before tucking a strand of hair behind Liz's ear.

Even to Liz, the scene was sweet, almost romantic.

Liz watched A. J. watch her. Liz glanced at her own pale face as she blinked slowly. That's when A. J. released his gentle hold on her hand and started rubbing both shoulders, adjusting the thick blanket. They spoke for a moment, but she didn't remember what about. Then she watched as he placed a firm hand under each elbow and helped her to her feet, standing close. He didn't let her go.

A. J.'s solitary focus was touching. "Wow!" Liz whispered. She lifted her hands to hide her hot cheeks.

"Wow, is right!" Pam sat back. "You're right, Claire. Detective Hottie definitely likes our Liz."

Claire agreed.

Liz snapped out of her daze. "Oh, come on. Stop it! You two will make me a bumbling mess the next time I speak with him!" Her eyes flitted back to the screen where the video was still playing. "Wait, did you see that? Rewind it."

Liz studied the screen as the video played in reverse. "There, stop."

On the screen, the video panned across the crowd. The person who filmed it had been standing on the far side of the river, so they were able to get a close up shot of Rosemary Travers walking quickly away hand-in-hand with the young man they know only as Frank.

"Isn't that Frank?" Claire asked.

Liz nodded. "Brittany Cabot's ex-boyfriend. Another tiny detail Rosemary had failed to mention."

"Oh, that doesn't look good, does it?" Pam piped up.

"No, Pam, it really doesn't." Liz agreed.

Chapter Seventeen

Liz woke early the following day, more refreshed than she'd felt in weeks. Her mind was calm. She hadn't dreamed, but neither had she experienced any nightmares.

A big stretch and yawn took over, and Liz felt the smooth lavender satin sheets slide over her bare legs. Her pajama bottoms legs were bunched uncomfortably around her thighs. Kicking off the bedding to free her feet, it fell off the bottom of the bed in a big clump.

Liz swung her legs reluctantly over the side, allowing the momentum to pull her into a seated position. The moment her feet touched the thick purple rug next to her bed, habit and routine took over. Bathroom, dress, brush hair. She became more alert as she cleared away the remnants of girls' night, while one of her mother's breakfast burritos heated in the microwave.

She made a single cup of coffee using the multi-purpose coffee maker in her kitchen. Before long, Liz was carrying her breakfast into the living room. She set her ceramic mug bearing the Texas star logo on the coffee table, making sure to use one of her mother's coasters—crocheted, of course. Liz propped her feet up and took a big bite out of her burrito. Her eyes drifted closed as she savored the combination of fluffy scrambled egg, crispy bacon, and melted cheese, all wrapped in a soft burrito shell. Delicious.

She turned on the television for noise as she reached for the phone to call the locksmith company.

"Morning, Camila!" she said cheerily into the phone.

"Morning, Liz." The older woman's voice was gruff. "I'm still waking up, so please take it easy on me."

Liz smiled. That was how they began every early morning phone call.

"Sure. I'll make it easy for you. No calls last night. You know what that means, don't you?" Liz took another smaller bite of her breakfast.

A low laugh floated through the phone. "Saturday night is going to be insanely busy. Sorry."

Liz giggled. Such was the life of an on call locksmith. They spoke for a few minutes before Liz bid Camila goodbye.

She finished her breakfast and headed upstairs to prepare for the day ahead. Her thoughts drifted to the upcoming visit to the apartment of the victim and her client. Rosemary had a few questions to answer. Secretly, Liz liked the young woman. She earnestly hoped the guilt she felt emanating from her had nothing to do with the murder of her roommate.

Before long, Liz was padding through her apartment, shoes in hand, jacket over one arm, purse strap across her torso. She took a deep breath to ready herself for the transition from home to work. Liz swung open the door that was the final partition between work and home and stepped into her office. She smiled at Claire and then froze.

Mac Murphy, sporting a pair of dark sunglasses, sat in the waiting area across the room.

"Oh crap!" The heavy door swung shut behind her, locking automatically as it did so, cutting off any possibility of a quick escape.

Mac peeled his lanky form off the couch. "You!" He pointed an accusatory finger at her.

Did he get taller since yesterday? Liz thought, dropping her shoes and jacket by the door and raising her hands as she sidestepped toward Claire's desk. "Mac. Good to see you. Claire?" Liz dropped one hand on her friend's shoulder as she stepped behind her chair. "Can you give Mac back his key card? Please?"

"Certainly." Claire opened her desk drawer to retrieve the card before sliding it across the desk.

"You picked my pocket!" Mac said, his voice rising with each word, grabbing the card and shoving it into his back pocket.

"I did. I really did. I'm sorry. I just didn't want you listening in on my interview. You have it back now," Liz said weakly. Liz stayed behind Claire, knowing her friend was safe from the irate reporter's wrath.

"I had to flirt with Laurie at the front desk to get a new card!" Mac braced his large hands on Claire's highly polished desk. His knuckles popped loudly as the fingers spread.

"I'm sure she enjoyed that," Liz teased lightly.

"Wow, you smell good!" Claire piped up from her spot between the two combatants. "Is that cedar?"

Liz squeezed her shoulders lightly.

"Sorry," Claire mumbled, sliding down in her chair.

Mac threw a quick, lopsided grin at Claire before returning his focus to Liz. All signs of mirth disappeared from his face. "She wouldn't give it to me until I agreed to take her out for dinner last night." His voice rose again.

"Hey, so now you're a happy couple." She raised her fists in the air. "Yay!" she cheered weakly. Liz stepped past Claire as Mac circled the desk, sliding Claire in her chair out of the way so he could pass.

"You'd think so, wouldn't you?" Mac asked, sarcasm dripping from every word. "Do you know what her interest is? That's interest, singular." He held up his index finger to demonstrate.

"We're in suspense. Aren't we, Claire?"

"You're on your own, stranger," Claire responded, muffling a laugh.

"Reality shows. All. Of. Them!" Mac continued stalking Liz.

A giggle escaped the assistant.

Liz backed away from the irritated reporter, bumping into the edge of the small counter holding the coffee maker. "Ouch!" She rubbed her hip. "So, she's, uh, studying the human condition. That's, um, interesting." Liz backed away from Mac now that he had entirely circled the desk. She bumped her leg into the coffee table. "Dammit. The office is trying to kill me today." She raised her hands. "Look, Mac, I'm sorry you had a crappy night."

Mac stopped in front of her and removed his dark sunglasses.

She hesitated when the overhead light illuminated his face. "Uh, what's wrong with your eye?" Liz gulped.

Mac gingerly touched the dark purple bruise that was swelling the skin around his left eye, wincing as he did so. "Ouch! This? Guess who has a boyfriend? Come on, guess!"

"Laurie?" Liz responded meekly.

A muffled giggle escaped Claire now that she wasn't physically in the middle of the argument.

"*Bingo*! She tells me all about the family of her favorite reality show star but not a peep about her boyfriend! Her huge, college football offensive tackle, boyfriend!"

Claire's laughter got louder. "Oh my God!" She grabbed a tissue and dabbed at her eyes as the tears began to flow.

Mac threw a glare at Claire over his shoulder.

Which only made her laugh harder.

"Everything okay in here?" A. J.'s calm but firm voice came from the open doorway behind Liz.

Liz jumped at the interruption. She hadn't heard the door open. "A. J.! Thank God! So glad you're here." She pulled him into the office, swung the door closed, and hid behind him. She placed a hand on each shoulder, keeping him as a shield, gripping the soft leather of his jacket in her hands to hold him in place.

A. J. nodded to Mac. "Murphy." He held out his hand. "Nice shiner."

Mac accepted his hand in a firm handshake. "Sowell. Thanks."

"She give you that?" A. J. asked, gesturing to Liz with a jerk of his thumb.

"In a way. Can I press charges?" Mac glared at Liz over A.J.'s shoulder.

"Hey, now!" Liz protested from her position behind A. J., straightening up.

"I don't know. Maybe. I think I need to hear more details." A. J. slipped out of Liz's grasp and moved to greet Claire. "Ms. Henderson. How are you this fine morning?"

Claire smiled brightly through her tears of laughter. "Just fine, Detective. You going to do anything to stop this?" She waved a hand at the pair as Mac backed Liz toward the closed front door.

A. J. shrugged. "From what I heard coming up the stairs, a little yelling may be justified in this case." He pushed the flowery, square pen holder to the side and propped one hip on the edge of Claire's desk.

"Good. I haven't laughed like this in ages! Coffee?"

"Sure, thanks."

Claire jumped out of her seat and poured the detective a cup of hot, black coffee. She resumed her seat after placing it in his welcoming hands. "I feel like we need popcorn."

Mac glared at the pair.

Liz pleaded, hands clasped together in front of her. "Help!" she called feebly to the spectators.

A. J. smiled. "Please continue. The intermission is over." He lifted his cup to her before taking a sip.

Mac grinned evilly and returned his focus to Liz.

"Traitors!" Liz saw that she'd have to try and talk her way out of the mess she'd made. "Look, Mac. I'm sorry. Really sorry. I'll..." She struggled, trying to think of an appropriate peace offering while the doorknob pressed painfully into her lower back.

Mac straightened up to his full height and crossed his arms. Tapping his foot while he waited. "You'll what?"

"I'll..." She looked to Claire and A. J. for assistance and got nothing.

"I'll..." Liz dropped her hands, suddenly knowing the only offering he'd accept. "I'll give you an exclusive," she muttered.

Mac placed a hand behind his left ear and leaned in. "What was that? Loud enough so our witnesses can hear, please."

"I'll give you an exclusive." Liz raised her finger in the air. "*After* the case is over."

"Deal." Mac held out a hand to shake on it.

Liz took it, her shoulders dropping in defeat. "Deal," she said, her voice low.

Mac looked at Claire and A. J., keeping Liz's hand in a firm grip. "You two are my witnesses."

Claire nodded while she dabbed at her eyes gingerly with a tissue trying not to ruin her eye makeup any further.

A. J. grinned in between sips of coffee.

Mac released Liz's hand, spun on his heel, crossed the room, and resumed his earlier position on the couch in the waiting area. "So, how are y'all doing today?" he asked sociably as he got comfortable, propping his feet on the table, crossing them at the ankles, all signs of irritation vanished.

"Great." Claire grinned.

"Fine," Liz grumbled.

"The coffee's good. How 'bout you?" A. J. scratched behind his ear, stood up, shifted on his feet, and glanced at Liz.

"What's going on, Detective?" Mac asked, commenting on the detective's sudden awkwardness.

A. J. glanced at Liz again. "I, uh, need to speak with Liz."

A big smile crossed Mac's face. "By all means, go ahead! I have an exclusive, remember?" He draped his long arms along the back of the couch, demonstrating that he had no intention of leaving.

"Not until *after* the case, remember?" She grabbed a throw pillow as she passed the low chair and did precisely as its name described: she threw it. Straight at the irritating reporter's face.

Annoyingly, he caught it with one hand and put it behind his head. "Thanks!"

She stuck her tongue out at her still giggling assistant, retrieved her keys from her purse, unlocked the door, took A. J. by his arm and dragged him into her apartment.

Chapter Eighteen

Closing the door behind them, she put a finger to her lips and didn't let A. J. speak until they were in the living room. She stopped next to the tall bookshelves. "That wall is soundproofed, but I don't believe Mac is above listening at keyholes. Not that Claire would let him get away with it." Liz paused and grinned wickedly. "Now, I *want* him to try. I bet she'd blacken the other eye."

A. J. chuckled. "My money's on Claire too. I'm sorry, I'm a little distracted here. I can't get over how much space you have in here!"

He looked up and all around.

Liz watched as he turned slowly and took in the apartment. He studied the high ceiling, the long slats of the wood floor that gave the apartment the appearance of length, and how each area changed color even though they were technically one large single room. The living room walls were a soothing pale blue. Meanwhile, the open kitchen and dining area were a cheery yellow, and framed paintings of sunflowers adorned the walls. White trim, attached vertically to the wall, covered the transition between the colors.

A. J.'s gaze followed the stairs against the wall on the left up to the small loft area above the kitchen. "I like it!"

"Thanks, it's home." And just like that, Liz was aware of what had just happened. She had dragged A. J. Sowell into her apartment. Ruggedly handsome A. J. Sowell. Not that he had struggled or anything. Of course, she would have been much more comfortable if her friends hadn't spent the night before teasing her about him. Liz patted her cool cheeks. Relief filled her that she wasn't blushing. Yet.

A. J. nodded and turned back to Liz. "It's really soundproofed?"

Liz nodded. "Mostly. In the apartment anyway. I can still hear traffic and sounds through the windows, but yes. The goal was to muffle as much sound as possible from the crowds of the street, bar, and River Walk."

"That must have been some favor you did for the building's owner!"

The praise caused a faint flush to creep over her face. She shrugged one shoulder. "I found his teenage daughter. She ran away to meet some stranger she met on the internet. Thankfully, I got to her first." Liz omitted the huge part her extrasensory abilities had played in that case.

A. J.'s eyes grew big. "No way! Wait a minute. I don't remember that. Something like that would have made the local news at least." His brow wrinkled.

"I caught up with her in Arizona before the news caught wind of anything. The owner knows my dad. They were talking. Well, he was talking, and my dad was listening. Originally, my dad went to speak with him about office space when I was first starting up my own PI business. The building owner offered to set me up in this building if I'd take his case first." Liz grinned. "Let's just say he was extremely grateful when I not only found her but convinced her never to run away again."

A. J. walked over and sat down in the low dark blue armchair. His ankle rested on his knee, ready to hear the story while he continued to sip his coffee. "Now, how did you manage that bit of magic? It can take a lot to get through to a teenager, especially a teenager who thinks she's found true love."

"I asked her to stay with me and give me time to run a background check on the man she was leaving her family for." Liz shuddered, dropping onto the couch, twisting to place an arm along the low back. "He was the front man for a human trafficking syndicate. Very handsome, very charming, but a total sleazeball. I showed her enough evidence that she was grateful that her father and I intervened."

A. J.'s jaw dropped, and his foot fell to the floor as he leaned forward, an elbow on each knee. "What happened to him?"

Liz smirked. "Let's just say the FBI was extremely grateful to receive an anonymous tip with the man's precise location and the evidence I had collected proving his involvement."

A. J.'s eyebrows knitted together. "I don't understand. Why would you do that anonymously? That could have been a huge feather in your cap! Your private investigator business would have been a success from the start, and—"

"And a sixteen-year-old girl would have had to testify against an international crime syndicate. No." Liz shook her head.

A. J. took a sharp breath, his lips pressed to one side of his rugged face, signs of five o'clock shadow evident even that early in the morning. He nodded, understanding Liz's decision.

"The cowardly scumbag turned state's evidence almost from the moment he was in custody. I'm not happy he's hiding somewhere in the country, but..."

A. J. agreed. "That's how it goes sometimes. And the girl?"

Liz smiled. "She's working on her Bachelor's in Psychology. She wants to be a family therapist. Her father told me during our monthly rent dance that she got engaged at Christmas." Liz always felt proud of her part in changing that young lady's path in life.

"That's wonderful! But, monthly rent dance?" A. J. sat back, fiddling with the soft fabric on the seat.

"Yes, that's what we call it. Each month I go into my landlord's office to pay my rent. And each time, he tears up the check." Liz smiled. "I've even given it to his secretary before, who deposited it once. He transferred the money back into my account."

A big smile lit up A. J.'s face. "That is one extremely grateful daddy."

"And stubborn. So, what did you want to speak with me about?" She changed the subject, a little embarrassed talking about her first big success as an investigator.

"Yeah, well, I am hoping to compare notes. You spoke with Jim Stephens yesterday?"

"I don't think he did it, but..." Liz commented, curling her legs up on the couch.

A. J. sat back, resting his arms on the armchair. "Wow, that was easy. I thought you'd fight me at least a little." He lifted a finger. "Wait. But what?"

Liz smoothed the bright, striped, crocheted ripple blanket draped along the back of the couch. "But he lied to me about what he was doing the night of her murder. He didn't care for Brittany, that's for sure, but I don't think he's capable of hurting anyone."

A. J. nodded. "Me too. We're following up with the bar he claims to have been at, but so far, nothing."

Liz's eyebrows crinkled. "Nothing?"

"Nothing. So far, I can't find anything that proves where Jim Stephens was on the night of the murder."

"Oh," Liz said as reality dawned. "That doesn't look good for Jim."

"No, it doesn't." Silence fell between them. A. J.'s gaze dropped to the small end table to his left. His brow furrowed. He set down his coffee mug and picked up the item that had grabbed his attention. "What's this?" he asked, holding up a deck of cards.

Liz blushed slightly. "Tarot cards."

"You mean like fortune-telling?" A. J. looked at her quizzically.

"I learned how to read tarot in high school." She didn't mention that she learned how to read it because she was curious how tarot and her psychic abilities would work together.

"Really? That's not something I would have thought you'd be into."

"You don't know my mother very well. It's right up her alley." Liz grinned, thinking of her new-age, old-world mother. "I was curious, so I learned it. I got good enough to use it to earn some spending money. At parties, school fundraisers, that kind of thing. It's fun."

"Fundraisers, really? You know…" A. J. moved to sit on the couch next to her, placing the deck on the table. "There's a committee putting together a fundraiser that will happen in a couple of months. Some of the proceeds will go to the preservation of the five missions. But the majority goes to local food banks and homeless shelters. I don't know all the details yet." His brown eyes met hers. "Would you consider running a, what do you call it?" He waved a hand at the deck he set on the coffee table. "Fortune teller booth?"

"Tell you what." Liz tapped his arm. "Get me the details, and I'll see if Madame Esmeralda wants to come out to play."

A. J. pulled back a bit. "Madame Esmeralda?"

Liz giggled. "My alter ego. When I was first hired to entertain at a birthday party in tenth grade—" Liz cringed, thinking how long ago that was, "—I realized I should have an alter ego to add to the fun. And so, Madame Esmeralda was born."

A. J. grinned. "Fun. Yes, absolutely. Bring Esmeralda too. I'll get the info for you."

"Great. Returning to the case, Claire and I are off to meet Rosemary Travers, Brittany's roommate, at her apartment this morning." Liz glanced at her watch. "Shoot, we have to get going!" Liz stood. "Sorry."

"Not a problem." A. J. stood up, bumping into Liz as he did so. "Sorry to make you late. Want a police escort through traffic?"

"Oh, yeah. That would go over *really* well! No thanks." Liz felt a little lightheaded at his proximity and the faintest hint of cologne.

A. J. laughed, a deep throaty chuckle. "Yeah, bad idea." He turned and walked around the couch, pausing next to the back of the couch, waiting for Liz. "Nice blanket. Did you crochet it?"

Liz gave him a lopsided grin, her eyebrows raised. "Wow, most people assume it's knitted."

A. J. shrugged. "My mom and sister both knit and crochet. I'd be in deep trouble if I couldn't tell the difference!"

"That's awesome. And no, my mother made this one for me. I can crochet, but I don't do it nearly as often as my mom." A stretch took over her entire body. "Sorry! Late night."

A strange look passed over A. J.'s face, and his eyes grew big. "Oh. Is that why Murphy is here so early in the morning? Is he...are you?" The police detective stammered, suddenly looking extremely uncomfortable.

A burst of laughter escaped Liz, and her stretch collapsed. She grabbed his arm for support. "No. Definitely not. He's just annoying." Liz straightened up, her eyes bright with humor. "I mean, he seems like a good guy, don't get me wrong, but dating, no."

"Oh. Good." A. J. held an arm out, gesturing for Liz to lead the way.

Liz stopped and turned to say something more but bumped into A. J. instead. "Oh, sorry." She stepped back a bit, and she tripped on, well, nothing. *Why am I so clumsy this morning*?

"Graceful." A. J.'s hand snaked out and grabbed her elbow while she regained her footing.

"Thanks." His oak-scented cologne fogged her senses momentarily. "Um, do you want me to call you this evening to compare notes? About Rosemary?"

A. J.'s hand stayed on Liz's arm a little longer before sliding off. "Sure." A slow smile crossed his lips. "I've got an appointment to speak with her this afternoon. You beat me to her." A. J. shifted on his feet. "If you want—" he cleared his throat, "—maybe we could meet for dinner? I'll be able to give you more details on the fundraiser by then too."

Liz lit up. "Sure, where?" The fact that her heart started racing at the thought of spending more time with A. J. didn't escape her notice.

"Casa Rio? At seven?" he suggested, their eyes meeting.

"Sounds great!" Liz turned, and A. J. followed her to the door. Liz reached for the handle.

A. J. placed a hand on her shoulder to stop her.

She turned toward him. "Wh-?"

He winked. "Play along."

"Uh, okay," Liz agreed, opening the door, completely clueless as to what was happening.

"I can't believe we've solved this case with one conversation!" A. J. announced as they stepped into the office.

Claire turned her head. "Really? How did that happen?"

Liz giggled. The couch in the waiting area was empty. "It didn't. A. J. wanted to mess with Mac, apparently. He is gone, right?"

"Yes, I think he was disappointed," she wiggled her eyebrows suggestively at the pair as A. J. closed the heavy door behind them.

Liz laughed and waved her hand. "He'll be fine. Ready to go?"

Claire quickly gathered her belongings. "Absolutely!" She grabbed the folder with the printouts of the high-end items the victim had been obsessed with for comparison.

The trio headed out, setting the alarm and locking up behind them.

They walked together through the breezeway and across the street. Liz's car was parked in the same parking structure used by the police department. When the police department opened a substation at the heart of downtown, sharing the parking structure became the best option for both the police and local business owners.

"See you tonight," A. J. said. He waved and walked through the main doors to the station.

Chapter Nineteen

"See you tonight?" Claire squealed after the door closed behind A. J. "See you tonight!" Her eyes were enormous. "You have a date!"

"Shhh!" Liz took Claire by the arm and dragged her into the parking garage, her face fiercely hot. "It's *not* a date." She released Claire's arm when they got further into the garage. "We're meeting to compare notes about our interviews with Rosemary. That's all. It's not a date."

Liz turned and led the way to the elevator in the brightly lit parking structure so she could hide her red face from Claire's prying eyes.

Claire giggled as she followed. "Sure. So what are you going to wear? Never mind, it's wrong anyway. I'll help you find something suitable."

"It's *not* a date!" Liz repeated before stepping into the elevator.

Claire stopped teasing her friend until twenty minutes later as they walked up the path to Rosemary's apartment complex.

Liz pressed the doorbell for Rosemary's ground-level apartment.

"I'm just happy he's finally asked you out," Claire commented under her breath.

"Hmph. It's *not* a date," Liz muttered, unable to stop the ghost of a smile from crossing her lips.

"Sure, Liz. You keep telling yourself that." Claire patted her friend on the shoulder with her immaculately manicured hand.

"You're fired, Claire."

"You never hired me, honey."

"Dammit."

"Um, hello?" Rosemary's voice interrupted through the door.

Both ladies jumped. "Rosemary, hi. It's Liz and Claire."

"Oh, okay." The familiar sounds of a door bolt opening and a chain being released floated through the door.

Rosemary greeted them with a weary smile. She looked different, younger. She was wearing faded jeans, a bright red sweatshirt, and fuzzy blue slippers over bare feet.

"Hi." Rosemary stepped to the side to allow them entry to her home.

Liz shook Rosemary's hand as they entered. "Thanks for letting us come over." A heavy weight formed in her chest, distress and worry. "You okay?" Her eyebrows creased together, as she studied her client's face.

Rosemary nodded. "This is all still so upsetting. You know?"

Liz gave her hand a little squeeze in response before letting go. The weight in her chest vanished. "You remember Claire?"

Rosemary nodded, closing the door as an awkwardness fell over the small group.

Liz scratched her chin as she experienced that moment when she entered someone's home for the first time and didn't know where to sit or what to do.

Rosemary chased the awkwardness away and gestured to the small round kitchen table on the other side of the living room. "I made coffee."

"Perfect," said Liz. "I'm running on only one cup."

They approached the small, bright kitchen. The smell of hot coffee with a hint of vanilla and chocolate drifted through the air. Rosemary's open design kitchen was a pale yellow with white cupboards. A few photos of sunflowers adorned the walls in the dining area, carrying along the kitchen's colors. A matching set of salt, pepper, sugar, and creamer with small sunflowers painted on the high-gloss ceramic sat on a dark wooden lazy Susan in the center of the table.

"I have sunflowers in my kitchen too. Ooh, these are cute!" Liz commented as they settled at the table. She picked up the salt shaker to take a closer look. "Where did you find them?"

Rosemary blushed slightly. "Thanks, I found them at one of the little artisan shops in La Villita. I can't remember which one."

"Good find! I love perusing those shops. The only problem is they're always opening and closing, so you never know if a shop you love will still be there the next time you go."

The ladies agreed, sipping coffee. After a few minutes of small talk, Rosemary cleared her throat. "You wanted to see Brittany's room?"

"Yes. If that's still okay?" Liz asked.

Rosemary stood in response. "It's okay. It's just odd for me still. I haven't been able to bring myself to go in there since she went missing."

She led the way through the kitchen to the small hallway. They stopped in front of three doors. Two doors were wide open. In the bedroom on the right a mixed bouquet filled a clear vase on a shelf near the large window beside the bed. The décor was a mix of creams and pinks, a nice contrast to the dark wooden furniture. The other door led to a small, tidy bathroom done in creamy white.

"Pretty flowers," Liz commented, gesturing to the bedroom.

Rosemary blushed. "Thanks. They're, uh, from a friend." Her blush deepened.

"That's nice." Liz didn't have to be a psychic to suspect the person who sent the flowers was more than just a friend. She changed the subject. "And—" she nodded at the closed door, "—that's completely normal, Rosemary, not wanting to go into her room. I see it with missing person cases all the time. It's sad but completely normal."

Rosemary gave them a feeble smile. "That's good to know. Um, what are you going to be looking for?" Her hand rested on the brushed-nickel doorknob.

Claire held up a bright red folder and a legal pad in her hand. A pair of bright blue nitrile gloves flopped against the folder. "Brittany posted many photos of haute couture items on her social media accounts. We're curious if she ever managed to buy any of them."

"In the business, we call it, 'follow the money,'" Liz interjected.

Rosemary gestured at the folder. "I don't care for that stuff, but Brittany was wild for it. No matter what it was, big or small."

"It depends on the person and the item," Claire explained. "For some people, even if an item is hideous, they'll buy it solely based on the designer. From what I can tell, your roommate had good taste."

Not responding, Rosemary swung open the door. The air was dusty, and the room was dark. "See for yourself." She reached past the doorframe and flipped on the overhead light.

"Oh my God!" Liz and Claire gasped in unison.

Chapter Twenty

Aghast, Liz and Claire entered the room. The bedroom could be best described as a closet with a bed. Shelves adorned the walls displaying purses and shoes in a rainbow of colors. Small jewelry boxes filled racks next to the vanity table. Clothing racks on wheels held shirts, dresses, slacks, and skirts. A display of accessories, scarves, and belts covered the back of what they assumed was the actual closet door.

"Wow! I've never seen anything like this." Liz stepped further into the cramped room.

Claire grinned. "This could be my closet. Almost." She set the folder and legal pad on the bed, pulling on the nitrile gloves as she crossed the room. She reached for one of the purses high on a shelf over the dresser and studied it for a moment. "The only difference is that mine are real." She gently replaced the purse on the shelf. "Knockoff," she declared, turning back to Liz and Rosemary. "Still, I stand by it. She had good taste."

"I reiterate, wow!" Liz turned to Claire, professionalism replacing her initial shock. "Would you please take pictures first? I'm curious if where things are in the room will have any meaning to the case. Also, as you look, please set everything back where you found it." She looked around again, shaking her head. "Just wow!"

"I know, right?" Rosemary followed them inside. "She brought most of this with her when she moved in, but it's only grown since then. Oddly, this was the only space she kept neat and organized." Her eyes dropped, and a single tear ran down her pale cheek. "I'm sorry to say, it was the source of a lot of arguments. Sometimes she'd come home with a new pair of shoes or a vintage handbag but couldn't help with the monthly grocery bill. Ya know?"

Liz knew this information already, having learned it from the hotel manager, but she liked that Rosemary was being a bit more forthcoming. "That would be annoying." Liz walked around the room, touching random items with the back of her hand so she didn't leave fingerprints. No visions. Liz stopped, shrugging imperceptibly at Claire, then smiled brightly at Rosemary. "How about we drink more of your wonderful coffee while Claire looks around?" Liz handed Claire the small digital camera she pulled out of her purse. "*Lots* of pictures, please."

Claire accepted the camera and turned her attention to the room. "This will take a while."

Rosemary and Liz returned to the kitchen. When they sat, Rosemary refilled Liz's cup automatically. She blushed and returned the carafe to the hot pad. "Sorry, habit. You wanted to ask me some questions." The nervous young woman resumed her seat.

Sitting in the chair across from her suspect, Liz pulled out her notepad and pen and set her phone on the table. "Do you mind if I record this?" Even though Rosemary agreed to that request the first time they spoke at the office, Liz liked to ask each time she interviewed a client or suspect.

Rosemary shook her head, absently stirring her coffee with a spoon.

"Thanks. I spoke with Jim Stephens yesterday. I'm assuming you know?" Liz looked at her client expectantly.

"That the police brought him in for questioning? Yes. Gossip travels fast around the hotel." Rosemary gulped. "Do you think he...?"

Liz reached across the table and patted Rosemary's hand. "I don't know. Both the police and I are looking into him. His alibi is proving a bit of a mystery."

"I don't think he did it, but I'm glad you are looking into everything." Rosemary sipped her coffee. "At least, I hope he didn't do it. All the times I've been alone in the fitness center with him. I never got that vibe from him. Do you know what I mean?" The young woman looked Liz intently in the eye.

Liz offered her a lopsided grin. "Yes, I know what you mean." She knew better than most the value of listening to a vibe.

"Jim mentioned that Brittany had a boyfriend?" Liz noted the question on her pad, remembering the young man she saw Rosemary with on Sunday night. She looked back to Rosemary. She didn't need to be psychic to know that question caused a reaction.

Rosemary's face flushed, and she sloshed coffee onto the table. She set down her mug with a hard thud. "Sorry," she mumbled, rushing to the kitchen for paper towels.

Liz watched in silence as Rosemary cleaned up her mess.

"They weren't dating," she muttered, tidying the table.

"What was that?" Liz asked, taking her eyes off Rosemary's fidgeting hands.

"When she disappeared—was murdered," Rosemary corrected herself, shuddering visibly at the word, "they weren't dating. Brittany and Frank."

Rosemary returned to the kitchen. She was jittery, unable to sit still. She threw away the paper towel and tidied the neat kitchen.

"Do you know his full name? Do you know when they broke up?" Liz asked. She left her pen on the table, letting her phone record everything. She wanted to watch Rosemary's body language.

Rosemary slumped, resting her hip against the counter in front of the sink. Arms crossed over her chest. "Frank Stanley. And they broke up months before the...you know. At least three months." Her right foot tapped on the floor.

"Rosemary?" Liz took a deep breath, unsure if her next question would end the interview. "Why are you so agitated?"

Rosemary tried to smile, but it came out as a grimace. "Agitated? I'm not agitated. They broke up, that's all. Look." Rosemary returned to her seat at the table. "Frank Stanley is a nice guy." She jabbed the table with her index finger. "A guy who didn't deserve what she did to him. He is nice, and she, honestly, wasn't."

"Okay, he's a nice guy. But do you think he could have done this? Could Frank Stanley have killed Brittany? Since she mistreated him?" Liz asked bluntly. Murder among couples had happened for less.

Rosemary's eyes grew large, and her hand flew to her chest. All the color drained from her face. "No. Absolutely—no!" She shook her head adamantly.

Liz switched her angle of questioning. "I also spoke with Mr. Moore."

If there was ever a question about whether a person could turn as white as a sheet, Liz now knew the answer was yes.

"Oh," was all that came out of Rosemary's mouth before she tumbled out of her chair, fainting dead away, falling to the floor with a thud.

"Holy crap! Claire!" Liz jumped out of her seat and ran to Rosemary's side. Kneeling, she checked her pulse. It was strong. "Whew! Thank God!"

Claire ran out of the bedroom in response to Liz's yell. "What's...? Oh!" She dashed to the kitchen sink and wet a dish towel with cool water. She handed it to Liz, who folded it and gently patted Rosemary's pale face.

Seconds passed, each one felt like an eternity. Claire started dialing 911 when Rosemary's eyes fluttered. At that positive sign, Claire ended the call before she finished dialing. An audible sigh of relief escaped Liz and Claire simultaneously.

"Wha-?" Rosemary's eyes darted around as they flickered open.

"You fainted," Liz explained. "Does anything hurt?"

Rosemary closed her eyes for a moment. "No. I don't think so. Just my pride. Can you help me up, please?"

The two women got their hands under each shoulder to support her, until she was upright again. They allowed Rosemary time to get her bearings before helping her back into her chair.

"Would you rather lie down?" Claire asked, gesturing to the couch.

"No, thank you. I'm so sorry." Rosemary slowly shook her head. "Wow, I can't remember when, or if, I've ever fainted before. Weird." She covered her forehead with her right hand, as if checking for a fever.

"Is your head okay? You went over so suddenly, I don't know if you hit it or not," Liz asked, sitting in the chair next to Rosemary so she could catch her if she fainted again.

Rosemary felt her head gingerly. "No. I don't think so. I'm so sorry I frightened y'all."

"That's okay. Take a moment to collect yourself," Liz offered, dragging her notepad, pen, and phone over to her new spot at the table.

Claire retrieved a glass of water from the kitchen and set it in front of Rosemary. "Drink. Slowly," she ordered, placing one hand gently on her shoulder.

Rosemary did as she was told. She sat quietly, taking slow breaths, and sipping water.

Liz took her focus off her client and turned to Claire. "How's it going in there?"

Claire's bottom lip popped out exaggeratedly as her shoulders dropped. "Nothing so far. I'm starting to think this is a dead end."

"Have you had time to look everywhere?" Liz asked, a little surprised. Her eyes flicked over to check on Rosemary.

The young woman quietly sipped her water as the color gradually returned to her face.

"Not even. There's a lot of stuff in that room. I mean a lot!" Claire exclaimed. "Sadly, while she had good taste, she didn't have a very good eye. Most of the items, while beautiful, are knockoffs. She has a few authentic vintage items but nothing from our list so far."

"You said something about that earlier. How can you tell which are the knockoffs?" Liz was intrigued.

"If you know what to look for, it's easy. If you already own the real deal, it makes it even easier. There are four basic identifiers: materials, construction, hardware, and markings. What to look for varies. It depends on the designers and even the period the item was made. There's an entire industry now in the authentication of high-fashion clothes and accessories. Certain designers only use solid gold hardware. On knockoffs, it's typically painted gold leaf. For other designers, if the designer's logo is printed on the fabric and is cut off at a seam, that's a big no-no. Even making sure the stitching is lined up the way it should be can tell an authenticator whether an item is real or fake."

"Wow!" Liz remarked.

"Knockoffs are big business. But, as I said, there are a few authentic items—a small clutch from the 1950s. A bracelet with real gems from the 1920s, I'd guess. Brittany could have easily found those at antique stores for a good price if the seller didn't know what they had."

"So, do you think there's a chance she knew she had a bunch of knockoffs?" Liz tapped her pen on her notebook, resting her chin in her hand.

"Maybe," Claire answered, shrugging.

"Absolutely," Rosemary interjected.

Liz and Claire turned to her in surprise.

"Why do you say that?" Liz dropped her pen on the table.

Rosemary nodded in Claire's direction. "Listening to Claire just now. Suddenly, it felt like Brittany was back in the apartment. She knew *all* of that about knockoffs. When she'd bring home a new purchase, and it wasn't a time when she forgot to help with the bills, she'd point out all the parts that made it a fake. But she was still happy because it looked authentic to the untrained eye. And appearances were all that mattered to her."

Claire nodded. "She's right. Not about appearances, that's just, well, sad. But a knockoff can look like the real deal to the general public. If she wanted to *look* like she was carrying a five-thousand-dollar purse, she could pull it off in the right crowds."

Rosemary agreed. "Brittany used to say that exactly. Almost verbatim."

Liz turned to Claire. "I think you should keep looking then, if that's okay with you, Rosemary. Do you want us to come back another time? After you're feeling better?" She studied her client's face.

"No, no. I'm fine now. I promise. Go ahead." She gestured to tell Claire that it was okay to return to Brittany's bedroom. A healthy glow had returned to Rosemary's face.

Claire left the table and disappeared through the kitchen.

Liz returned her attention to Rosemary. "I'm half-afraid to start. Do you remember what we were talking about before you fainted?" Liz asked, ready to catch Rosemary if she fainted again.

Rosemary nodded and her gaze dropped to the table. "You said that you've spoken with Mr. Moore. So, you know?"

"What do I know?" Liz wanted Rosemary to tell her the whole story. She wanted to allow her client a chance to come clean about the argument and confirm the manager's statement simultaneously.

A tear rolled down Rosemary's nose. She was unable to meet Liz's gaze. "That I kicked Brittany out of the apartment the day she was murdered!" The words exploded out of her, followed by a flood of tears.

"Oh dear." Liz reached for Rosemary as sobs racked her slender body.

Rosemary leaned into Liz's open arms.

"Is everything okay?" Claire called out, sticking her head around the corner.

Liz nodded. "Yes. I've got it this time." She caressed Rosemary gently on the back as warm tears flowed down her client's face.

"If I hadn't kicked her out, Brittany would still be alive." Rosemary hiccuped, as more tears poured down her cheeks.

"Maybe, but we don't know that yet," Liz said quietly.

Rosemary straightened up. "But, if I hadn't kicked her out, she would have come home and been safe!" Rosemary insisted, picking up the damp towel from the table and patting her flushed face.

"You don't know that. Think about it. Brittany had it pretty easy here with you as a roommate. You let her slide for months at a time on the rent and groceries. Something tells me she would have fought to stay."

Rosemary shook her head slowly. "But—"

"But nothing. Let's not invite trouble or guilt until we have all the answers, okay?" Liz offered sage advice.

Rosemary sniffed, rose, and grabbed a tissue from the small table by the couch. She blew her nose loudly. "I've been racked with guilt ever since that argument. When I told her she had to move out...I never meant *immediately*." Rosemary walked to the kitchen, where she threw away the dirty tissue before returning to the table. She dried the last of her tears with the towel after she sat. "I just didn't get a chance to tell her that before...you know."

"I'm sorry you've been dealing with that, Rosemary, because I have to ask. What were you doing the night Brittany, um, disappeared?" Liz purposely chose a less upsetting word than murdered.

Rosemary took a ragged breath. "I was too tired to cook, so I grabbed dinner and came home." She stood and returned to the kitchen, setting her mug in the sink.

"Did you eat out, or did you get takeout?"

"I ate out."

"You weren't with anyone?" Liz asked, studying Rosemary's movements closely.

Rosemary washed and dried the mug, then fiddled with a clean towel while she hung it on the oven door.

"No." Rosemary tidied away all signs of having made coffee.

Liz watched her client. Rosemary's responses were getting shorter.

Before she could draw her client's attention to it, though, a commotion from the bedroom drew the women's attention.

"*Jackpot*!" Claire yelled.

Chapter Twenty-One

"Liz! We were right!" Claire called from the bedroom, her voice muffled. "We were right!"

Liz and Rosemary dashed into the room to join Claire. They found her on her hands and knees, pulling boxes from under the bed. An open box sat on the quilt, where a small, black, quilted clutch with a gold chain rested on a pillow of white tissue paper. Three more boxes joined it. Claire opened the second box revealing a pair of black leather shoes bearing a famous designer's trademark bright red sole.

After all four boxes were open in front of them, Claire announced, "These four boxes are probably worth as much as her entire collection. Minus the handful of authentic vintage items I found."

Something caught Liz's attention. "Look at this." She pointed to the small slip of paper.

Claire gingerly pinched the paper at the corner, pulling a receipt with a gentle tug from under the black clutch.

The rest followed. The tally added up to a little more than ten thousand dollars.

On a whim, Liz asked Claire to arrange them in order by date of purchase. This told the women a bigger story. Brittany had bought those items with cash between July and November of last year. The least expensive item, the shoes, had been purchased first.

"You mean to tell me Brittany had nearly ten thousand dollars last year, and she couldn't help pay the rent in July, September, or November!" Rosemary's voice trembled. She reached out to pick up one of the shoes but stopped before touching it. She closed her hand into a tight fist and straightened up. Her lips pressed into a tight line before she turned on her heel and stormed out of the room.

Claire took pictures of everything without saying another word.

Liz touched the side of the shoebox with the back of her hand. A flash of Brittany appeared in her mind. Alive, happy, and hugging the shoebox in one of the high-end malls Liz recognized as being on the north side of San Antonio.

Snapping out of the brief vision, Liz glanced at the shoe receipt, confirming the store's name and location. She smiled happily at Claire.

"You saw something, didn't you?" Claire whispered, lowering the camera.

Liz nodded, unable to hide her excitement. "It was of Brittany right after she bought the shoes, but yeah."

Claire dashed around the bed and hugged her friend. It was the first sign that Liz's psychometry ability was returning. Claire bounced on her toes next to Liz as she touched the remaining boxes.

Liz shrugged off her disappointment when the touches revealed nothing more. "That's okay. I imagine the first item she bought had the most emotion and energy attached to it. Do you think this is the last of it?"

"Absolutely. I haven't looked at everything yet, but I feel that I can reasonably say this is it," Claire confirmed. "Other than those vintage items I found earlier, everything else I've looked at is a knockoff, or at the very least, a reasonable facsimile."

"Okay. I better call A. J. I don't think this can wait until this evening. Don't touch anything else and leave it all on the bed." Liz started to leave the room, but Claire stopped her.

"Why did she hide them?" Claire spread her arms to encompass the room. "She put the knockoffs on display, but the real items, the jewels of her collection, she hides under her bed. It doesn't make sense."

Liz looked at the receipts instead of the boxes. "I think..." She paused. "I think it has more to do with *how* she got the money to buy them in the first place. That's a lot of money in a short time, and we haven't seen any sign of her having a second job. This tells me that we must consider our victim's extracurricular activities."

Claire made a face. "Oh, dear."

Liz agreed. She left the room, looking for her client. She found Rosemary in the kitchen. "Are you okay?" Liz asked quietly, crossing her arms and propping her shoulder against the open doorway.

Rosemary was leaning against the counter, using a fistful of tissues to dab at her eyes. "I'm sorry. I'm just..." She blew her nose and stomped on the pedal to open the trash can. The lid slammed into the wall with a bang. She flung the wad of damp tissues into the garbage. She faced Liz, fury bringing color to her tear-stained cheeks. "I'm just so angry! Last year, we were surviving on bologna and cheese sandwiches because most of my money was going to the rent to keep a roof over our heads. I thought..."

She hesitated, taking a deep, steadying breath. "I thought we were struggling together!" She pointed violently toward the bedroom, her voice rising with every word. "Meanwhile, she's literally sleeping on top of thousands of dollars!"

"I know. I'm sorry, Rosie," Liz used Jim's nickname for her, draping a comforting arm around her back. "I know you aren't exactly in the mood, but I have a few more questions. First, I have to call A. J."

Rosemary looked at Liz, her brow furrowed. "Who?" Her gaze followed Liz to the table, where she picked up her phone.

"Detective Sowell. He's the lead investigator on Brittany's case," Liz explained, not looking up as she navigated her contacts list with her thumb. "He needs to see that." Liz jerked her head toward the victim's bedroom.

"Sowell," A. J.'s deep voice brought an unbidden smile to Liz's lips.

"Hi, A. J. It's Liz," her voice dropped as she walked into the small living room. The sound of her client blowing her nose drifted out of the kitchen.

"Hey, Liz. You aren't calling to cancel, are you?" The detective's voice held a tinge of disappointment.

Liz smiled, tilting her head. "No. Nothing like that. Of course, *you* may need to cancel on *me* after this call. I found something. Well, more accurately, Claire found something. Can you come to Rosemary Travers's apartment?" Liz summarized Claire's discovery. A low whistle drifted through the phone.

"Son of a—Please ask Claire not to touch anything else. In fact, can she come out of the room? I'll arrange to have a couple of crime scene technicians on standby if we need to inventory that room. I'll need to speak with all of you and get signed statements and elimination prints from Claire and Ms. Travers. We already have yours, of course."

Liz nodded, agreeing with everything he suggested. "You don't have to worry about Claire. She wore gloves the entire time she was in the room. See you in a few minutes."

"Hey, Liz?" A. J. called out to her before she hung up.

"Yeah?" Liz brought the phone back to her ear.

"Thanks for calling me on this," he said quietly.

Before she could respond, Liz heard him yelling for someone named Wilson before the line went dead.

"The police will be here shortly. Claire?" Liz called out.

"Yes?" Claire asked, walking into the hallway.

"A. J. asked that you come out of the room and not touch anything else."

"Sure." Claire disappeared for a moment and returned with the camera and her file. She pulled the blue gloves off her hands when she joined her friend. "Eww!" Claire made a face when she looked at her sweaty hands. She gingerly placed everything on the kitchen counter before washing her hands at the sink.

The women chose to sit in the living room to await A. J.'s arrival. Rosemary took the pale green overstuffed armchair while Liz and Claire sat on the matching couch, side by side.

"Rosemary, um, I know this is an odd question, but was Brittany exceptionally busy outside of work at the hotel? Did she have a second job?"

"No. Brittany was home more than usual after she and Frank broke up. Why?"

Liz shifted uncomfortably. "Well, we need to figure out where and how she got the money to buy those things. Did she..." Liz paused, trying to find a tactful way to ask her next question. "Did she go out on many *first dates*, to put it bluntly?"

Rosemary looked from Liz to Claire, her face blank. "I don't think so. As I said, she was home a lot. Oh!" Rosemary's eyes grew big. "Oh!" she repeated. "You want to know if she did...if she was a..." Rosemary couldn't even bring herself to say the word. "No way. Never. I didn't like her at the end, but I don't see her prostituting herself so she could buy things!" She shook her head vehemently.

"It's okay, I believe you. So you know, Detective Sowell will ask the same question." Liz slid her small purple notebook and pen across the coffee table to Rosemary. "Do you have Frank Stanley's contact information handy? I will need to speak with him as soon as possible."

Rosemary picked up the items and jotted down his name, phone number, and place of work from memory. "He's a mechanic," she stated, sliding the pen and notebook back to Liz after she'd finished writing.

Liz picked up her belongings, getting a slight hum from the items but no clear feelings or visions. Taking a deep breath, she decided to ask about Frank. "Um, Rosie, are you and Frank close?"

Her client paled slightly, but there was no sign that she would faint again. Her lips formed a tight line across her face. She took a sharp intake of breath through her nose.

"I saw you walking together, past the crime scene, on Sunday night."

Rosemary nodded, reaching for the tissues. "I didn't know that was what we walked past until you told me Monday morning. I still can't believe it."

Liz found the non-answer to her question intriguing. "And Frank?"

"We became friends after he and Brittany broke up. He's come by to check on me from time to time since her disappearance." Rosemary cleared her throat and dabbed her eyes.

"That's nice of him." Liz didn't believe the explanation, but decided to abandon the tactic for the moment. "What was Brittany's relationship like with your boss?" Liz asked, her pen poised over her notepad. She studied Rosemary's face as she waited.

"With Mr. Moore? Honestly? She used to complain about him constantly. He's an extremely strict boss, but he's fair, because he's equally strict with everyone. But, starting last summer, it looked like they were getting along better. I don't know why, though, and Brittany never said. I secretly wondered if they were having a sordid affair!" Rosemary giggled and shivered exaggeratedly. "That's the first time I've ever said that out loud. God, I hope it wasn't true!" A look of horror blended with her amused expression.

"Can you think of anything or anyone else? Any topic that Brittany spoke of frequently? Besides, fashion, of course."

Rosemary started to deny the question, then stopped, raising a finger. "You know—" she waved the thought away with her hand. "No, it's silly."

Both Liz and Claire leaned forward eagerly.

"What's silly?" Claire asked.

"Well, there's the mystery guest," Rosemary said matter-of-factly.

Liz straightened up. "What mystery guest?"

"*The* mystery guest. Sorry, they are the talk of the hotel. You haven't heard about them yet?" Rosemary asked, astonished.

"No. But I'd love to hear all about this mystery guest. Please. Who are you talking about?" Liz asked, writing

Learn more about mystery guest in her notebook before turning her full attention on the young woman opposite her.

"That's just it. I don't know. No one does. I take that back. Mr. Moore knows, naturally. He's the only one who does anything to help the guest, as far as I know, from check-in to checkout. They have stayed for a week, every month for the past year," Rosemary explained.

"You keep saying 'they.' Are you telling me you don't even know if this guest is male or female? Or is there more than one person?"

"No, I don't know. And as far as the grapevine knows, it's only one person."

Liz turned to Claire next to her. "Was there anything about this on Brittany's social media?"

"No. Everything was about fashion." Claire jerked her thumb toward the bedroom. "And early last year, there were the 'I hate my boss' posts. But nothing about any guest at the hotel."

Rosemary sat back in her seat, pulling her feet up to sit sideways in the armchair. "Really? I'm surprised! She was obsessed, and I do mean obsessed! At one point, that was *all* she spoke about. The curiosity was killing her. Oh."

"What?" Liz asked, curious about what made Rosemary stop speaking.

"That expression never really meant anything to me before. It's just something you say. You don't think...?" Rosemary stopped again.

"That she discovered the mystery guest's identity and was killed for it?" Liz finished for her. "I'm certainly going to find out! How do we see them? Do you know when the person will be at the hotel? Do they request the same room every time?" Liz's fervor grew as she fired off her litany of questions at her client.

Rosemary straightened up at the stream of questions. "The Alamo Suite. That's not true. They take the entire top floor—both The Alamo and The Mission suites. So I honestly don't know which one they stay in."

"Really? Wow!" Liz turned to Claire. "There's no chance that you know who they are? I mean traveling in the same circles, that kind of thing."

Claire bit her lip while she thought. "I can't think of anyone I know coming to town. But, honestly, from Rosemary's description, it's probably *not* anyone I know."

"What makes you think that?" Liz's forehead wrinkled.

"Honestly, people in my circle tend to ensure *all* the staff knows they are there. They crave, and typically *seek*, attention. My family never does that, but we know plenty who do." Claire shrugged her shoulders.

Rosemary looked back and forth between Liz and Claire. "What are you talking about? What circle?"

Liz scooted forward on the couch. "You don't know who Claire is? Claire Henderson?" Liz enunciated her friend's last name.

Rosemary shook her head, pursing her lips.

Claire giggled. "It's fine. Liz likes to poke fun at my, well, lifestyle. I come from a wealthy family."

Liz sighed and rolled her eyes. "A wealthy family! That's putting it mildly. That's like saying Matthew McConaughey is just a little famous. Geesh!" Liz elbowed her friend gently in the ribs.

Rosemary looked back and forth between them. "So, if you'll forgive the question, why do you work for Liz? If I was rich, there's no way I'd want to work." Rosemary looked at Liz with a smile. "No offense."

"None taken," Liz said happily and sat back to let Claire respond.

"It's how my parents raised me. They never wanted me to have the jet-set lifestyle when I grew up, so I went to university. I'm an accountant, a CPA. But when my grandmother died unexpectedly a little over a year ago, her will put me in charge of the Henderson family trust. Since I didn't have to work anymore, my mother suggested I find some volunteer work." A devious smile crossed her lips. "She just didn't specify what *kind* of volunteer work."

"No way! Really?" Rosemary looked to Liz for confirmation.

Liz nodded. "I tried turning her down, but she kept showing up. Now, I don't know how I ever managed without her."

"Awww!" Claire hugged Liz.

Rosemary grinned at their exchange. "Oh." Her eyes grew large, and she sat up straight. "Oh! They're here!"

Liz looked confused. "Who's here? A. J.?" Turning, her gaze moved toward the door behind them.

"No. The mystery guest. They're here, I mean, they're at the hotel. Now. They arrived over the weekend. The only reason I know is that the order to not go to the top floor was up on the bulletin board in the locker room when I got to work yesterday morning. I read it just before the police called me."

Liz tucked her notebook and pen into her purse. "How do I get to the top floor?"

Rosemary shook her head. "You can't. Not without a keycard."

Claire grinned wickedly at Liz. "Gee, Liz. Too bad you don't know someone staying at the hotel. Someone who has an extra keycard." She put a finger on her chin and looked to the ceiling. "Too bad."

Liz's shoulders slumped and her face dropped into her hands. "Crap."

"What's going on?" Rosemary's head tilted to one side, her eyebrows meeting above her nose.

"My friend has just realized she has to eat some humble pie." Claire rubbed Liz's back as she grinned at Rosemary. "I imagine it's going to taste like crow."

"Okay?" Rosemary's voice trailed off, still in the dark.

Liz looked at Rosemary through her fingers. "Um, odd question. You say you need a keycard to get to the top floor. Can a keycard be reprogrammed to give a person access to that floor?"

"Yes, I've been training to work at the front counter, so I can pick up some extra shifts. Oh, I know how to do that!" Excitement filled Rosemary's voice now that she could do something to help. "We can meet at the hotel in the morning, what, about nine?"

"I'll be there."

The sound of approaching sirens cut through the air and interrupted their conversation.

"A. J.'s here. He's so dramatic!" Liz joked, rolling her eyes.

A nervous giggle escaped Rosemary.

Liz stood up. "I'll get it." She walked over and opened the door.

The detective greeted her with a warm smile. "Hi." His cowboy boots thudded on the concrete path as he approached.

Warmth flowed over Liz as she basked in his attention. "Hi." What was it about him that caused her to smile every time she saw him?

He stopped in front of her, his hands in the pockets of his open brown leather jacket, the collar turned up against the cold wind. All business, he cut to the chase. "Thanks again for calling me, Liz." His voice was low but friendly. "Wanna show me what you found?"

"Sure, come on in." Liz led the way into the living room, wishing she could stop blushing whenever he was around.

"Claire. Ms. Travers." A. J. nodded to each woman in turn. "I understand Ms. Henderson made something of a discovery this morning," he stated simply.

"In here." Liz escorted him to the bedroom, the items in question on the bed, exactly where Claire had left them.

A low whistle escaped A. J. as he stepped into Brittany's room. By the time he reached the bed, his phone was already coming to his ear. "Hey, it's Sowell. I'm definitely going to need a team over here."

Chapter Twenty-Two

More than an hour passed before Liz and Claire could leave Rosemary's apartment. While A. J. interviewed Claire regarding her discovery and a technician fingerprinted Rosemary, Liz took the opportunity to set up an appointment to meet with Frank Stanley that afternoon. Leaving behind signed statements, specialists were busy inventorying the room when they bid Rosemary and A. J. goodbye.

Dropping Claire off at the office with strict instructions to enjoy a good lunch, Liz navigated the busy streets of San Antonio, heading to Frank Stanley's place of business, just beyond the historic downtown area.

A man dressed in dark blue coveralls stood outside the auto shop's office door. He was holding a large, blue, insulated lunch box in one hand when Liz pulled into the parking lot. There was no question. He was the man Liz saw walking with Rosemary on Sunday night.

"Frank Stanley?" Liz called out as she locked her car and walked across the lot toward the man squinting into the afternoon sun. Already Liz could see why Brittany had been attracted to Frank. He could be a poster boy for the description of "tall, dark, and handsome."

A bright white smile flashed at her question. "Yes. You must be Liz Pond, the private investigator Rosemary hired." Frank stepped off the sidewalk, his hand outstretched, his blue eyes glittering in the sunlight. "Do you mind if we eat outside?" He gestured to a small metal table with an umbrella next to the shop. "It's nice out again, and I've been under a pickup all day."

"Sure. It feels like spring, doesn't it?" Liz fell into step next to him. "I guess we should take advantage of it now. It'll probably be winter again in an hour."

Frank grinned. "Can't trust Texas weather, that's for sure."

Liz set a water bottle on the table and pulled packaged jerky and a nut-filled protein bar from her purse, items she kept stashed in her car for stakeouts.

"Is that all you're eating?" Frank commented, opening his laden lunch box. Two thick sandwiches rested on top of an apple, the same protein bar Liz brought, a baggie of store-bought cookies, and two water bottles.

"I've had a busy morning," Liz grinned, settling into a seat opposite him.

Without hesitation, Frank placed one of his sandwiches in front of her.

"Oh no, I couldn't," she resisted, but her body had other ideas. A loud, slow rumble escaped her stomach, making Frank laugh and Liz blush. "Excuse me. Okay, so maybe I will. Thank you. What are we eating?" She unfolded the wax paper wrapped around the thick sandwich. Half-expecting a simple bologna and cheese sandwich,

Liz was pleasantly surprised at the sight of the stack of sliced turkey.

"You're in for a treat. Hickory-smoked turkey breast with cheddar cheese, lettuce, mayo, spicy mustard, a dash of salt and pepper, and a touch of cranberry sauce on fresh bakery bread. Sorry, I ran out of bacon."

Liz's stomach growled again. "That sounds heavenly. I've never had cranberry sauce on a sandwich before."

"It's a great touch. I had it at a deli once and have been hooked ever since." Frank looked from side to side secretively. "I make a mean sandwich, even if I say so myself. Just don't tell these guys. Or I'll never eat alone again." He jabbed a thumb in the direction of the busy auto shop where a pair of mechanics, dressed in the same dark blue coveralls, stood on the bumper of a large pickup truck, wrenches in hand as they worked on the engine. His bright eyes twinkled as he winked. "Dig in."

Liz eagerly took a bite out of the sandwich. Her eyes closed as the combination of flavors met her taste buds. "Mmmm."

A low chuckle escaped Frank as he bit into his own sandwich.

They ate in companionable silence for a few minutes before Liz remembered why she was there. She wiped her lips with the paper napkin Frank had placed in front of her only a moment before.

"Thank you. This is delicious! I'm a terrible cook, but I'm pretty sure I can make this!"

A half-grin broke out across his face as Frank chewed. "I'll email you a shopping list and directions," he said after swallowing.

"Thank you. Okay, now I really should ask you a few questions." She took a quick sip of water. "First, do you mind if I record our conversation?"

Frank shook his head as he chewed.

Liz placed her phone on the table and started the recording app, reciting the usual details of when and who. "As I'm sure you are aware, the body of Brittany Cabot has been found."

Frank's gaze dropped to the table between them as the mood shifted dramatically. He nodded slowly. "I saw it on the news, and Rosemary called and told me. That's too bad. I thought she'd just decided to take off." Frank fiddled with his napkin.

"Unfortunately not. Brittany was likely murdered the same night she disappeared." Liz took a quick drink. "I know this is difficult, but I must ask, why did you two break up?" She took another bite, studying Frank's face, waiting for his response.

"Which time?" A series of emotions passed quickly over his face, anger, sadness, and finally, resignation. "The first time, honestly, it was because I just couldn't afford to date her anymore," he said simply, nibbling on a cookie. He held the bag out to Liz, but she declined.

"I don't understand." Liz's eyebrows wrinkled, and she set down the bottle in her hand.

"I, uh, well, she…" He paused and sipped water, followed by a deep breath. "She had extravagant tastes. Every time we went out to dinner, it had to be at a fancy restaurant. Never, well, frankly, a sandwich at a table under an umbrella." Frank gestured to the table where they were sitting. "Not to mention the nightclubs she liked to go to because she heard someone famous was in town or some local rich hoity-toity would be there. Anytime I bought her a gift, it resulted in an argument if it was anything less than jewelry. Flowers that weren't roses weren't good enough." Frank took another bite and gazed into the distance as he chewed.

Liz nodded, not surprised at this answer. "Why 'the first time'?"

"Huh?" Frank asked, returning his gaze to meet Liz's.

"You said 'the first time.'"

Sadness poured off Frank in waves.

It was so strong Liz didn't have to touch him to pick up on it.

His gaze dropped, and his hand fiddled with the wax paper he'd been using as a plate. Several moments passed before he spoke again. "When I first broke up with Brittany, she…" He paused, unable to lift his gaze from the table. "She told me that she was pregnant."

"Really?" This news came as a complete surprise to Liz. "I didn't read anywhere that she was pregnant when she…" Concern filled Liz. Currently, one of the most common causes of death of pregnant women in the US wasn't medical. It was murder, most often by the father of the unborn child. Her gaze drifted toward her parked car judging the distance as her thoughts spun out of control.

"She wasn't," Frank interrupted. His voice was low.

Liz's crazy train of thoughts came to a screeching halt. Her eyebrows squished together as she gave her head a quick shake. "I don't understand. Did she lose the baby?" Liz asked quietly, gently.

"No. Brittany wasn't pregnant," he said, unable to hide the bitterness in his words.

"Now, I *really* don't understand. If Brittany wasn't pregnant when she died, and didn't lose the baby, what happened to the baby?" Liz watched as Frank struggled to gain control over his emotions.

Bitterness surrounded Frank like a balloon. "There *never* was a baby."

"What?" Liz asked incredulously, her hand dropping to her lap.

Silence fell over the table.

Chapter Twenty-Three

Liz cleared her throat and straightened up. "Excuse me. But what do you mean there was never a baby?"

Frank shrugged his broad shoulders. "She lied to me so I wouldn't break up with her."

"That b-" Liz stopped the epithet before it could escape her lips. "Sorry!" she apologized, shame coloring her cheeks.

A half-smile graced Frank's sad face, and he nodded in understanding.

The waves of anger Liz could feel from him slowly morphed into sadness.

"That's okay. That's pretty much on par with what I said to her. Only a lot louder. Even though the baby wasn't real, I still feel like I lost someone. Is that silly?" A single tear rolled down his cheek. He didn't bother brushing it away.

"That's just, well, honestly, I can't even begin to imagine." Liz shook her head in disbelief. She reached across the table and gave his hand a quick squeeze. A flash of Frank and a woman filled Liz's vision. It was choppy, like an old flickering movie. It was so fast that Liz didn't see the woman's face. And then it was gone. But not before she heard a long, high-pitched wail.

Returning to the present, she pulled her hand back to her lap. To distract herself from the wave of excitement washing over her, Liz took a bite of her thick sandwich, allowing Frank time to collect himself.

Frank cleared his throat. "That makes me a pretty credible suspect, doesn't it?" he asked, his voice low.

Liz placed the sandwich on the wax paper, her joy abating. Swallowing, she nodded. "Do you have an alibi? What were you doing the night Brittany disappeared?" Liz asked bluntly.

And just like that, Frank Stanley couldn't meet Liz's gaze. He fiddled with the wax paper, his paper napkin, and the condensation on the bottled water. "I was out," he mumbled lamely.

On a whim, Liz decided it was an excellent time to hazard a guess. "With Rosemary," she stated, studying his face closely.

Frank's gaze flew up to meet Liz's, his eyes wide, and his jaw fell. That was all the answer Liz needed.

"I saw you together Sunday night on the River Walk. How long have you two been dating?" She didn't allow Frank any opportunity to backpedal.

His shoulders dropped.

Liz could tell that he knew there was no getting out of this.

"Since mid-October last year. I didn't see Rosemary for a few months after Brittany and I broke up, especially not after that scene at the drugstore and—"

Liz interrupted him by lifting her hand. "Sorry, what scene?"

Frank cleared his throat. His jaw worked back and forth slightly. "I was at a drugstore on Navarro when I found out Brittany lied about the baby. Or, to be more accurate, I bumped into Brittany at the drugstore when I discovered that she lied."

"How did seeing her at a drugstore tell you she was lying?" Liz helped herself to one of Frank's cookies in the center of the table. She took a bite out of the chewy chocolate chip cookie and waited.

"It was what she was buying that told me. It was, as she calls it—called it—'girlie supplies.' You know." Frank gestured at Liz.

Understanding dawned on Liz quickly. "Oh. So how did that tell you that she lied? Maybe she'd lost—"

Frank shook his head slowly. "It didn't. She confessed after I asked her about it. It was bad. I'll never be able to show my face in that store again." Humiliation colored his handsome face. "I'm positive they caught the fight on their security cameras. We were, uh, asked to leave by the store manager."

"You said 'fight.' Did you hit or hurt her in any way?" Liz asked, hating to ask such a question of the heartbroken man opposite her.

He met her eyes calmly. "Not even when she told me she'd never have a baby with a lowly mechanic."

"Wow, that..." But Liz caught herself that time.

A faint smile passed over Frank's lips.

"Sorry. So, how did you and Rosie start dating?" Liz finished off the cookie in her hand.

"We bumped into each other at Bill Miller's Bar-B-Q on the north side of town in October last year." His shoulder lifted in a half-shrug.

Liz nodded, recognizing the popular local restaurant chain. "Plenty of their barbecue has graced my kitchen table over the years. And, as you said earlier, Brittany had such expensive tastes that you knew you wouldn't run into *her* there. Anyway, you and Rosemary bumped into each other." Liz gestured to Frank so he could continue.

"Yes, exactly. Rosemary doesn't share Brittany's proclivities toward fine dining and expensive clothes. We ended up eating together. At the end of the meal, Rosemary told me that she had some of my belongings. She had rescued them when Brittany tried throwing them away. So we arranged to meet again, without Brittany knowing, and it happened gradually. We realized we were dating when we ran out of excuses to meet up and saw that we didn't need or want excuses anymore. We kept it secret to protect Brittany's feelings. But when she went missing..." Frank shrugged. "It seemed tactless to go public."

Liz nodded. "I can see that. So, where were you and Rosemary the night Brittany disappeared? Really?" Internally, Liz hoped it was somewhere public with lots of witnesses. She liked her client and her handsome beau.

"At Bill Miller's again. They know us at that location. Here's the receipt." Frank pulled the folded receipt out of his wallet.

Liz raised an eyebrow at him as she took it from his hand, studying him suspiciously, her head cocked to one side.

"It's nothing bad. I dug it out of the glove box in my truck when Brittany's body was found. I've been carrying it around in my wallet, just in case the police questioned me."

Liz nodded, reading the receipt and taking a picture of the front and back with her phone. The date and time on the receipt showed he was at the location. The restaurant's address confirmed he was in a neighborhood far away from downtown. She handed it back to Frank. "Hang on to this. Detective Sowell will want it, and I'd prefer that you are the one to give it to him." She bit her lip.

Frank returned it to his wallet. "You seem sad. Isn't the receipt our alibi?"

Liz looked into his blue eyes. "I assume that is your partial credit card number at the bottom of the receipt?"

Frank nodded "But...?"

"And the receipt shows 'dine-in,' so you ate there."

"Yes, but..."

"That proves where *you* were the night Brittany disappeared, but not that Rosemary was with you. I'll need something more that shows she was with you and not at the hotel murdering her roommate to clear the path to you. That's how the police will see it, too, I'm afraid."

"Oh wow!" Frank's jaw fell open. "That looks bad. But she was with me, isn't that enough?"

Liz shook her head sadly. "Police like evidence. Irrefutable proof that Rosemary was nowhere near the hotel when Brittany was murdered."

Frank's eyebrows went up, and he reached for his phone. Lots of tapping and swiping later, he stopped, tapped a couple more times, and smiled. A deep breath escaped him. "Will this do?"

A selfie of Frank and Rosemary filled the screen on his phone, and a sign displaying the restaurant's name was on the wall behind them. Liz tapped the screen for more details, and the date and time stamp, complete with the restaurant's GPS coordinates, appeared.

Liz smiled broadly. She had never been so happy to see that long series of numbers before. She took a picture of his phone with the display of information. "That'll do. Rosemary is speaking with A. J., Detective Sowell, right now. I'm sure you'll be hearing from him soon. Just be sure to show him that picture and receipt. That should be enough to clear suspicion from you both!"

Liz could feel the stress falling away from Frank even across the table.

"Do you think? I mean, do they know what time she was murdered yet?" Frank asked, his voice low.

"No, not that I'm aware of. But since she was still wearing her uniform when the police identified her, she was at the hotel. What did you do after dinner?"

Frank grinned. "Went back to my place and streamed a rented movie."

"Anymore selfies by any chance?"

His grin widened. "Just one." He swiped at his phone again and handed the phone back to Liz. Once again, the date, time, and GPS coordinates confirmed when and where the photo had been taken.

Liz looked at the photo and couldn't hide her smile. Frank had taken a selfie of himself and Rosemary on the couch. She was sound asleep, her head on his shoulder, her mouth gaping wide open. "Awww!"

Frank grinned. "Yeah, I love this picture. It's a pity it's not a video though."

"Why do you say that?" Liz asked, taking a sip of water.

"Because she was snoring like a buzzsaw!" Frank laughed.

A snort and a cough escaped Liz as she nearly spewed water across the table, making Frank laugh even more.

The dam of stress was broken, and Frank and Liz laughed together. "You can't tell Rosemary that I told you that. She'd kill me. Then your police detective friend will *have* to arrest her!"

Liz giggled. "I won't say a word," she promised, wiping water from her chin and tears of laughter from her cheeks.

After the laughter subsided, Liz took a bite of her sandwich when another question came to her. She raised an index finger, chewed quickly, and swigged some water. "Odd question. Do you know anything about this mystery guest? More specifically, Brittany's obsession with him or her?"

Frank rolled his eyes dramatically. "Lord, she was obsessed with finding out who that was! Big actors would stay on occasion, and she'd barely say two words about them. But that one unknown guest drove her to distraction! It was constant! There was a point when her only two topics of conversation were complaining about her boss and theorizing about that mystery guest! It got really old, really fast." Frank grabbed another cookie, gesturing for Liz to help herself.

Liz accepted one, nibbling on it thoughtfully. Her eyes raised to the sky beyond the umbrella.

"That's what Rosemary said," Liz said quietly. She returned her gaze to meet Frank's. "Do you remember a time when she stopped talking about this person?"

"No. I remember when Brittany stopped complaining about her boss though. We went out for dinner at a breakfast place, which was unusual, because it wasn't a fancy restaurant. Brittany said she was craving waffles." Frank's jaw set as his brow furrowed.

Liz heard his teeth grind.

"Wow! She really played me! She even faked cravings when she was faking being pregnant! Now I'm curious just how far she was planning on taking that whole act?" He shook his head. "Sorry." He returned to the topic at hand. "She wanted to celebrate getting a raise at work. She didn't complain about her boss after that. I honestly can't remember when she stopped talking about that guest. We broke up not long after that meal, so I don't know if she ever found out who the person was."

Liz finished the chocolate chip cookie. "You know, Rosemary thought Brittany stopped complaining about her boss because she was having an affair with him."

Frank choked, coughed, and pounded himself on the chest. He wiped up the cookie crumbs that had sprayed over his side of the table with a napkin. "What? No way! Rosemary's never said anything like that to me!"

Liz nodded slowly. "Well, that's probably because she was trying to protect your feelings. I'm assuming she knows all about the fake pregnancy?" Liz gestured to Frank. He nodded. "Then, would she want to pour salt on the wound? Really?"

Frank opened his mouth to speak but stopped. "You're right. She wouldn't. Wow, do you think they...Brittany and Mr. Moore? Really?"

Liz shrugged. "At this point, I honestly don't know. This morning, I would have said it was unlikely. But now, knowing how she treated you, I'm not so sure anymore."

They finished their lunch together, at ease now that the air was clear of suspicion, but Liz had more questions. None that Frank could answer though.

Liz stood, holding the snacks she brought out to Frank. "Do you want these for later? I don't want you getting hungry halfway through your shift because you gave me half your lunch."

Frank waved the gesture aside. "Thanks, but I'm fine. Just a few more hours and I'm done for the day." He held his hand out to Liz across the table. "It was great meeting you, Liz, and thank you! I feel *so* much better now!"

Liz took his rough, warm hand, feeling a light weight form in her chest. "I'm glad, and thank you for lunch. It was delicious. Please, take my card." She held it out to him with her free hand. "Don't hesitate to call if you think of anything else."

Frank nodded, sticking her business card into his wallet alongside the receipt. "I will." His eyes sparkled. "I'll email you the recipe for that sandwich too. Do you like tuna salad?"

Liz's eyes rolled back in her head. "Oh, yes, please!"

They threw their trash away and parted company.

One conversation successfully exonerated two of her suspects, at least in Liz's eyes. She drove away from the repair shop, waving to Frank as she passed.

Chapter Twenty-Four

"Oh, thank God, I was worried you would be late!" Claire stopped pacing when Liz entered the office.

"For what? What's wrong?" Liz asked, concern washing over her. She dropped her purse on the couch, her keys digging into her hand.

"A. J. called. He's finished at Rosemary's house, so he's still available for dinner tonight!"

Liz let out a deep breath. "Claire." Liz looked at her friend through lowered eyebrows. "Do we have to break out the dictionary to define an emergency again? And this is work. Not a date!" Maybe if she said it often enough, she'd start to believe it.

Claire raised her hand, gently patting the air. "Sure, sure. Not a date. Got it. He called asking if you could meet him an hour earlier. Still not an emergency?"

"What? Why didn't he...?" A brief flash of panic washed over Liz's face as her eyes opened wide. She dug her phone out of the side pocket of her purse. As soon as she turned on the screen, the notification appeared, a voice mail from A. J. Sowell. "He must have called while I was driving." Liz flushed while she listened to his husky voice. She tapped a text message back to A. J. before setting her phone aside again. "There. Still, not an emergency." Liz insisted, wishing she could stop blushing at every mention of the detective. "Do you want to hear about my interview with Frank Stanley or not? It may include my first clairvoyant vision in more than a month, but if you're not interested…" Liz made like she was going to walk away.

"What? Really? That's fantastic!" Claire's excitement for her was infectious. She dashed across the room, throwing her arms around Liz in a tight embrace.

Happiness washed through Liz. The most challenging part for a person with empathic abilities was that, sometimes, it was difficult to tell if an emotion was yours or the other person's, especially when you were both experiencing the same one.

"I know. I'm feeling so much better now that there are at least small signs of my abilities returning," Liz said into the cloud of Claire's hair.

Claire released Liz and collapsed into the small armchair, prepared to listen to the details.

Liz sat on the couch, kicked off her shoes, and rested her feet on the coffee table. She sighed happily before launching into a summary of the interview with Frank. This was the part Liz enjoyed the most. When speaking with Claire, since she knew Liz's secret, Liz could include *all* the details of an interview—both psychic and mundane. When Liz wrote her reports, they only contained mundane details, which sometimes involved a touch of creativity.

Claire gave all the appropriate responses as Liz recounted her interview.

"Well, it sure doesn't sound like Frank, or Rosemary, killed her," Claire said when Liz finished. "Although, no one would blame him if he had. Wow! I can't imagine!"

"I know, right? I was shocked when we discovered she was spending money on stuff instead of helping Rosemary with the bills," Liz agreed. "But this takes the cake! Even Frank was wondering how far she was planning on taking the pregnancy. He realized while we were talking that she even faked cravings! How messed up is that?"

"She was the worst! Do we even *want* to find the person who killed her? Or, would it be evil to send them flowers after they're arrested?" Claire asked, slapping the back of her hand to chide herself. A small grin softened the cruelty of her words.

"Yes, I have to agree. All the evidence shows that Brittany was the worst roommate and girlfriend. Yes, we want to find the killer, even if it's just to take suspicion off the suspects we like. And yes—" Liz wagged her finger at her friend, "—it would be evil to send the killer flowers!"

Claire returned to her desk, grinning and waggling her fingers above her forehead like little devil horns.

Liz shook her head before glancing at her watch. "Okay. I have enough time to type up my notes of both interviews before changing and meeting A. J. You can leave early if you want," Liz offered.

"You know, I'll take you up on that. My research was stalling out a bit anyway. I took care of some accounting while you were gone, by the way. The final invoice to the Masterson family is in the mail."

With those words, a knot formed in Liz's throat, and she froze in place. The memory of her last conversation with Regina Masterson's parents washed over her.

"No. I can't do that," Liz stated firmly, sitting on the dark leather couch opposite Mr. and Mrs. Masterson in their family room.

Phyllis Masterson dabbed at her eyes with a cotton handkerchief. She gave Liz a watery smile. "Yes, honey, you will." She reached for her husband's hand and he nodded.

"No. I can't. I didn't find Regina." Liz swallowed the sob that threatened her self-control. "Not in time anyway. I don't feel right about charging you after I failed so miserably." A single tear rolled down her cheek.

"Don't you understand? You're the reason we have answers. Even though you didn't get to her before…" Mrs. Masterson's voice caught in her throat. She took a shaky breath. "You brought her home to us. In this kind of situation, so many parents don't get that. We want to pay you." Mrs. Masterson moved over and sat next to Liz, pulling her into a tight embrace.

Ultimately, Liz agreed to bill them, but only if they let her spread out the invoices. She wanted to allow them some breathing room after the unexpected funeral expenses.

"Liz!"

Claire's voice brought Liz back to the present. Her friend was watching her with a concerned look on her face. Liz ran a hand over her eyes. They were dry this time. "Sorry, I'm okay. Thanks for taking care of that, Claire. I'm going to knock out this paperwork. Let me know before you leave!"

Liz pushed up and off the couch.

"Will do!" Claire called out as Liz walked the short distance to her desk.

The remainder of the afternoon flew by, and before Liz knew it, Claire appeared in front of her desk.

"I'm taking off now, but first, I'm running into your apartment for a minute!" Claire stated, a broad smile on her face, turning away before Liz had time to say anything.

"Um, sure. Huh?" Liz asked, looking away from her monitor, but her assistant was already gone. "Why?" She followed her, catching up as Claire opened the apartment door by her desk.

"Because I want to root through your closet and pick out something nice for you to wear on your date tonight," Claire responded simply.

"It's not a date!" Liz responded, not bothering to hide her frustration at her friend's insistence that her plans with A. J. were anything other than work.

"Whatever you say, honey. And what are you planning to wear for this non-date?" Claire asked, leaning against the doorframe, her fashionable purse dangling from her crossed arms.

Liz glanced down at her worn jeans and purple t-shirt. "Well—"

"No. Absolutely not. Come on up to your room as soon as you're done. Hopeless!" Claire ended the conversation with a wave and turned on her heel.

"But..." Liz called lamely after her friend. She returned to her desk and tried to focus on her reports. After the third attempt at writing and rewriting the same sentence, she saved her work and logged off. *Could this be a date?* she wondered, even as she shook her head. *Surely I'd know if...*

Liz looked at her clothes. Suddenly, the jeans seemed old and the shirt was just wrong.

"Fine!" Liz pushed away from her desk and shut off the floor lamp behind her chair. "You win!" she yelled as she walked through her apartment. "Nothing too over the top, okay?" she called out as she headed up the stairs leading to her loft bedroom.

"It's about time you saw things my way! Get in here!" Claire's voice was muffled.

Liz entered her bedroom, her eyes took in the disaster that greeted her. Her bed was completely covered with clothes. "Claire? Holy crap!"

Claire stepped out of the closet with hangers hooked over each finger. "Liz! You can't spend your entire life in jeans and t-shirts! Trust me. We can put a nice outfit together without going too over the top. Look, I found this nice forest green blouse. It'll bring out the green in your eyes. Do you own slacks? You know, pants made from something other than denim?"

Liz made a face at her friend. "Of course I do. I just don't know where they are," she finished weakly. Dragging her feet, she joined Claire in the closet. "They're here somewhere, I'm sure." The two women rooted around. "You know, I swear, I had no clue that I owned this many clothes! For crying out loud! Aha!" Liz held a pair of black slacks above her head in victory.

"Finally!" Claire cheered from amidst a cloud of shirts and hangers. She and Liz laid the two items next to each other on the bed. "Perfect. Now go to the bathroom and put this on. Then I'll help you with your hair."

"You know, sometimes you can be very bossy," Liz teased, picking up the outfit from the bed.

"Yep. Now scootch!" Claire chased Liz out of the room with a hanger.

Liz couldn't help but smile when she looked at her reflection after changing into the clothes Claire had picked out for her. The tapered slacks showed off her slender waist and made her legs look longer. And, as her friend predicted, the blouse did bring out the green in her eyes. That was something Liz had never noticed before.

When Liz returned to her room, Claire had miraculously tidied away most of the mess.

"Wow! Look at you!" Claire exclaimed as she stepped out of the closet. "Beautiful. Now let's work on your hair and makeup."

Claire took Liz by the elbow and guided her back into the bathroom. By the time Claire was finished, even Liz had to admit she looked pretty. Not too dressed up, but nice enough for a non-date.

She and Claire finished tidying away the last of the clothes on her bed before heading downstairs. Grabbing purses, keys, and jackets, they cut through the office, locking up behind them as they headed out into the cool night air. Winter was making its presence known again this evening.

Liz and Claire walked to the intersection to cross when Liz froze in place on the sidewalk.

"What's wrong?" Claire stopped in the crosswalk and turned around.

"Oh my God, I think this might be a date!" Liz answered suddenly, not meeting Claire's eyes.

Claire followed Liz's gaze and saw A. J. stepping off the curb to meet them. His hair was combed, and he was even wearing a tie.

"I told you so." Claire teased before offering a bright smile to the handsome detective. "Detective H-, Sowell. A. J., how are you this evening?" Claire gave Liz time to collect herself.

"Fine, thanks. And thank you again for your help today." The three of them finished crossing the street together. "I still can't believe the original officers missed those items!"

Claire dismissed his words with a wave of her hand. "They were looking for signs of foul play. I was looking for signs of haute couture."

"I appreciate the help all the same. Are you joining us for dinner?" A. J. asked, glancing over at a quiet Liz.

"Oh no. I don't want to intrude! You two go, enjoy!" Claire walked the short distance down the street to the parking structure. With a wave, she disappeared around the corner.

Chapter Twenty-Five

"She is something else, isn't she?" A. J. commented with a grin.

"That's for sure," Liz responded, nervously touching her hair. Claire had put a small *flip* of a curl at the ends and which was more effort than Liz normally put into her hairdo. Mostly because curls wouldn't last in her hair.

A. J. smiled at her. "Hi. You look nice."

A faint blush warmed Liz's face. "Hi, thanks. Uh, so do you." She glanced up to meet his gaze, but he was already looking away.

They fell into step side by side, walking down the stairs to enter the popular restaurant from the River Walk level.

"Thanks again for calling me this morning. I don't know how it will help our case, but I believe there's a connection. By the way, I've already put my name down for a table. It's a little chilly this evening, so we're eating inside," A. J. explained as they approached the hostess stand.

"Perfect. You know." Liz stopped walking and touched his arm. "I've never eaten inside Casa Rio before! I eat here regularly, but it's always been outside by the river." Liz gestured to the row of tables with brightly colored umbrellas interspersed with outdoor heaters that bordered the normally flowing river.

"Really? I have a lot, usually with my family."

An awkward silence fell over them while they waited in the cool January air.

Liz fiddled with her keys in her jacket pocket.

A. J. pulled his phone out of his back pocket to see if the restaurant had texted him that their table was ready.

The awkwardness got to Liz until finally, she spoke up. "I kept telling Claire that this isn't a date." Liz heated a bit when she looked into A. J.'s ruggedly handsome face.

A. J. relaxed visibly, his shoulders shifted, and a boyish, lopsided grin crossed his face. "I kept telling my partner the same thing. It's just dinner. We're two colleagues comparing notes over a meal. Right?"

Liz smiled. "Right!"

"Yeah, he didn't believe me either."

Liz laughed, her nervousness dissipating. At least they were in this together.

A. J.'s phone buzzed. He pulled it out of his back pocket and read the text message. "Our table is ready." He placed his hand on Liz's lower back to guide her toward the man wearing a bright white server apron coming down the stairs to meet them. He was an older gentleman and his face lit up as they approached. "Oh, aren't you a handsome couple? Wonderful. My best table for you! Very romantic!" His voice reverberated off the buildings around them with the faintest trace of a Hispanic accent. He whispered something to a waitress as they passed.

Liz and A. J. shared a smile and a low laugh as they followed their escort into the dining room.

The interior of the restaurant was brightly lit. Creamy white paint covered the rough-hewn stone walls. Splashes of color abounded, from designs painted onto the large wooden tabletops to the multicolored heavy wooden chairs. A brilliantly striped sarape was draped over a chair in a corner. Large, oversized paintings of women, young and old, dancing in colorful Jalisco dresses adorned the walls. Photos of the restaurant throughout the decades were nestled among the paintings.

The gentleman stopped at a table in the corner, holding the chair for Liz as she sat down. He laid the menus on the table between them as A. J. took his seat.

"I have a confession to make," the elderly man stated. "I'm not a waiter but one of the owners. We are short-staffed this evening, so I'm helping out. Please have patience with me. I'm a little rusty."

Liz and A. J. smiled up at him.

"Of course. We feel honored, don't we, Liz?" A. J. smiled at Liz across the table.

"Absolutely."

The kind man patted Liz on the shoulder. "I'll let you look at the menus and be right back with glasses of water and our wonderful chips and salsa."

Neither Liz nor A. J. reached for their menus.

"It's beautiful in here! I can't believe I've never come inside before! Then again, I typically enjoy eating out by the river and sharing chips with the birds."

A. J. didn't have time to respond before the man reappeared, carrying a tray in his hands.

The restauranteur set the tray on a nearby empty table and winked at them. "Arthritis. I can't carry the trays over my head, on one hand, the way I used to." He set glasses of iced water with lemon wedges perched on the rim in front of them, followed by a large metal bowl of chips and small bowls of salsa. "Have you decided on your drinks yet?" He looked to Liz first.

"Unsweet tea for me, please."

"Sweet tea for me, please," A. J. chimed in.

"Excellent!" He turned away, scooping his tray off the table.

"Actually," Liz spoke up, "I know what I want to order already. How about you, A. J.?"

"Yes," A. J. agreed, his raised eyebrows showed his surprise.

"Wonderful!" The gentleman returned the tray to the table and pulled an order pad from his apron pocket. He jotted down their drink order and waited.

"The chicken fajita dinner for me, please," Liz ordered, sliding her menu to the edge of the table.

"Excellent. And for you, sir?" He turned to A. J.

"The beef enchilada dinner, please."

"Wonderful!" He scooped up the menus and tray before hurrying away, stopping to greet other patrons as he wove his way through the dining room.

"I hope I have nearly as much energy as he does when I'm his age!" A. J. commented as the older man disappeared into the kitchen.

"I know, right? I say the same thing every time I'm around my mother. Energy pours off her in waves. He's the same way." Liz smiled at A. J. "What would happen if we got them in the same room together? Nuclear blast?"

A. J. grinned in response, shaking his head. "I'm thinking a spontaneous party incorporating every business along the River Walk that would go down in history." They shared a laugh.

Liz nodded. "You're exactly right!"

A young, pretty server showed up with their drinks. She set them down, blushed, and ran off.

"Well, that was different," Liz commented, reaching for her glass. She took a sip, and the sugary tea hit her taste buds like a freight train. She set the glass on the table, forced herself to swallow, and made a face. She looked across the table and saw A. J. making, what she imagined, was the same expression. She giggled. "Unsweet?"

He wrinkled his nose.

Without hesitating, Liz swapped their glasses. "Bottoms up!" They clinked their glasses and sipped again. Sighs of satisfaction floated into the air.

"I don't know how you can have all that sugar!" Liz commented, happy now to have rinsed the sugary taste from her mouth. "Don't get me wrong. I like sugar in cookies, ice cream, and donuts. I add it to my coffee on occasion and certain hot teas. Things I want to be sweet. Not iced tea, though, unless it's been steeped too long. I'll add a little sugar to mask the tannins," Liz stopped, embarrassed. She hadn't meant to prattle on about tea or sugar.

A. J. smiled. "So you're saying you don't like things that are too sweet. And that you are a tea snob. Gotcha."

Liz opened her mouth to argue but caught herself. She grinned instead. "I never realized it before, but I am. It's my mother's fault. This time of year, she's all about hot teas mostly. Irish breakfast is her current favorite. Loads of caffeine."

"It sounds like you and your mother are close," A. J. commented, toying with the condensation on his glass. "That's nice."

"It is. Mom is a complete nut at times, unpredictable with her interests, but has a great sense of humor and is an amazing mom."

"Wow, that's the best description of a mother I've ever heard. What about your dad?" A. J. asked, crossing his arms, leaning forward to rest them on the table. His brown eyes focused on Liz.

Liz warmed to the attention. "He's awesome too. Super supportive, has a sense of humor to rival my mother's, and is just about the worst repairman around. Matched only by his best friend, Pam's dad. He wants to be good at it—has all the tools, watches all the videos—but, without fail, something goes horribly wrong. We're never sure what. He's a genius at the grill though." Liz allowed her eyes to drift closed while she remembered. "He makes the most amazing ribs! You have to try them sometime." Liz stopped and took a sip of her tea. She hoped she wasn't blushing or sounding like she was making future plans for them together.

He ignored the implication. "Sounds fantastic. I am pretty good at barbecuing too. If I do say so myself." He grinned, blew on his fingers, and polished his nails on his shirt.

Liz set her glass on the table. "Really? To quote my dad and Uncle Tommy, 'Them thar are fightin' words,' which results in a challenge to a cookoff. Once a month, at least, from about April to September, they try to outdo each other on their barbecues."

A. J. nodded. "My brothers and I are the same: beef, pork, chicken. Steaks, ribs, chops, you name it. Sometimes I wonder if it would be easier to just hand my paycheck over to the butcher."

Liz laughed, nodding. "I've heard my dad say the same thing!"

All this talk about barbecue made the pair ravenous. First, Liz's stomach rumbled loudly, followed immediately by A. J.'s. They laughed together.

"What does your mother do?" A. J. asked, taking a sip of his sweet tea.

"She is co-owner of the Alamo Bells Yoga Studio. You've probably noticed it. It's next to my office." Liz did nothing to hide her pride in her mother and best friend's enterprise.

"Really? Some of the female officers go there. One or two of the men, too, after recovering from injuries. They all swear by yoga now. I've heard nothing but good things."

"I'll be sure to tell Mom and Pam. They'll be thrilled!" Liz responded, delighted at the unsolicited praise of their business.

"Pam? As in your best friend, Pam, from Sunday night?"

Liz nodded. "The studio used to be co-owned by my mom and Pam's mom, Susan. Aunt Susan passed away when we were teenagers. Mom's been teaching yoga to Pam and me since we were kids. Pam took to it way more than I did. After high school, she got her certification and partnered with my mother. They are planning to expand into the space next door. Then they will be able to hire another couple of teachers."

"That's a shame about her mother. But on the business front, wow, that's impressive!" A. J. opened his mouth to say more, but their waiter returned with the nervous young lady in tow.

The restauranteur set the tray down, while the server placed fresh glasses of tea in front of them before dashing off with their empty glasses.

"My granddaughter. She was nervous about carrying the pitchers," the older man explained, resting his hand on the back of A. J.'s sturdy chair. "She's timid, so I thought I'd help her get over it by having her work at the restaurant." He and A. J. watched as she disappeared into the kitchen.

"How's that going so far?" A. J. asked, winking at Liz. A smile spread across his face.

A low sigh escaped the kind man. "Not so great. Oh well, we'll find something to draw her out of that shell. You've not eaten any of your chips and salsa. Is there something wrong?" Without hesitating, he grabbed a small chip, scooped up some salsa, and popped it into his mouth. Chewing and swallowing quickly, he shook his head. "No. It's fine."

Chastened, A. J. looked up at the man with a broad smile. "We've been busy talking. I forgot it was there. We'll do better, we promise."

"No, talking is good. Getting to know each other better is good. Make sure to eat your dinner though. I can't have my patrons leaving hungry. It just won't do!"

They each ate a chip heaped with fresh salsa to appease the man. Happier, the owner set their entrées on the table. "Enjoy!" He held his arms wide before walking away, whistling with the tray under his arm.

"Thank you!" Liz and A. J. called out in unison.

They ate in companionable silence for a few moments before Liz spoke up.

"How did your interview with Rosemary go? Did you find more high-end items?" She constructed a fajita with the collection of ingredients spread across three plates before her. Spanish rice, seasoned grilled chicken, pico de gallo, and creamy guacamole all made their way onto the small warm flour tortilla in her hand.

"No, we didn't find anything else, but we're arranging to take a look in her hotel locker. The interview went well overall. She was a little stressed over Claire's discovery. She broke down a couple of times, I'm afraid."

Liz's eyes opened wide in shock. "You made that sweet young thing cry? How mean of you!" Liz paused and grimaced. "Come to think of it, so did I! And she fainted. I suppose she has been under extreme stress this week." Liz topped her fajita with a generous dollop of snowy white sour cream and took a bite.

"Possibly. Did you know Ms. Travers has a boyfriend?" A. J. asked.

Liz's eyes drifted closed as she savored her first bite of the fajita. The flavors combined perfectly. She opened her eyes after she swallowed and smiled. "Sorry, I don't know why I'm so hungry. I had a great sandwich at lunch." Liz paused to take a sip of tea while A. J. cut into his queso-smothered enchilada. "Which was made by Rosemary's boyfriend. So, yes, I know. I can give you his contact info if you want it."

A. J. stared at Liz, his eyes wide. "What?" his question was muffled as he concealed his mouth with a cloth napkin.

"I arranged to meet Brittany's ex-boyfriend over lunch while you were speaking with Claire this morning. Frank Stanley and Rosemary Travers have been dating since mid-October. It came up during our interview." Liz set her fajita down and reached for a chip.

"Wow!" A. J. exclaimed, drinking some iced tea. "We must have found out at the same time then. Weird. Poor Rosemary. She was so convinced that their relationship made her look guilty. Which, in reality, it does. At least until we have corroborated their shared alibi, does he look good for this?" A. J. asked before cutting another piece of his beef enchilada with his fork. He dragged the forkful of food through the sea of queso before putting it into his mouth.

Liz shook her head. "When he told me the story of his and Brittany's breakup, I had my concerns. But, now, after seeing the evidence of their alibi, no, definitely not."

A. J.'s eyes lit up. "Proof of an alibi. That's perfect. Please say he'll readily provide this proof and it's solid."

Liz nodded again, eating some of the toppings for her fajitas with a chip. "I'd still like to confirm it with the restaurant they were at, but, yeah, I think it's solid."

"Great!" A. J. ate another chip with salsa, winking at Liz.

"Oh, and I told Frank that it would be better if he gave you their alibi himself." Liz popped the last bite of her first fajita into her mouth.

"I have to say, Liz, your investigation has helped us a ton," A. J. complimented her ability sincerely. "Are you sure you don't want to become a police officer?" he teased.

"Thanks, but no. I'm glad I can help. After our last case together, I had doubts..." Liz's voice drifted off. Her gaze dropped to her hand as it fiddled with the corner of her napkin.

To her surprise, A. J.'s hand gently covered hers.

A quick flash of vision overtook her mind and a shiver ran through her body. In Liz's mind she saw A. J. standing in an office. Feet planted wide. Gun held steady in both hands. His firearm pointing directly at her!

Chapter Twenty-Six

"Liz, are you okay? I don't know…you kind of went away for a second there." A. J.'s gaze ran over her face.

"I'm fine. I promise," Liz said woodenly, unsure how to reconcile her vision with the man sitting across from her.

"You sure?" A. J. asked, his forehead wrinkled, dragging his hand back across the table.

"I'm sure." The vision faded. She gave herself a mental kick and a reminder, *A. J. would* never *hurt you*! "Sometimes remembering how wrong that case went, it still bothers me, you know?" She cleared her throat. "How's your food?" Liz asked, steering the conversation to a neutral topic.

"Yes, I know. And, uh, great." A. J. took the cue, picking up his fork again. "Yours?"

"Wonderful. Would you like to try some?"

A. J. declined, allowing the serious mood to dissipate. They ate in silence for a few minutes. Tejano music played by a wandering three-person mariachi band drifted through the restaurant.

"So," Liz asked, after regaining her self-control, "when you made Rosemary cry, did you learn anything else?" she teased, mentally working to shrug off the remnants of the vision. As she well knew, what she saw wasn't always a certainty until seen in context. Why would A. J. point a gun at her? There had to be more to the story.

"You made her cry too." He pointed his fork at her. "And at least I didn't make her faint!" A. J. chided gently.

"Good point. I wonder what the deal is? I've never had a client or suspect faint on me before!"

"Really? I have. Just this week, in fact. One second, we're talking, the next she slides to the ground and..."

"No way!" Then it hit her. He was talking about her on Sunday night. "Hey!" She threw a chip across the table.

A crooked grin spread across his face as he scooped up the chip from the table and threw it into his mouth with a quick wink. "And no, I don't think I've learned anything new. She was something of a mess after she revealed the identity of her boyfriend."

Liz smiled, relaxing once more. "No problem. After all, we're in this together, again."

A. J. grinned before taking another chip and stealing some of Liz's guacamole.

"Hey!" she protested, playfully shielding her plates with her hands. "Get your own!"

A. J. winked at her. "Delicious! Next time."

"Did she say anything about this mystery guest at the hotel? Brittany was completely obsessed with finding out who it was." Liz nibbled on her food, playfully slapping away A. J.'s hand each time he tried to steal more guacamole from her plate.

A. J. nodded. "Yes, I can't imagine who that might be. I am seriously considering asking the hotel manager to take me up tomorrow afternoon."

Liz grinned. "Oh really? Rosemary offered to help me get up there in the morning. And Mac is going to help, although he doesn't know yet. Do you want to tag along?"

A. J.'s eyebrows went up, and he gave her a lopsided smile. "You know, I'll take you up on that. What time?"

"I'm meeting Rosemary in the lobby at nine tomorrow morning. Um, can I suggest you *not* look like a police officer when you show up?"

A. J. agreed, his eyes twinkling. "Oh, I almost forgot." He reached into his jacket pocket, hanging on the back of the chair next to him, and pulled out a folded sheet of paper. "Here are the details about the fundraiser. It's a couple of months away, so you have time to figure out anything special you may need for your booth."

A vision flashed through Liz's mind as she accepted the paper. An old green army tent in stark contrast to her glittery fortune teller décor. The future, obviously. A quick thrill ran through her body. "Thanks! I can't wait. That will give me plenty of time to practice. It's been a while since I have read Tarot." She wiggled her eyebrows.

They lingered over the end of their meal. The kind owner came over to check on them. "How is everything? More tea? Chips?" His shy granddaughter waited for him near the staging station, rolling cutlery into cloth napkins, pitchers of iced tea on hand. She glanced furtively at her grandfather as she placed each napkin roll in a waiting basket.

"Oh no. Thank you. It was wonderful," Liz replied. She looked to A. J. as he agreed wholeheartedly.

"Everything was perfect, as usual. Liz, do you want dessert?" A. J. asked.

"No. I can't eat another bite. You can if you want. I don't mind."

A. J. declined. "I think we're good, sir. Just the check, please."

The older man nodded and started to step away from the table.

"Split the check, please," Liz piped up, stopping him.

The older man turned back to them, his eyebrows raised in surprise.

"No. One check, ignore her." A. J. winked at the gentleman while he circled a finger at his temple.

Recognizing the argument that was about to ensue, the man smiled brightly, and left. He returned with a single check leaving it on the table between them with a sly wink at A. J.

"A. J., I can pay for mine. I don't mind," Liz protested.

"No. I invited *you* out for dinner. I'm paying."

"But…"

Wrestling his wallet out of the back pocket of his dark jeans, A. J. pulled his credit card out and began tapping it quietly on the table.

Seeing that she was fighting a losing battle, Liz ceded defeat. "Okay, I give up. This time. Next time, I pay."

"Deal." A. J. lifted a finger to their server standing next to his granddaughter, whispering, sharing a private laugh.

Liz sat back and bit her lip.

"What's wrong?" A. J. asked as their waiter's granddaughter walked over to accept his credit card, unable to raise her gaze off the floor.

"Nothing." Liz grinned. "I just feel a little guilty now that I didn't share my guacamole with you."

"That'll teach you," A. J. teased.

After they left the restaurant, they stood on the River Walk level, A. J. gestured to the right instead of left in the direction of Liz's apartment. "Want to take a stroll and walk off some of our meal?" he invited with a shy smile.

Chapter Twenty-Seven

"Sure." Liz zipped up her jacket, shoving her hands into the pockets as they fell into step next to each other.

They walked past the line of empty tables with their brightly colored umbrellas. The temperature was cooler now, and there weren't any brave souls eating outside that evening. Even the bubbles of heat generated by the large portable heaters weren't enough to entice customers to eat under the clear night sky.

"So, I realized today that I've never asked you how you became a private investigator?" A. J. asked as they strolled along, passing couples, some hand in hand.

"That's an interesting story, to me anyway." Liz stepped behind A. J. and allowed another couple approaching them to pass. "I went to college like most of my friends and was studying to get my Bachelor's in Criminal Justice. One night, as a sophomore, I was out on a locksmith call when I saw a broken window. The person who called us had already showed me proof that they lived there. He was pretty embarrassed that he'd broken a window while trying to find another way in. But when I started working on the lock, I realized he was an abusive husband, and his injured wife had locked him out."

"Wow! That's a heck of a guess. What tipped you off?" A. J. asked, placing his hand on Liz's waist, guiding her past a lone pedestrian more fixated on his phone than his surroundings.

"Thank you." Liz's heart thudded in her chest at his touch.

A. J.'s hand slipped from her waist.

Liz resumed her story, even as her heart continued to flutter. "One clue was seeing the big cut he was trying to hide on his arm. He'd already told me he'd broken the window. So why hide it? The second was seeing his wife inside the house. There were these tall, skinny windows on each side of the door. Like at my office."

A. J. nodded.

"When I knelt to pick the lock, I could see her inside, curled up in a corner, sporting a decent black eye and cradling what turned out to be a broken arm across her chest. A large kitchen knife was lying on the floor next to her. She shook her head at me. I tell you, incompetence isn't a valued trait to me, but it can be a useful ploy. I feigned a need for tools from my car and called the police. I returned to the front door and faked having trouble with the lock, dragging it out until the police arrived."

"You got lucky. That could have gone bad quickly. Domestic disturbance calls are among the most dangerous situations for a police officer." A. J. looked at her sternly, lowering his eyebrows.

Liz shrugged. "I know, but once I realized the woman on the other side of that door was in danger, I did what needed to be done."

"Do you know how it all turned out?" A. J. asked quietly.

Liz gave him a small smile, remembering the woman. "As soon as the police had him in custody, I was through that lock in seconds. She cried when I told her it was all over. He had kept her prisoner in the house for two days after she locked him out. Every time she tried to escape, he'd block her path."

"What about a restraining order? Why didn't she call the police?" A. J. asked.

Liz could tell from the stern expression on his face that A.J. was fully invested in that woman's safety and well-being now.

"There wasn't time. Since her husband had her trapped in the house, she couldn't go to the police to get a restraining order. Plus, he managed to cut the phone lines to the house so she couldn't call for help. Before you ask, she couldn't afford a cell phone."

A. J.'s mouth formed a firm line. "You probably saved that woman's life that night."

"The police officers who arrested him told me the same thing. I tell you, that was a heady feeling for a twenty-year-old. When all was said and done, he went to jail for unlawful imprisonment and assault. She didn't fight any of the charges. I sat next to her in court for every session. I was even there when she testified against him. She told me later that I helped her stay strong. After that, I considered becoming a police officer for a while, but then I met a private investigator on a locksmith job one day. It sounded more intriguing to my independent nature."

"I'm glad it ended so well for her. Hopefully, the husband kept away from her when he got out."

Liz's gaze lowered to the ground. "Reports were that he still thought he was the biggest, toughest guy in the room, even in prison. He was killed by another inmate a month into his sentence."

"Oh, wow." A. J. looked sideways at Liz. "You don't blame yourself for that, do you? Obviously, he brought that on himself."

"I know," Liz stated simply. There was a brief time that she'd blamed herself, but then she remembered his wife's testimony. He had tortured that poor woman for years.

As they approached the quiet Arneson River Theatre, A. J. steered Liz with his hand at the small of her back, and they turned left to walk up and over Rosita's Bridge, the only officially named footpath bridge on the River Walk, so that they could cross to the other side.

Liz looked up at him. "Don't you want to keep walking... Oh!"

They paused at the bridge's apex and saw the crime scene in the distance.

"Thank you," Liz said quietly.

"No problem. So," A. J. resumed their conversation as they stepped off the bridge on the other side. "You were a locksmith in college. How did that come about?"

"Am," Liz corrected. "I *am* a locksmith. Only part-time, but still, it comes in handy with my work. Don't worry." She raised her hand to ward off a lecture from A. J. "I'm not breaking into places to gather evidence or anything like that. But if a client needs their locks changed to keep out an unwanted person, usually an ex who doesn't want to let go, I take care of that for them. I decided to get licensed the summer before starting college, because I thought it'd be an interesting job to have while going to school."

"So, you're saying, the next time I lock myself out of my house or need any locks changed...?" A. J. looked at her questioningly, his eyebrows raised.

"Sure, give me a call." Liz grinned, her shoulder bumping into the arm of A. J.'s soft brown leather jacket.

They fell silent as the noise from a cluster of restaurants and bars grew louder as they rounded one of the many curves of the River Walk. Outdoor heaters and hundreds of twinkle lights dangling across the walking paths made this busy section of the River Walk popular, even with no water in the river and the cooler temperatures. A combination of music and cheering blasted through the open doors of the sports bar they were approaching. Based on the sign outside the bar, a mud pie-eating contest was happening inside. The mud pie recipe used was a combination of chocolate pudding and whipped cream. Alcohol helped spectators stay warm as they cheered from outside the open doors. Each bar entered its own contestant into the mud pie-eating event during the Mud Festival, so they held competitions the week before to pick their champions.

The crowds got denser as they walked. A. J. reached for Liz's hand. They wove past pedestrians, patrons, and around outdoor heaters and tables.

Liz was grateful not to experience a second vision from A. J.'s touch. The warmth of A. J.'s hand on hers was distracting enough.

When they broke free of the crowd, A. J. stopped walking and turned to her. "Wow, your hands are freezing!" He took her chilled hands and rubbed them with his warm ones. "Do you want to go back and stand by a heater for a bit?" He nodded to the crowd they just came through.

A little frazzled at their sudden closeness, and the feel of his hands enveloping hers, Liz didn't answer right away. Her brain was so overloaded she was grateful that no visions tried to push in. She looked up at him and shook her head. "I'm good, thanks."

"Here, wear my gloves, at least." A. J. pulled a brown leather glove from each of his jacket pockets. Like one helping a child, he held each glove so Liz could slide her hand inside the soft fuzzy warmth. The gloves swam around her smaller hands.

"Thanks! Shall we keep walking?" She forced a smile as her psychic abilities took hold. The effects of wearing A. J.'s gloves were immediate and strong. His honesty, sense of self, and even fleeting thoughts of the affection he felt for her washed over Liz. She felt the warmth of a blush creep up her neck. "It's not much farther to my place."

They resumed their walk, closer now, their shoulders occasionally bumping as they moved.

"So," Liz asked, "how did you become a police officer? Have you always lived in San Antonio?"

"Yes, I've never lived anywhere else. And for how I became a police officer, honestly, it goes all the way back to the Alamo."

"Oh, come on!" Liz exclaimed, positive he was teasing her. She looked at his serious face and realized she was wrong. "No, wait, you're serious. The Alamo? Really?"

"Really. One of my ancestors was there," he stated simply. Stories of a connection to the historic battle were not uncommon statements from people born and raised in the area.

"Oh, I didn't know. Sorry for your loss." Feeling a bit odd offering condolences for a man who died so long ago but at a loss for what else to say.

"Thanks, but he didn't die there." A. J. smiled at the sentiment. "People often forget there were a handful of people who survived the events of the Alamo. He wasn't there during the siege. He and a couple of friends volunteered to help defend the mission. But, they were hunting and foraging for food to feed everyone when the siege began. They weren't able to return."

"Oh wow, I never thought of that before. Someone had to make sure there was food for all the people there. It makes perfect sense now that I think of it. Most of the Alamo's stories focus on those lost in the siege. Not the people who were a part of it and survived because they simply weren't there when everything happened."

They walked under the Commerce Street overpass. "From what I have learned, it was hard on my ancestor. He suffered from what is referred to today as survivor's guilt. Eventually, he chose to make a good life for himself and his family to honor the people and friends he lost at the Alamo."

"That doesn't explain why you are a police officer, though," Liz said, still curious about the connection.

"I'm getting to it, Pushy." A. J. winked at her, jabbing her playfully with his elbow. "My ancestor, who is also my namesake, became a Texas Ranger when the organization was around thirty-five years old. As a kid, I knew I wanted to be a Ranger when I heard that. The best way to become a Ranger is to be a police officer first, to gain experience before applying."

"Okay, that's pretty cool." Liz's shoulders slumped as she stared off to the side. "But that means you're going to leave San Antonio, doesn't it? I know the Rangers are all over Texas, but there's no guarantee you'll be working at the local office." Liz was surprised at how sad the idea of A. J. leaving made her feel.

"I'm not leaving. I haven't applied yet. My entire family is here. I love this city and the Alamo. I volunteer there on one of my days off every week. Plus, I take a week of my vacation time during the annual commemoration so I can volunteer and take part in the reenactments. Sometimes I consider leaving and joining the Rangers, but

I haven't pulled the trigger yet. Does that make sense?" He glanced at her from the corner of his eye.

"You don't want to leave everything and everyone you love behind. I get it. I was born and raised here, too, and I have never wanted to leave." Liz nodded as she spoke, rubbing her gloved hands up her arms.

"There was a time this winter when I seriously considered it." He hesitated. They stopped at the footbridge nearest to Liz's building. "I didn't want to leave the SAPD with a stain on my record."

"A stain. What stain? Oh." She had been so wrapped up in how bad last month's failure had been on *her*, she didn't think of how hard it must have been on A. J. He was right beside her for that case, the failed rescue attempt, the gruesome discovery in the barn, breaking the news to Regina's parents, the funeral, all of it. Guilt washed over Liz. "I haven't been a very good friend, have I?" She reached out and awkwardly took his hand in her gloved one. "I've been so focused on how that case affected me…" Liz caught herself before she added, *and losing my abilities.* "I didn't stop to think how it affected you. I'm sorry. I guess I assumed that as a police officer, you are used to that kind of thing. Are you okay?" She studied his handsome face, seeing the sadness in his gaze.

A. J. squeezed her hand. "I am, thanks. I've had cases end badly before, but something about that case was hard to get past. Probably because we were hopeful that we would rescue Ms. Masterson. Most of the time, the victim is beyond rescuing by the time I get there. You know?" His gaze dropped to their joined hands. "I haven't been a very good friend to you either. I should have checked on you after the funeral. I was worried I'd remind you of that night too much."

Liz was surprised at his words. "No. I mean, yes, of course, you were a part of that, but I don't associate you with it negatively or anything." Liz saw A. J.'s shoulders relax like a heavy weight had been lifted.

"Really?" he asked, raising his gaze to meet hers.

"Really. And I'm doing better too. I'm still trying to decide whether I want to continue being a private investigator, but I'm—"

"What? You're thinking of quitting! Why? Wait, silly question."

Liz stepped up onto the first step of the bridge when A. J.'s voice stopped her in her tracks.

"Don't," he said quietly. "Don't quit." A. J. stayed on the sidewalk, their hands still joined.

She smiled at him. "Thank you. That's sweet. But I'm still not sure. I've lost faith in myself. I'll keep you posted on what I decide. I promise." Liz crossed her heart with her gloved hand. "You're not going to leave for the Texas Rangers without telling me, are you?" Her eyes locked onto his.

"No, ma'am." A. J. grinned. He gave her hand a quick squeeze before reluctantly releasing it.

They crossed the busy plaza and were inside Liz's cozy office within minutes. She placed A. J.'s gloves on the back of the armchair. She turned on the floor lamp next to the waiting area and sighed happily as she unzipped her jacket. "I didn't realize how cold it was going to get tonight. Take off your coat and warm up while I find Frank's contact information."

Liz hung her jacket on the coat rack next to the door.

She left A. J. and stepped around the corner into the semi-privacy of her office. She leaned against the wall and took a quiet, slow breath.

When they worked that last case together, she'd admit, she had developed a slight crush on him. A fondness she still had, apparently. Until this evening, she never dreamed there was the slightest chance he might return any of those feelings.

Liz brushed her hand, the one he'd held briefly to lead her through the crowd, against her cheek. Allowing time for a final sigh, she got to work. She quickly located Frank Stanley's contact information in the purple notebook she'd left on her desk and jotted it onto a notepad she kept handy. Even with all the current technology at her fingertips, sometimes nothing beat good old pen and paper.

A last quick breath and Liz was ready to face A. J. again. She only hoped she didn't blush as she stepped around the dividing wall.

"I've got it!" she called out, not seeing A. J. at first. She saw his brown leather jacket on the coat rack next to hers, so she knew he was still there. "A. J.?"

"Over here," he replied from the space behind Liz's office. Liz found him standing next to Claire's desk, his arms crossed, his muscles straining slightly at the cotton fabric of his dark blue dress shirt. He was studying their whiteboard, covered with details of the case.

"Oh, we forgot to cover this up before leaving this evening." She flushed, a little embarrassed, feeling like she'd just caught A. J. reading her diary. She moved toward the wall to pull the curtain across it, but A. J.'s words stopped her.

"This is impressive. Your layout is almost exactly like mine."

"Really?" Her hand dropped from the curtain, stepping back to stand next to A. J.

He nodded, studying it closely. "I still can't believe you and Claire found the expensive fashion items she bought. How did you think of that?"

"That was all Claire. She spent a lot of time reading through the victim's social media feed and recognized the value of some of the items she posted about. All I did was wonder if she'd bought any of the items. Honestly, I wouldn't recognize a haute couture accessory anyway. I would have just thought, hey, a purse, or a belt, or whatever."

A. J. grinned boyishly. "I know. That's what I thought when I spent some time doing the same thing."

It made Liz feel good, knowing that A. J. also saw the value of the wealth of information available on social media. She felt a little silly when she first started using the sites as an additional resource for a case, but she couldn't deny that it had proven helpful repeatedly.

"Yes, it amazes me how much personal information people put on their social media accounts for all the world to see! It's probably why my social media usually consists of crochet posts and complaining about the weather."

A. J. nodded, still studying her board. "Mine is all about Texas history and barbecue recipes."

Liz giggled and bumped his shoulder playfully. "People probably say we're doing it wrong."

A. J. shrugged. "Yeah, oh well. I lived most of my life before social media was even a 'thing,' so I think I'll survive." A. J. turned to Liz.

The darkened office was lit only by the floor lamp next to the couch. She smiled at him, enjoying the way the low light made his eyes appear darker.

He cleared his throat. "Um, did you find the boyfriend's contact info?" he asked distractedly.

Liz looked into his warm brown eyes and held out the paper in her hand. "It's right here."

Their fingers brushed when he took the note from her hand. Warmth spread from the weight in her chest but disappeared before she identified anything.

"Thanks," he said, his voice gruff. "Um, well—" he cleared his throat again, "—I should probably get out of your hair. I'll meet you at the hotel in the morning?"

"Works for me. Let's meet in the lobby. Thanks for dinner, and next time it's on me," Liz said, wishing she could make up an excuse for a hug just to feel his arms around her.

Liz dragged her feet as she led A. J. to the door.

He grabbed his jacket from the rack on the way past. He pulled it on and shoved his gloves into the pockets as he approached the open door. Flipping the collar up, A. J. leaned in and dropped a quick kiss on Liz's soft cheek. "See you tomorrow," he said quietly before heading out.

Suddenly unable to speak, Liz could only nod as the door closed behind him.

Lifting her hand to her cheek, she could still feel the gruffness of his five o'clock shadow on her skin. She closed the door and put her weight against it. A happy sigh escaped her.

"See you tomorrow," she whispered to the empty office.

Chapter Twenty-Eight

The next morning, Liz walked to the hotel along the busy River Walk, humming happily, memories of last night giving her plenty of reason to smile. As a bonus, she slept great and experienced no nightmares. That was two nights in a row. She did enjoy a few dreams that made her a little weak in the knees, even now that she was awake. A. J. was walking through her dreams all night, and she'd love to be able to say they were clairvoyant. But Liz knew wishful thinking had more to do with creating those particular dreams. A girl could hope though.

She had a busy but productive morning before leaving to meet A. J. and Rosemary. Of course, she couldn't go until after Claire and Pam invaded her apartment and relentlessly teased out details of her date with A. J., especially when Liz finally conceded that last night might have been a date.

Not long after she passed the yoga studio and made it down the curving stairs to the River Walk level, she heard more cheering behind her. Stopping and turning around, Liz grinned at Pam and most of her elderly, early morning yoga class cheering from the open balcony in front of the studio. She laughed and waved as she walked around the river bend.

Her friends were a little too over-zealous regarding Liz's social life.

Still humming, trying to rid herself of an overabundance of good humor before meeting this new, unknown suspect, Liz entered the hotel by the main entrance and stopped in her tracks. Mac was there, wearing an untucked khaki shirt, the sleeves rolled up, revealing surprisingly muscular forearms. He was interviewing a hotel employee unknown to Liz.

She raised a hand as she passed, to get his attention. He acknowledged her with a quick nod before returning his focus to his subject. He was so much taller than the person he was speaking with that he was standing with a hunch and his feet wide apart to bring himself closer to their height.

Poor guy must be so uncomfortable, she thought as she slipped past. A knot formed in her stomach at the thought of asking a favor of the reporter. *I wonder how bad his eye looks today?* She glanced over her shoulder, but that side of his face wasn't visible from that angle.

Liz headed to the dining rooms to wait for Rosemary. She checked her watch, and it was only ten minutes until her client was off from the breakfast shift.

As she approached the dining room, she heard a familiar booming voice. It belonged to the hotel manager, Mr. Moore. Since she had a few minutes, she decided to stop and follow up with him.

She entered the River Walk-level ballroom and found herself in the middle of a flurry of activity. Tiny bouquets in various shades of pink rested in small, clear, bubble-like

vases lined up along half the length of the dark, wooden
bar to her right. Crisp, white cotton tablecloths covered
most of the tables filling the room.

A slightly damp employee stood by the bar, one foot
propped up on the worn brass footrest running along the
bottom, a few inches above the floor. A gray container
was by her elbow, which Liz learned held cutlery when
the young woman pulled out a fistful of forks. She dipped
them in a pitcher of hot water, based on the steam, and
dried them quickly with a large white bar towel before
dropping them noisily into a second gray cutlery tray.
She'd been at this for a while, judging by the water spots
down the front of the oversized white apron protecting
her uniform.

"Ms. Pond."

The hotel manager's voice made Liz jump when he
appeared next to her.

"Wow." She placed a hand on her pounding chest. "You
managed to sneak up on me. Good morning, Mr. Moore.
How are you today?"

Literally and figuratively, the manager looked down at
her—where did he learn how to do that? And how could
he possibly be comfortable wearing a three-piece suit so
early in the morning?

"Extremely busy. Can I be of assistance?" Each word
was clipped as it came out of his mouth. "Again?" He
managed to squeeze impatience into a single word with
an abundance of skill.

"I haven't heard from you regarding the date of that
argument you witnessed. The one between Rosemary
Travers and Brittany Cabot." While Liz didn't consider
Rosemary a suspect anymore, she liked to be thorough.
She pulled out her notepad and pen.

"No, no, no!" Mr. Moore yelled, his eyebrows drew
down in annoyance.

Liz stepped back in surprise. Her question certainly didn't warrant being yelled at. Studying his face, she realized that he wasn't talking to her.

The hotel manager was looking past Liz's shoulder at a frazzled young man. "Wait to set up the chairs until *after* the tables are completely set!" He glanced around the room and pointed. "Go help Ms. Martinez with the cutlery. And, please, don't make me remind you again to wash your hands!"

The chastised young man crossed the room, dragging his feet, his head low, to join the young woman at the bar.

The banquet server handed him a clean towel after he washed his hands. A muffled, incoherent comment reached Liz's ears. She didn't know what was said, but it drew a laugh from the young man.

Mr. Moore's focus returned to Liz. "I am short-staffed today. The maître d' and two of her staff are out sick with this blasted flu working through the hotel. Can this wait?" Irritation flowed off him in waves.

To Liz, an irritated person usually made for a prime opportunity to get answers, so she changed her tactic. "Just a quick question then. Do you remember what you were doing the night Ms. Cabot disappeared?"

Mr. Moore directed an employee to move a table with sharp jabs of his finger in the air. "Yes." He pointed at another employee, who immediately grabbed a cloth to cover the new table. His gaze jumped from employee to employee as they worked. "I was taking a cooking class, and it met that night." His voice rose again. "Please, everyone! Table setup starts from the center, so you aren't leaning over the clean place settings. Follow the charts!"

He gestured sharply to the wall where, sure enough, large, laminated, full-color charts hung, instructing how to set a table based on its shape and size. The employee, who was the target of this latest outburst, returned the plates in his hands to the laden cart next to him.

Liz's eyebrows were raised when his attention returned to her. "Really? A cooking class?"

"I am a lifelong bachelor, Ms. Pond. I decided to expand my skills in the kitchen. Nothing nefarious about that, is there?"

Liz shook her head. "No, of course not. I am curious about the class though. I'm a terrible cook. Does it meet regularly?"

"I don't have the details in front of me. It's taught through Mission Community College. I have no clue how many classes there might be or how often they meet. Why don't you contact the school directly, if you are so interested?" His gaze moved from Liz to follow an employee as she crossed the room carrying a large bouquet.

"Yes. Thank you. Can I come to see you later to confirm the date of that argument?" Liz asked, tucking her notepad and pen away in her purse. "In your office, maybe?" Her eyebrows raised.

"Yes, yes." He nodded distractedly as more flowers were carried to tables. "Tomorrow morning, please. This wedding reception will keep me busy from eleven to well into the evening. In my office *before* that time. Now, please, I must return to the task at hand."

"Yes, of course. Sorry to have disturbed you." Liz zipped up her purse and held out her hand to the manager.

Mr. Moore looked down at her hand disdainfully. "Not to be impolite, but I don't want to shake hands at the moment. With three staff members out sick in this department alone, I just can't risk it. You understand."

Liz pulled back her hand, so much for seeing if she could psychically pick up anything from him. "Absolutely.

Have a great day. This is going to look beautiful!" she complimented, gesturing to the room around them.

He didn't answer as he walked away to straighten some flowers that apparently weren't at the dead center of the table.

Liz slipped out of the room to meet Rosemary.

***

Rosemary stepped out of the dining room as Liz hurried toward her. "Hi, Liz!" she called out.

"Rosemary. Hi!" Liz replied, stopping in front of the young woman. "I'm not late, I swear. I've been pestering your boss."

Rosemary grinned. "That's okay. I just finished." She stretched and yawned. "These early morning shifts really take it out of me lately. I swear, I could crawl into bed right now!" Another yawn took over, causing tears to run from her eyes. She swiped them away with the back of her hand and smiled sheepishly. "Excuse me!"

Liz smiled. "I run into a similar feeling on overnight stakeouts. Sometimes I breeze through an all-nighter and am raring to go the next day. Other times, I swear my coffee is defective, and I consider the value of an IV drip of caffeine to keep my eyes open."

The women shared a laugh as they fell into step next to each other and walked toward the lobby.

"I've heard from a friend of yours. Mac Murphy? He says he's a reporter," Rosemary commented as they passed the busy ballroom. Mr. Moore's sharp directions continued to reverberate off the walls. "Is he the one you have to eat humble pie for?" she teased.

Liz bit back the verbal jab that came to her automatically when anyone mentioned Mac's name. "Yes, that's him, and I do. He was there the night I found..." Liz didn't finish the statement. Rosemary knew what night she was talking about and who she found.

"Oh." The woman nodded slowly. "Is he a good writer? I haven't looked him up yet. He caught me as I walked into work at four-thirty this morning!"

They stepped into the busy lobby, and the dull roar of dozens of people speaking simultaneously ended their conversation. A handful of people were checking out to get on the road or catch early flights out of the city. Others were waiting in groups for shuttles to the variety of tourist attractions around San Antonio.

An elderly woman, wearing a bright purple knitted hat, waved emphatically at them. "Yoo-hoo!"

Liz recognized her coconspirator from the other morning. She waved with her whole arm, smiling brightly in reply, wishing she knew the older woman's name. The sea of tourists moved en masse toward the door, and the woman was swept along with them.

Liz turned to Rosemary with a grin. "That lady helped me out of a jam the other day. Yes, he's a good writer," Liz admitted, moving closer, so she didn't have to yell over the din. "Really good. Very thorough."

A. J. walked past a window.

"Look, Rosemary, I know you said you'd help me get up to see this mystery guest, but I have an even bigger favor. A. J., Detective Sowell, would like to join me. Am I horrible for asking?"

Rosemary bit her lip, her hands fidgeting with the string from the apron tied at her slender waist. "I don't know. I'm risking a lot helping you. I guess if it helps you figure out what happened to Brittany..." Her words were interrupted by yet another yawn. "For crying out loud!" Rosemary wiped the moisture away from her cheeks.

"Yes, I think it will. I don't know how I will convince Mac to let you recode his room key. He's a little peeved with me at the moment." Liz's shoulders bunched up around her ears as her mouth twisted into a grimace. "He's sporting a pretty decent black eye right now, and it's kind of, well, my fault."

"How is it your fault?" Rosemary's eyes opened wide in wonder.

"Well..." Liz lifted her hand to Mac when he looked up from his notepad. She gestured for him to come over.

A. J. came through the crowd by the front door at the same time, nodding to Liz as he navigated the lobby.

The memory of the brief kiss on her cheek warmed her face. "Detective Sowell is here." She touched Rosemary's shoulder. A wave of exhaustion and stress hit Liz. *Wow!* She looked Rosemary in the eye. "Are you okay?" The question came out before she could stop herself.

Rosemary nodded, swiping more tears of exhaustion from her face with the back of her hand. "Just nervous and hoping we don't get caught."

A. J. and Mac stopped in front of the women together. The detective, about a head shorter than the reporter, looked much like he did the night before, wearing worn jeans and his favorite brown leather jacket which he had unzipped as he walked, revealing a red plaid shirt.

"Morning!" the handsome detective said to Liz with a smile. "Ms. Travers, I hope you are doing well this morning."

Liz flushed.

Yet another yawn came over poor Rosemary. She nodded as she dabbed at her wet eyes with the corner of her apron. "Sorry. It's been a long day already. Morning."

"Murphy." The men shook hands. "What are you doing here? Oh, I forgot, so you are willing to help us out then? That's great!"

Mac looked between Liz and A. J. "I have no idea what you are talking about. Liz waved me over just now."

Liz gulped. She leaned toward A. J. "I haven't asked him yet."

"Oh, sorry." A. J. bit his lip and stepped aside.

Liz turned to the reporter, her cheeks heating in embarrassment. "Uh, Mac. I...we—" She gestured to the others in their group, "—have a favor to ask of you."

Mac tucked his notepad and pen away in the brown leather satchel hanging by his hip. "Oh, you do, do you?" He removed his glasses, scratching his face with his index finger. His black eye was a stunning collection of blues, greens, and yellows.

"What happened...?" Rosemary started to ask. "Oh, Liz!"

"I'm sorry, really!" Liz exclaimed to the group. "How could I possibly know that would happen when I stole your card? Seriously?" She looked to A. J. and Rosemary for help. Both were smothering grins and were of no help at all.

"Uh-huh." Mac nodded, replacing the glasses on his face. "You owe *me*, not the other way around. But, to add to your already considerable debt, what favor do you want to ask of me this morning?"

"I, um," Liz faltered, allowing a deep breath to escape as she swallowed her pride. Humble pie did not taste good. "Ugh. Okay, have you heard anything about this mystery guest staying on the hotel's top floor?"

"Maybe," he replied, crossing his arms across his chest.

"Well, A. J. and I want to get up there to speak with them, but we need a keycard. And it needs to be programmed to give us access to that floor. And," Liz made a face, "you're the only person we know who is a hotel guest and has an extra keycard." She stopped and caught her breath.

"I see. And what about me? Will I still be able to get into my room?" He looked at each of them in turn.

Rosemary cleared her throat. "Yes. Reprogramming one card won't affect the other. I don't think. If it does, I'll fix it."

A small sigh escaped Mac. "I'll say yes on one condition. I go with you." He straightened up, his lips forming a straight line across his face.

"But..." Liz started to argue.

"I go too, or it's no deal." Mac stood firm on his request.

"Deal." A. J. answered for Liz and Rosemary.

Rosemary looked at them, biting her lip. "But, I don't know."

A. J. patted her on the shoulder. "It'll be fine. I'll talk with your boss on your behalf if anything comes of this. He can't fire you if you are helping with an official police investigation."

"Okay, if you say so." Rosemary held her hand out for the keycard.

Mac removed the small card from the buttoned breast pocket of his khaki-colored, long-sleeved shirt, winking at Liz while he did so. "Fool me once..." he said as he handed the card to Rosemary.

Liz grinned. "I wasn't going to try to pick your pocket again, I swear!" She held up her right hand by her shoulder.

"Sure, sure," he responded, nodding slowly.

The trio watched Rosemary cross the lobby. She exchanged a few words with the young man behind the counter.

Within moments, Rosemary returned to the group, holding out the card nervously. "All you have to do is insert the card in the access terminal, and the elevator will take you straight to the penthouse floor without stopping. I'll wait for y'all in the coffee shop, okay?" Her hand shook as Liz accepted the card from her.

"Thank you, Rosemary. We'll come to find you as soon as we're back. I promise."

The woman nodded. "Good luck!" She glanced around the lobby before walking away toward the coffee shop.

"Ready?" Liz asked, looking at the two men next to her.

"Ready," A. J. replied, nodding.

"Are either of you armed?" Mac asked out of the blue.

"Why?" She looked up at Mac in surprise and saw how pale his face had gotten. "Are you nervous? You don't have to come."

He shook his head vigorously. "It's just... I'm used to press rooms and interviews when and where I choose them. Are you armed?"

Liz patted him on the arm gently. The familiar weight formed in her chest and felt like—butterflies. She smiled kindly. "No, I didn't bring my firearm today. A. J.?"

He looked at her, his gaze lingering for a moment where her hand was on Mac's arm. "I didn't either. Liz asked me not to look like a cop for this." A. J. started across the lobby. "If you're coming, we're going," he called curtly over one shoulder.

Liz and Mac hurried to catch up.

She reached A. J. first. "You okay?" she whispered.

"I'm fine. Just want to get this started, is all." He refused to look at her.

Liz wished she could ask him more questions, but Mac stepped in next to her, effectively ending private conversation.

She reached out and gave the detective's hand a quick squeeze. And there it was, twinges of anger and heartache. Which, to Liz, identified as only one thing. Jealousy.

She started to let go when, to her surprise, A. J. squeezed her hand gently before releasing. She looked up at his face and saw the corner of his mouth lift slightly.

Feeling better, Liz started to focus on the task at hand. *What are we about to walk into*? she wondered.

"What are we about to walk into?" Mac asked.

Liz looked up at him in shock. "How did you...?" she stopped herself before finishing the question. "Um, actually, we don't know. All we know is that this individual stays at the hotel in total anonymity and secrecy, known only to the manager. The victim was obsessed with finding out who he or she was. So..." she trailed off.

"We're hoping to find out if she found out who it was and was possibly killed for it," A. J. finished for her.

"Oh, great. So you're saying we may be walking into a murderer's lair." Mac dabbed his forehead with a plaid cloth handkerchief before shoving it into his back pocket.

"Yes," Liz and A. J. responded in unison. Their attention shifted to the elevator doors when a low bell dinged.

The doors slid silently open, and the pair stepped inside. They turned and faced Mac, who was still standing in the lobby.

"Wonderful. Just wonderful," he muttered, following them inside reluctantly. "Can I just say for the record that this could potentially be a horrible idea?"

Chapter Twenty-Nine

Elevator music played quietly from a speaker overhead. Liz recognized it as the song "Private Eyes" by Hall & Oates. The favorite theme song by most private investigators of her generation. She hummed along.

Mac elbowed her shoulder. "Can you not look so happy about walking into a potentially dangerous situation?"

"What?" She looked up innocently. "It's my theme song!" She pointed to the speaker in the ceiling.

A low laugh escaped A. J.

"What are you laughing at?" Liz asked, looking up at his amused face.

"Nothing. Your theme song. It's perfect. I just..." He stopped talking.

"You just what?" Liz asked, bumping the back of his hand with hers.

"Mine is 'Bad Boys'," he muttered, his cheeks red.

"Really?" Surprise filled Liz. "I thought it was just me. Do you have a theme song?" She looked up at Mac expectantly.

He shrugged. "Not really. There aren't any songs that have struck a chord with me. I have a favorite author who was originally a journalist." He stopped talking. His lips pressed together.

"Come on! It can't be *that* bad!" Liz coaxed.

"Fine. Ernest Hemingway," he responded. "I collect memorabilia, books. You name it. I even have a vintage typewriter that is the same model as the one he used most often." A blush colored his face as he tried to rein in his enthusiasm.

Liz snorted. *If Claire only knew how accurate her nickname for Mac was!*

"You snorted!" A. J. chuckled.

She elbowed the detective. "Yeah, yeah." She grinned and coughed to clear her throat. "He was a great writer."

"Are you kidding me? He *lived*! If he wanted to write a book about something, he went and did it—no matter what it was!" Mac's eyes lit up while discussing his idol.

Liz studied his face. "There's something more, isn't there?"

The redness on his cheeks deepened. "I have a white polydactyl cat named Snow White. She's named for his favorite cat."

"Awww!" Liz said. "Can I see a pic—"

The elevator stopped, and just like that, the congenial mood was put on hold.

Liz and A. J. stepped out first, their heads swiveling as they checked the hallway for threats. Mac fell into step behind them, his eyes wide. The doors slid shut behind him.

Watercolors of San Antonio's five missions painted by a local artist adorned the opposite wall. A colorful bouquet in a brightly painted adobe vase rested on a long, dark wooden table that ran under the paintings. Two doors at each end of the hall left them with a choice.

"Rosemary told me the guest pays for both suites for additional privacy. So I don't know which door to knock on." She glanced from left to right, listening for any signs of life.

A. J. solved the dilemma. He jerked a thumb to the door on the right. "I'll take this one."

Liz liked the simplicity of his solution. "I'll take the other." They parted company and approached the doors.

Mac stayed in front of the elevator doors, his hands twitching, fiddling with the keycard. "I guess I'll wait here."

Liz looked over her shoulder at A. J.

He looked at her. "Ready?" he mouthed.

Liz nodded.

They knocked on the doors simultaneously.

Liz heard shuffling inside the suite and what sounded like a door closing.

"A. J.! Mac!" she whispered. She waved them over. Liz dug through her purse for the black leather wallet that held her private investigator badge and credentials.

A well-dressed, middle-aged man opened the door. While handsome, with a smattering of gray sprinkled through his brown hair, he wasn't a movie star as many hotel staff hoped. Even Liz felt slightly disappointed. Although, he did look vaguely familiar.

"Can I help you?" the man asked, his eyebrows rising and eyes wide.

"I hope so, sir. My name is Elizabeth Pond. I'm a private investigator." Liz held up her badge and credentials. She gestured to A. J. "These are my partners, A. J. Sowell and Mac Murphy. We're investigating the death of a hotel employee and would like to ask you a few questions. May we come in?"

The man hesitated, glancing past the trio. "Okay, sure. I don't know how I can help, but come on in."

He opened the door wider, holding his hand out to Liz. "I'm Chuck."

Liz took his hand, and feelings of violence, pain, and hope immediately washed over her. The wave of emotions was accompanied by a brief flash of the man standing in front of her, lying in a pool of blood. Liz struggled to maintain her smile. "It's nice to meet you, Chuck. Please, call me Liz."

Liz stepped inside as Chuck and A. J. exchanged a firm handshake.

When Mac approached the man, his eyes widened as he studied Chuck's face. "It's, uh, nice to meet you," he mumbled, his gaze dropping to the floor when they shook hands.

Liz studied Mac curiously. She swore fear had replaced the reporter's nervousness.

The group followed Chuck into a decent-sized living area. He gestured for them to sit, waving to the pair of brown, soft leather sofas facing each other. A glass-topped coffee table holding current and past issues of *Texas Monthly* magazine sat in between. Chuck walked with a slight limp in his right leg as he lowered himself awkwardly to the couch, facing the door.

Seeing the limp, Liz believed the flash of vision she just had may have been in the past.

They settled on the couches, Liz, A. J., and Mac squeezed together on the one facing their suspect.

Liz spoke first. "Are you familiar with Brittany Cabot?" She pulled a notepad and pen out of her purse, instinctively believing that a recording of their conversation would be out of the question.

Chuck shook his head. "No. Sorry. The only people in the hotel I have met are Bill and Jim."

"Jim Stephens?" Liz asked, her interest piqued.

"Yes." He didn't explain further.

"Okay." Her eyebrows wrinkled while Liz considered the other name. She made a quick note: Bill? "I don't believe I've met Bill yet. Do you know his full name?" She looked at A. J. and Mac to see if the name rang any bells for them. They each shrugged and shook their heads.

Chuck offered them a lopsided grin. "Oh, I'm positive you've met him. William Moore, the hotel manager. It annoys him when I call him Bill. Which, you know, adds to the fun to keep saying it."

Liz giggled and wholeheartedly agreed. "It's going to be hard *not* to call him that now. Even if it's just to watch his blood pressure go up."

A. J. smothered a laugh.

Mac nodded, but didn't laugh. He wiped his forehead with the back of his hand.

"So, I have to ask, because it's unusual for any hotel guest to interact solely with the manager and hotel trainer. Why do you need Jim? Is he helping you with your physical therapy?" Liz asked bluntly, nodding to Chuck's right leg sticking straight out under the table.

Chuck grinned at the bluntness of her question. He glanced at A. J. "I like her. She doesn't beat around the bush, does she?"

A. J. smiled. "Not that I've ever noticed."

Chuck turned back to Liz. "Yes. Finding a hotel with a massage service is easy, but finding one with a fitness trainer like Jim isn't. He helps me keep up with my physical therapy whenever I'm in town and has even added exercises to my regimen. Plus, he gives a heck of a therapeutic massage."

Chuck leaned forward, his expression turning serious. "Oh, wait, there was one other person I've met here. I don't know her name, though. Do you have a picture of this young lady you're asking about?"

Liz pulled up a picture of Brittany on her phone and handed the device to him. She saw Mac's eyes grow large out of the corner of her eye. *What is wrong with him?* she wondered at the reporter's odd behavior.

"Yes!" Chuck nodded, his eyes on the picture. "Definitely. I did see her once. It was, what, about five, six months ago? I didn't get her name, but Bill was furious with her. From what I gathered at the time, she sweet-talked a security guard into giving her access to this floor. She knocked on the door and announced herself as housekeeping. Unfortunately for her, Bill was here at the time. He apologized profusely and practically dragged her into the elevator. That was it. The only time I ever saw her. I don't think I even spoke to her." He glanced down at Liz's phone again. "A shame. She was a pretty young thing." He handed the phone back to Liz, reaching awkwardly across the table.

Liz accepted her phone, set it on her lap, and made a quick note.

Chuck cleared his throat. "Not that I'm not enjoying the company, but I pay Bill and Jim a lot to maintain my privacy during my stays. Why—"

Liz raised a finger. "Do you mind if I ask how much money you pay each of them? I'm assuming it's what, a tip?"

"I guess you could call it that. I pay them ten thousand dollars each every time I'm in town."

A low whistle escaped both A. J. and Liz.

Chuck resumed speaking. "The privacy is worth it, and I'd pay Jim more if I could make him take it. He turned me down originally. Can you believe it? He kept telling me it's part of his job!"

Mac's silence continued, his leg bouncing so much that he shook the couch.

Liz reached across A. J.'s lap and placed her hand on Mac's bouncing knee.

He stopped. "Sorry."

Liz straightened up and returned her attention to Chuck. "My apologies. Mac is new to our investigation team."

"Not a problem." Chuck smiled at Mac before returning his focus to Liz. "Now, a single interaction with someone I didn't even speak to doesn't typically raise questions. Why are you here? Really?" His gaze ran over each of them in turn.

Liz took a deep breath. "Honestly, your request for anonymity has made you something of a curiosity among the hotel staff. But, for Brittany, discovering your identity was something of an obsession."

Chuck's eyes opened wide, and his jaw dropped. "Really? I had no idea!" He looked back and forth between his three guests and repeated his question. "Really?"

The group nodded simultaneously.

Chuck shook his head. "I don't know why. I never leave this room when I am here. I come into town for some private meetings, and that's it. I had no idea I was causing such a stir among the staff!"

Liz placed a hand on her chest. "I think they are more used to people who stay in these suites *demanding* attention and service rather than, frankly, avoiding it."

Chuck gave a small laugh. "Huh. I never thought of it that way before." He stood, manhandling his leg to bend it properly. "I wish I could help you more. Other than that extremely brief meeting, I never saw that young lady before or since."

Mac stood up, too, obviously eager to leave. He furtively stepped behind the couch.

Liz and A. J. remained seated.

"I understand that you pay for both suites on this floor. Do you mind if we ask what brings you to town?" A. J. asked quietly.

Chuck's eyes darted to Mac. His gaze swept around the room, checking the doors and the windows. He stepped back from the trio.

Liz could feel his anxiety increase and the stress filling him from where she was sitting.

He limped across the room and poured a drink. He signaled to them with the bottle, but all three declined.

Standing by the small bar, Chuck stared into his glass but didn't drink.

Liz watched him take, hold, and release his breath, yogi-style. Interesting.

"Just business. Nothing more. I pay for the second room for the added privacy, that's all."

Liz opened her mouth to ask another question when a low thud came from the next room. Liz's head turned toward the sound.

Mac twitched.

A. J. stiffened. His hand instinctively reached for the gun in the holster that wasn't there. He stood and stepped past Liz, placing his body between her and the door.

Chapter Thirty

"Someone else is here," Liz stated simply, leaning back to keep her gaze on the door, looking past A. J. She glanced up and saw A. J.'s gaze pivot between Chuck and the door.

Chuck swore under his breath.

The door opened, and a tall man limped out. His dark hair was kept short and his tanned skin showed up well against the white dress shirt he wore. He was wearing black trousers, highly polished black dress shoes, his sleeves rolled up, a plain black tie pulled down and away from his neck.

"Oaf," Chuck chided the man as he limped to join them. A half-smile crossed Chuck's face. His shoulders dropped, and he leaned against the bar, setting down the untouched drink.

A. J. continued to guard Liz with his stance.

Liz's head tilted as she studied Chuck's transition from stressed to relaxed. But she didn't understand the reason for the change.

Mac's eyes were huge, and his face paled. He gulped and gripped the back of the couch.

"I kicked one of those damned weights the trainer leaves up here. I hope I didn't break a toe!" The man dropped onto the couch and untied his shoe to check for injury.

"Yeah, they are *such* a secret! They are only stored in the same place every time I'm here!" Chuck responded sarcastically, his grin softened his words.

Liz turned to Chuck as the pieces fell into place in her mind. "You're Charles McIsaac."

A. J. looked down at Liz. "Who?"

Chuck nodded at Mac. "He knows who I am." He looked Mac in the eye. "Don't you? Recognized me the moment I opened the door." He moved back to the couch, propping his stockinged foot on the table, massaging his thigh.

Liz kept her gaze on Chuck.

A. J. turned to look at Mac.

He nodded, nervous sweat beading on his forehead. "Head of the Irish Mob in Boston." His voice was low and hoarse.

Without further hesitation, A. J. took Liz's hand and brought her to her feet to stand behind him at the end of the couch next to Mac. He kept his body between Liz and Mac and the criminals seated on the couch. "How do you know who he is?" he asked Mac without turning.

Mac took his full attention off Chuck and the mystery man who was still busy inspecting his foot. "How do you *not* know who he is? You're the—" he caught himself before he finished.

A. J.'s stress washed over Liz. She wasn't picking up any threat from the two men opposite them. She squeezed

A. J.'s hand. "It's okay." She turned to Mac, accidentally bumping into him as she moved. His fear and anxiety washed over her after the brief contact. She patted his arm gently.

She stepped around A. J., turning her focus to Chuck, ignoring the man who just joined them. From Liz's unique vantage point, the new guest's stress level was as high as A. J.'s.

Liz struggled with the waves of emotion coming at her from so many directions. It appeared that, while her empathic abilities have been slowly returning all week, now, during the span of this visit, they were back, and stronger than ever. Unfortunately for Liz, after a month of not having them, her ability to control feeling the emotions of everyone around her was a little rusty. It was a struggle to gain control as A. J.'s guilt and concern for their safety slammed into Mac's anxiety and nervousness.

She wished she could leave the room to get a break, but she couldn't. Not yet.

Liz took a steadying breath. "Someone tried to kill you, what, a year, a year and a half ago?" Liz asked Chuck directly, an old news report springing to mind. Chuck's gaze stayed steady on her, but she felt no threat. Instead, Liz felt a rising sense of concern from both A. J. and the other man. She understood it from A. J. He was a cop worried about her and Mac's safety. But what would the other man be so concerned about?

The tall man stood, his shoe and sock forgotten on the floor next to his bare foot. His hand reached behind his back.

Liz's heart leapt into her throat. *How could I have been so wrong?* Blood pounded in her ears.

A. J. pushed Liz behind him as the man's hand swung around.

Chapter Thirty-One

A flat black leather wallet was in his hand, similar to the one Liz carried her credentials in. He opened it for their examination.

Liz nearly fainted from the rapid change in her blood pressure. She gripped A. J.'s coat to steady herself. She looked back and smirked at the sight of Mac on his knees hiding behind the couch.

She returned her attention to the man opposite them. "You're FBI?" she choked out. The shift in Chuck's feelings now made sense. The FBI was there to protect him.

And just like that, Liz felt the overall mood in the room shift. A. J.'s shoulders relaxed.

"What?" Mac's head popped up from behind the couch. He got back to his feet, embarrassment coloring his neck.

Liz glanced back and forth between Chuck and the agent. "Ohhh," escaped her quietly. "A. J., Mac, it's okay. Chuck's retiring. Am I right?"

All four men stared at Liz, mouths agape.

"How did you...?" the agent asked.

"You can put it that way," Chuck responded simultaneously.

Chuck jerked his chin at A. J., but his question was aimed at Liz. "These law enforcement types need coddling sometimes, don't they?"

Liz grinned. She was patting A. J.'s shoulder. Liz didn't know when she started doing that. She looked up at A. J., his strong jaw working back and forth. Liz could hear his teeth grinding.

"I told you not to look like a cop." She smiled up at A. J.'s serious face. She turned back to Chuck. "Seriously, how hard is that?"

Chuck and Liz shared a grin.

A. J.'s jaw relaxed, but he was still on alert. He stepped away from Liz and held his hand out to the agent. Introducing himself properly this time. "Detective-Inspector A. J. Sowell with the San Antonio Police Department. Sorry for the deception and intrusion."

"Not a problem. I'm Special Agent John Smith. Yes, that's my real name. My parents have a terrible sense of humor."

Chuck stood. "Now that we're all in on my little secret, we need to talk about how to keep this quiet."

While the air in the room had relaxed considerably, Chuck was still under a great deal of stress. He paced slowly behind the second couch, rubbing his lower back, his limp was more evident now. The rest resumed their seats.

"Ms. Pond—Liz—is right. I am retiring, as she puts it. Once the FBI is through with me, I'll be handed over to the US Marshals to enter the Witness Security Program." Chuck stopped pacing and sat, stretching out his aching leg. "Look," he said, "ever since the last boss went to prison, I've been trying to take the, uh, *group* legitimate. We even make sure to pay taxes!"

Agent Smith grinned. "Yeah, well, there's some creative accounting there, that's for sure. But that's for the IRS to worry about."

Chuck gave Agent Smith an amused look. "The only problem is, while some of my business associates are happy with this new arrangement, taking away the shadow of criminality hanging over their heads and their families, others are not excited about the change. This opinion was demonstrated to me quite clearly when one of my own men tried to kill me." Chuck stopped massaging his leg. "He nearly managed it too. I spent months recovering, and I'm still not a hundred percent. The attempt left me with a back problem and this damned limp. If one of them tries again, I doubt I'll be so lucky next time. So, it's time to retire if I want to live."

As dangerous as her job could be on occasion, Liz couldn't imagine speaking about a murder attempt so matter-of-factly.

A. J. scratched the back of his neck, looking at the table for a moment. "Not to be a pain about this, but—" he looked up at Agent Smith, "—have you checked in with the SAPD about your guest here?" He gestured to Chuck with a subtle tilt of his head.

John Smith nodded. "My supervisor at the local field office spoke with your chief. Don't worry. We followed all the protocols. But, only the chief of police, and now you, know of Chuck's presence in the city."

A. J. nodded slowly. "Good. I won't put this visit in my report, but I will let the chief know we met."

"Of course, and I appreciate your discretion." Agent Smith gave Chuck a sideways look. "Normally, we'd be doing this at an FBI safehouse, but Chuck needs to keep up his physical therapy during his trips here, so this hotel is our compromise. I'm sorry, Chuck, but now we'll have to change hotels."

Chuck looked crestfallen. "I know. I wish I could hire Jim and bring him with me. He's been indispensable. But, I understand."

"What can we do to help?" Liz asked, leaning forward.

"Keep our secret. Don't put this meeting in any paperwork," Agent Smith stated simply.

"That's all well and good," A. J. commented, "but there is still a matter of this murder investigation. We haven't exactly cleared Mr. McIsaac here from suspicion. What can you offer as an alibi for the night of the murder? Some proof that you didn't pay someone to *take care* of her, so to speak?"

Chuck shook his head. "The only proof I can offer is that I spend nearly every waking minute with either Agent Smith or Jim when I'm in town. And, of course, Bill when he brings up our meals. Other than sleep, I'm never alone. I can't risk letting the local 'criminal element' know I'm here. Word will get back to someone in Boston. It always does. Which is why we're being so careful."

Agent Smith slid business cards across the table. "Here is my contact information. If you have any questions about Chuck's actions on specific dates related to your case, I'll check my reports and tell you what he was doing. Deal?"

Liz knew the truth of the matter. She, and A. J., would be stuck with an unsolved murder if Chuck was involved. The FBI would value the information he was giving them over the murder of one young woman.

Liz tucked the card in her notebook while A. J. slid one into his back pocket.

Mac picked up the card, staring at it like a prized jewel. A contact in the FBI was a gem every reporter dreamed of having. His shoulders dropped and he cleared his throat. "Um, I guess I should introduce myself too."

Chuck and the agent turned their attention to him.

"Okay," the agent said.

Mac rubbed the back of his neck. "I'm Mac Murphy. And, I'm a reporter."

Chuck's eyes bulged.

Agent Smith's head dropped into his hands. "Son of a—"

Liz apologized profusely. "I'm so sorry. He was our way of getting up here. He won't be writing anything about this." Liz focused her gaze on Mac. "Will he?"

"No," he mumbled, tucking the agent's business card in his back pocket. "It would make for a great story too! But no, I won't write anything, I promise. At least not until after your case is finished." Poor Mac looked like someone just kicked his cat.

Liz patted him on the leg, his despondency pouring out of him and slamming into her. She felt like an anvil had just dropped onto her chest. "Just remember, if you do, the world will learn about your bravery in an emergency." Liz gesticulated to the couch. "I'll make sure of it." She winked at him.

Low laughter filled the room while Mac glowed bright red.

With the mood relaxed again, Liz held her hand out to Chuck. "Will you swear to me that you didn't have anything to do with the death of Brittany Cabot, or pay anyone else to do it?" She looked him squarely in the eye.

Chuck accepted her hand, returning her straight gaze. "I swear, I had nothing to do with the death of that young woman," he replied.

It wasn't his words that convinced Liz. She picked up no malice or deception from him through their contact.

"I believe him," she announced to the room. "I have a sixth sense when someone is lying to me." She winked at Agent Smith. "Women's intuition."

Chuck grinned at Mac. "Oh, I like her." He turned to Liz, "Will you come work for me?"

John Smith and A. J.'s gazes flew to the mob boss.

"I'm kidding!" Chuck held up his hands, smiling broadly. "Wow, this is a tough room," he said to Liz, gesturing to both law enforcement officers.

Liz grinned. "I won't come work for you, but thanks for the offer." She looked to Agent Smith. "Is it okay with you if I give you my card? Both of you? Just in case."

Agent Smith agreed reluctantly. "Chuck will only be able to keep it until the marshals take him, but sure, I guess so, for now."

Liz handed her business cards to each man. A. J. and Mac followed suit.

"Thank you for your assistance. This is a huge RICO case for the bureau. Chuck is helping us take down some of the other local crime bosses, who will move in to fill the void when he's gone. We're hoping this will weaken many of the crime families in the area."

A low moan escaped Mac as he dropped his head into his hands.

Liz understood his disappointment. "Wow, that's something else! It's very courageous of you, Chuck," Liz complimented him.

Chuck shrugged his shoulders. "I never wanted this life to begin with. My father and uncle brought me into it. That's why I worked so hard at taking us legitimate. I'm no saint, but I *never* killed anyone. I know a lot of secrets though." He winked at Agent Smith.

John nodded. "That's for sure. Well, we all have each other's contact information. Detective, give me a call with those dates, and I'll be able to confirm our activities for you. As long as—" he held up a finger, "—it doesn't go into any reports or beyond the five of us. Deal?" His gaze fixed on the top of Mac's head.

"Deal." The threesome replied in unison, although Mac's voice was muffled behind his hands.

A. J. and Agent Smith stood and shook hands again.

Chuck's mirth disappeared as his mouth fell open in mock surprise. "What? No secret handshake among law enforcement? How disappointing!" He winked at Liz.

They made their way to the door and parted company at the elevator.

Liz stopped the doors from closing. "Oh, please don't tell Bill." She smiled at Chuck. "Or Jim, that we were here. This is still an active investigation."

Chuck and Agent Smith agreed before the doors slid closed.

A moment or two after the elevator began to move, Liz and A. J. looked at each other and said, in unison, "Holy crap!"

"Oh crap!" Mac said. His disappointment at having to sit on the biggest story of his career was undeniable.

"That's not what I expected at all!" Liz declared.

"Me either! Wow! How did you figure out that he's retiring so quickly?" A. J. asked, impressed.

Liz shrugged. "What other reason is there for an FBI agent and a crime boss to meet in secret?" Liz giggled.

"What's so funny?" A. J. asked, grinning.

"I won't be forgetting this one—" she elbowed Mac in the side, "—on his hands and knees hiding behind the couch anytime soon."

Liz and A. J. were laughing when the doors opened on the main floor. Poor Mac looked depressed as he dragged himself out of the elevator.

"Cheer up, Murphy," A. J. said, pounding the writer on the back, "there will be other stories."

Mac groaned exaggeratedly.

Liz patted him on the back. "Come on. Let's go find my client."

The trio found Rosemary sound asleep in a small corner booth of the coffee shop.

Liz gently shook her awake.

"Huh?" she mumbled, coming around.

"Hey, are you okay?" Liz asked, studying her client's face for signs of illness. "You aren't coming down with that flu that's making its way through the staff, are you?"

Rosemary straightened up. She ran her hands over her hair, tucking loose strands behind her ears. "I hope not. I have been more tired lately." She looked at each of them in turn. "How did it go?" She reached for her coffee cup.

Instead of answering, Liz gestured for her to follow them outside so they could speak more freely.

Rosemary gathered her belongings.

The small group left through the external door of the coffee shop. A handful of café tables were set up under the cypress trees so guests could sip their drinks by the River Walk. They sat around a table farthest from the door.

"First, we're sorry to say, but we promised the guest we wouldn't say who they are," Liz stated, patting Rosemary's hand. A strong wave of exhaustion hit her. "I'm sorry we can't cure your curiosity. Second, we believe—" Liz looked at the others and received nods of agreement, "—the mystery guest didn't kill Brittany."

Rosemary let out a short breath. "Well, that's another suspect removed. This is so frustrating. We know who *didn't* kill Brittany. I just wish we could figure out who *did* kill her!"

"Look, why don't you go home and get a good long nap? Even if you aren't getting sick, exhaustion can make you more susceptible when illness is going around. At least, that's what my mother says. I'll keep working on this, I promise."

Rosemary nodded and yawned simultaneously. "I think I will. I wish you could tell me who is up there, but I understand. I guess all those months of Brittany's curiosity rubbed off on me. Thank you, all of you." She stood as another yawn took over. She grabbed the back of her chair for support. "Excuse me!" she exclaimed. "I need to get some sleep!" She consulted her watch. "If I leave now, I'll just make the next bus."

A. J. joined her. "Tell you what, Ms. Travers— Rosemary—let me give you a lift home. My truck is just down the way at the SAPD garage. You'll get home a lot faster than taking the bus."

Rosemary smiled gratefully. "Thank you. I'll take you up on that! Oh, Mr. Murphy, your keycard. We need to reprogram it!"

Mac waved her off. "Call me Mac, please. Don't worry about it. I'm checking out today, anyway. I'll sweet talk a staff member to get me inside. Laurie definitely owes me one."

Liz smiled at the reporter. "Thanks for your help, Mac. I wish you could, you know..." She made writing motions on the air. "But, we really appreciate your assistance today."

Mac smiled. "You're welcome. Anytime."

Mac and A. J. shared a firm handshake before the group left him at the table.

The trio walked in contemplative silence along the River Walk, cutting through Casa Rio, where the staff was busy preparing for the lunch crowd. They stepped onto Commerce Street at the top of the stairs and parted company at the crosswalk.

Liz waved goodbye before A. J. and Rosemary disappeared into the substation's parking garage. She turned into the breezeway below her apartment.

Chapter Thirty-Two

Later that evening, Liz struggled to shove work aside as she pulled into her parents' driveway. She stepped out of the car just in time to be tackled.

"Hi, Yogi. Down!" Liz fought off the large dog's affections. The oversized black lab had a leg on each side of Liz, hugging her and wagging her tail so hard that her entire body was shaking. Her tongue darted out of her mouth, trying to lick Liz's face.

Her dad stood at the door, laughing at the scene they were creating. He'd dressed for an evening of gaming, in jeans and his favorite Metallica concert t-shirt.

"Hey, kiddo," Gerry called out as he walked down the path to the driveway, scratching his salt-and-pepper goatee.

"Hey, Dad," Liz said between laughs, pushing the dog off her, only for Yogi to jump, hug, and wag her tail again. "Some help here, please?" Liz managed to get the dog off her, only for a second. Rinse and repeat. Jump, hug, and push off. "How do you stop this? I think her dog programming is stuck!"

Her dad laughed and clicked his tongue, slapping the side of his leg as he walked toward them. Yogi stopped the cycle and sat. She looked up, tail wagging across the concrete, her head turned, watching Liz's movements expectantly.

"Wow, neat trick," Liz said. She hugged her dad.

But the hug was too much for the affectionate dog. Yogi jumped up, a leg on each of their backs, and she crammed her head in between their stomachs. Father and daughter broke apart laughing.

Discipline was entirely out the window as both adults were now fending off the lovable canine's affections. She had them pinned to the side of Liz's car when Audrey pulled into the driveway.

"Hi! What a nice surprise!" Audrey closed the car door. Popping the trunk lid, she retrieved her duffle bag and purse.

"Hi," Liz said in between giggles. "Can you help us? Dad's lost all control of Yogi!"

Audrey snapped her fingers and patted the side of her leg, and Yogi was at her side in a flash. She leaned against Audrey's leg, almost smiling, while Audrey patted her head. "Good girl. Stay." She walked over, handed her bag to her husband, and gave Liz a warm hug.

Then Audrey took her duffle from her husband and gave it to Liz. She greeted Gerry with a hug and a kiss.

"Ewww, gross, old people kissing!" Liz teased, wrinkling her nose.

"Yeah, yeah, yeah!" Audrey released her husband, snapped her fingers for Yogi to follow, and led her family into the house.

The group came to a screeching halt when they stepped into the kitchen.

The room was in total disarray. Tools were everywhere and the dishwasher was in the middle of the room. Tom Whitlow's blond-bearded face popped up from behind the machine. He stood, wrench in hand. "Hi, Aud! Hey, kiddo."

"Hi, Uncle Tommy." Liz saw that he was also wearing a concert t-shirt from his favorite Swedish heavy metal band, Sabaton.

"I think we got it, Ger." Tom looked to Gerry. "That thing back here was loose. And the other thing. Well, it came off, but I think I got it on again."

"Really?" Gerry asked. "Let me see!" He joined his friend behind the dishwasher.

Audrey closed her eyes, took a deep breath, and let it out slowly. "What was *wrong* with the dishwasher? It was working fine last night!"

Liz stifled a giggle. She turned and reached for the drawer in the small kitchen desk where her mom kept her address book. She saw a line through the repairman's name that she was looking for. "What happened to Mr. Doug, Mom?"

Audrey stood in front of her stove, a hand on each side.

To Liz, it looked like her mother was protecting the appliance from Gerry and Tom.

"Doug retired, honey. Junior took over the business from him. Guys, did you have to do this on game night?"

"It made a weird noise, so I thought I'd check it out," Gerry offered in defense.

"Gerry," Liz's mom said, the warning obvious in her voice.

"Babe, we're not cooking tonight anyway. And see, we're done." Gerry quickly packed away his tools and moved the bag out of the way so he and Tom could push the machine back into its proper space. The dishwasher stopped three inches shy of going in all the way. "Huh?"

"It fit before, right?" Tom asked, scratching his ear.

"It came out just fine," Gerry said, studying the machine.

Another giggle escaped Liz. It felt so good to be home. This exact situation was a perfect example of what her childhood had been like. Liz stopped giggling when she noticed the giant puddle on the floor.

"I'll get the mop. Here's the number, Mom." Liz handed her the open address book.

Audrey accepted it. "Thanks, sweetie. I have it programmed into my phone already." She reached for her purse to dig out her cell phone.

Liz dashed to the garage and returned to the kitchen, mop and bucket in hand. She quickly dried the floor but realized it needed cleaning as well. Dumping the small amount of dirty water down the drain, she placed the bucket in the empty sink. She turned on the faucet, but no water came out. Liz bit her lip. "Um, Dad, the water?"

"There's no water!" Audrey glared at her husband, her voice got higher with each word.

Tom dove into the pantry next to him, closing the door behind him.

Gerry held up his hands and straightened up to face his irritated wife. "I can fix that! We turned off the water before pulling out the machine so we wouldn't get water everywhere."

Liz coughed, subtly holding up the mop and bucket in her hands.

"Oh." Gerry turned to his wife with a big smile. "Remember, you love me!"

Audrey rolled her eyes and left the room. "Don't fix anything else while I'm changing! Please!" she yelled as she entered the bedroom, closing the door behind her.

Gerry opened the door to the pantry to find his friend with one hand in a package of cookies. "You're sure it's connected before we turn on the water?"

Tom nodded, munching on a cookie. "Yes, I'm sure. Liz, keep that mop and bucket handy, okay?" Tom winked, following Gerry out the front door to turn on the water at the main.

Liz kept a wary eye on the dishwasher.

"Is it okay?" Tom called from the front door.

"So far," Liz answered back. She, her father, and Tom quickly cleaned up the kitchen.

By the time Audrey returned, the only sign that anything was wrong was the dishwasher sticking about three inches out of its space.

"Junior will be here in the morning!" she called out as she left the sanctity of the bedroom, phone in hand, looking less irritated. Now dressed in worn jeans and a soft yellow t-shirt, she padded barefoot to the pantry and pulled out a bag of pretzels and a stack of paper plates and napkins.

After placing their usual pizza order, the group gathered around the kitchen table to chat while they waited.

"So, Liz, how's the case coming?" Tom asked, reaching for a pretzel from the bowl Audrey placed in the middle of the table.

Liz rolled her eyes and let out a groan of frustration. "Great! I'm finding plenty of people who *didn't* kill her. I just haven't found the person who did yet."

"Is there anyone who stands out?" Gerry asked, grabbing a pretzel.

"Only the trainer and that's got more to do with the fact that he keeps lying about what he was doing that night."

Audrey cleared her throat. "Honey, if he killed her, he would lie about his alibi. Doesn't that just make sense?"

"You'd think that, wouldn't you? The only problem is I don't think he did it. I'm worried he will be arrested before he stops lying and then no one will believe him." Liz threw a small pretzel into her mouth.

"Too bad you don't know his mom. She'd make him tell the truth quick enough," Audrey commented, sipping her iced tea.

"I'd love to see that! Maybe that's the trick. I'll go see him in the morning and tell him I know he's lying. Demand that he tells me the truth." Liz brightened up as the idea took hold. "And if that doesn't work, I'll threaten to call his mother!" She winked at her mom.

"I can come with you if you'd like. Put the fear of the mom-look into him?" Audrey offered, swiping a pretzel from Gerry's grasp.

"If he doesn't 'fess up, I'll take you up on that." Liz grinned at her mother, already picturing her going toe-to-toe with the large trainer. "On a different note, I have some good news to share. It looks like my abilities are returning!"

"Wow!"

"Fantastic!"

"That's wonderful!"

Liz grinned at the response. If every person in the world had this absolute acceptance of what made them different from everyone else, the world would be a better place. "My empathic abilities are stronger than before I lost them, which is, frankly, weird."

"That is weird. They were always your weakest. Maybe the rest did them good?" Tom suggested. He pulled the bowl of pretzels toward himself and grabbed a fistful.

"That's what I'm thinking. I went into a meeting this morning, they were iffy, but by the end of the meeting, they were back in full swing."

"Hi, sorry I'm late. Pizza's here!" Pam called out. She entered the kitchen laden with a stack of pizza boxes.

After greetings, Audrey zeroed in on Gerry and Tom. "Why didn't we hear the doorbell ring when the pizza arrived?"

Gerry raised his hands into the air. "We didn't touch it, I swear!"

Audrey and Gerry argued good naturedly as they walked to the front door.

"I met the pizza guy in the driveway." Pam looked at Liz and her father, crestfallen. "Oh, come on, what did I miss?"

Liz didn't answer. She was too busy laughing as the ringing doorbell echoed through the house.

Chapter Thirty-Three

Re-energized after a fun night with her family and another dreamless night's sleep, Liz had already had a productive morning. She got in her run, which her numb face regretted when she climbed into a hot shower after to warm up. Liz ate another of her mother's breakfast burritos at her desk while researching the cooking class Mr. Moore offered as his alibi. It was too early to contact the school to confirm registration or attendance for the night of the murder, but she'd ask Claire to make that call later. Reading the details of the class intrigued Liz. Maybe she *should* look into signing up for it. Stop eating out so much or relying on meals provided by her mother. Even as she thought about the cooking class, she knew dinner would consist of a store-made salad and cold pizza from the night before.

Liz was pulling on her coat to head to the hotel to confront Jim when Claire breezed in.

"Morning, Liz. Off already?" Claire asked, hanging her bright purple wool coat on the rack. She sat to remove her fashionable knee-high black leather winter boots and replaced them with more comfortable shoes. More comfortable for Claire anyway.

"Yes." Liz got distracted as she stared at the three-inch heels. "I don't know how you can walk in those. I can barely manage not tipping over in a one-inch pump!"

Claire's tinkling laugh filled the air. "Practice, darlin', years of practice! So where are you off to so early?" She rose and carried her boots to set them next to the coat rack. She dropped a short pool noodle in each boot to keep them from flopping over.

Liz filled Claire in on her plan to convince Jim to confess what he was doing on the night of the murder. "I left a note on your desk. Could you please contact that community college and ask if William Moore was registered as a student there in December? He told me that he was taking a cooking class. I don't have a real reason to doubt him, but still, I like to follow up on all alibis."

Claire settled at her desk, her eyes flitting over the note written in Liz's neat handwriting. "Will do. So, should I sign you up when I call?" Her eyes twinkled while she muffled a giggle.

"Very funny. Thanks!" She turned back at the door. "Maybe ask them to email me some details?" Liz requested.

Claire laughed.

Liz waved and headed out into the freezing Texas morning.

She walked quickly, eager to get out of the cold, so focused on her thoughts that she was standing in front of the locked door to the hotel gym before she knew it.

Taking a deep breath, Liz knocked on the heavy glass door.

Jim Stephen's handsome face popped around the doorframe of his small office. His lips spread into a broad grin when he recognized Liz. He strode across the room to let her in.

"Morning!" he greeted her warmly, welcoming her into his quiet domain.

"Morning, Jim. How are you today?" Liz asked, peeling off the scarf she had wrapped around her neck. Removing her brown leather gloves, she dropped everything on the table, glancing around the empty gym. Pulling off her purple hat, she ran her hands through her hair to tidy it.

She reached out for Jim's hand. "Thanks for letting me in. I'm hoping I can ask you more questions?"

Jim gave her hand a firm but gentle squeeze.

The brief handshake triggered a vision that brought a smile to Liz's lips. She saw Jim sitting on a couch, a small dog sitting by his side, and a tiny kitten napping, perched on his broad shoulders. Jim was sharing popcorn with the dog while watching television, his feet propped on a coffee table.

"I'll do what I can!" Jim replied, gesturing to a chair. His eyes flitted around nervously.

Liz decided the direct approach was best and cut to the chase. "Jim, what were you *really* doing the night Brittany was murdered?"

Jim's jaw dropped open at the directness of the question. "I told you. I was at a bar watching a pay-per-view event." He sat down, his gaze not meeting hers.

Liz cut him off with a wave of her hand. "Yeah, I don't believe you." She sat opposite him, crossed her arms, and watched him stoically. "The truth. Please."

His shoulders slumped. "The real answer could get me fired," he said quietly.

"The lie could get you arrested. You see, I haven't been able to clear you as a suspect. I like you, Jim, but if you can't give me a real, verifiable alibi, I can't help you. How bad can it be? Really?" Liz implored.

Jim nodded slowly, anxiety pouring off him in waves. "Mr. Moore will fire me if he finds out."

"If it has no bearing on this case, he won't find out from me," Liz offered calmly.

Jim pushed away from the table, his chair scraping across the floor. He stood and walked into his office. He returned with his phone in his hand, his thumb sliding quickly across the screen.

When he set the device on the table in front of Liz, a picture of Jim surrounded by a group of smiling young ladies looked up at her.

"I don't understand. What am I looking at?" She tapped the screen and saw the date and time the photo was taken. "These four women are your alibis! Why wouldn't you show this to me before? And why do you think this will get you fired?"

"Flip back a few pictures," he offered as an answer.

Liz swiped her thumb across the screen a few times and stopped at another picture of Jim, with the same four women, and a stern-looking man, all wearing bright white chef's attire in a stainless-steel kitchen. Jim and the four ladies were each holding what looked like a certificate in their hands.

"They were your classmates?" She hesitated, confusion clouding her thoughts. "I don't understand how this will get you fired. Why didn't you just offer this as an alibi the first time we spoke? Oh!" Liz's gaze flew to Jim's face as realization dawned.

Liz glanced around the silent, empty gym and then back down to the picture on Jim's phone. "You're leaving your job with the hotel, aren't you?"

Jim nodded. "I've got a job offer at a local spa resort outside the city. But it doesn't start until the summer. They are giving me time to finish my certification as a nutritionist. I'm almost there. I took the cooking course the semester before Christmas and am now taking the last course to be a certified nutritionist and dietitian. I didn't want anyone to know, because every spare penny I've earned here has been paying for the courses." He opened his arms to encompass the empty room. "This job covers all my other expenses. I *need* to keep working here until the summer. I've been taking classes toward my certification off and on for the past few years. Last year, something came up that made it so I could finish sooner. When the job with the spa came up last month, they agreed to give me time to complete the certification, and I'm so close!" Jim pleaded with Liz as he grasped her hand. "Please, don't tell Mr. Moore!"

Liz patted his hand gently as a wave of desperation washed over her. "There's no need, except... Jim, how are you earning that extra income to pay for these courses?" She kept her voice low, even.

He swallowed and pulled his hands back. "Um, tips."

Liz's head tilted to one side, waiting for him to come clean with her. "Jim, come on, I already know about Chuck."

Jim's worried expression changed to surprise. His eyes opened wide. "What? How?"

"We met yesterday. He had nothing but great things to say about you, by the way. He also told me how much he's been tipping you whenever he comes into town. That is life-changing money. And you've been putting it all toward this certification to get a better job?"

Jim's shoulders dropped, and a sigh escaped him. He nodded, seeming grateful that his secret was finally out. "Yes. I've been helping him with his physical therapy when he's here. At first, I tried to refuse a tip of that size, but when I realized that I could use the money to help find a different, better job, I accepted it," he whispered, even though they were alone.

"But that's wonderful! I mean, I understand why you don't want Mr. Moore to know, because, you're right, he would fire you. But, getting certifications to further your career is fantastic!" Liz praised, smiling sincerely at the man opposite her. "Oh no!" she gasped, clapping her hands to her mouth. "Oh, Jim," she said, her voice muffled. She removed her hands from her mouth. "I am so sorry! He's leaving!"

"Who's leaving? Mr. Moore?" Jim's brow wrinkled.

"No. Chuck! At the end of our meeting yesterday, his…" Liz caught herself not knowing whether Jim knew about Agent Smith. "He told me he's leaving, and he won't be back! Did I screw up your plans?"

Concern came off Jim in waves. "He's leaving?" He jumped out of his seat. "But I've been researching new exercises to help him. I've got to run them up to him before he goes anywhere!" Jim stopped and turned back to Liz, a smile lighting up his tanned face. "No, you didn't mess anything up. Chuck's tip from this visit put me over the top. I am paying off the school this week. It's enough to finish. Can you excuse me for a minute?"

Jim didn't wait for a response and disappeared into his office.

Liz heard the quiet hum of a printer warming up. Looking at the class picture again, Liz zoomed in on the certificate in Jim's hand. It was fuzzy, but she recognized the name of the school. She should. She had spent the entire morning reading all about their cooking course. Singular.

"Um, Jim?" Liz called out.

He came to the door, leaning against the wall while the printer spits out page after page. "Yeah?" His arms were crossed loosely over his chest. His well-defined muscles strained at the sleeves of his black t-shirt.

"How many cooking classes are offered at this school?" Maybe the website was out of date.

"Only one. The chef who teaches the class runs a restaurant and can only teach the course during the fall semester. Why?"

"Have you ever seen Mr. Moore there?"

"What? No way. Why?" Jim's brow wrinkled at the question.

"He told me yesterday that he took a cooking class at this school last year. *This* cooking class. It's his alibi."

Jim shook his head. "I've been taking classes off and on at that community college for several years. There's only one. In fact, we're using the kitchen classroom for my nutritionist certification course this semester. There's been talk of adding another cooking class, but they haven't found a chef to teach it yet."

Liz opened her mouth to speak, but her phone rang, stopping her. "Excuse me, it's my assistant." She pulled her phone out of her purse. "Hello, Claire," Liz greeted her friend, nodding as she listened. "Thanks, Claire. That confirms what I just learned."

After she hung up, she stood, gathering her things quickly. "Um, I've got to go. Thank you, Jim. You've been a great help. Tell Chuck I didn't share his identity with anyone else, please?"

"Um, okay." Jim stopped short, confused by Liz's drastic attitude change. "Is everything all right? You're acting strange."

"Yes, sorry. I'm fine. I'll talk with you later. Don't worry about your job here. You won't be getting fired, or arrested, trust me."

Liz let herself out of the gym, dialing A. J. with her free hand as she looked for a quiet corner to talk.

"Hello?" A. J.'s deep voice came through the phone.

"A. J., it's Liz. I know who did it. I don't know why or how yet, but..." Liz sat in an armchair tucked away in an alcove.

"Liz, Liz. Slow down. What's going on?" A. J. asked.

Liz explained her theory quickly.

"Liz, don't do anything. I was just about to call you. I just spoke with a witness that corroborates your theory. Just wait at your office, and we'll head to the hotel to question him together." Liz could hear rustling through the phone and the sound of A. J. pulling on his jacket.

"I'm already here, A. J.," Liz responded, tucking her gloves away in her coat pockets. "I'm going down to find his office now."

"Liz, no, wait—"

Liz hung up on A. J. She squared her jaw as she headed down the stairs, following the signs to the office. The pieces continued to fall into place as she walked. His fury with Brittany, as described by Chuck. Lying about his alibi for the night of the murder. The sudden change in his relationship with Brittany last year. Brittany's unexplained windfall of money. Her expensive shopping sprees to buy the designer items found hidden in her room. What was it Claire called it? Mad money. It was definitely madness.

Even with all that, Liz still found it difficult to reconcile the strict, uptight man she'd been pestering all week with the image of a cold-blooded killer.

Liz saw another sign directing her to the manager's office. She slowed, working out what she would say, and, hopefully, allowing A. J. a few extra minutes to get to the hotel to back her up.

Liz stopped. Mr. Moore's office door was directly in front of her, and she took a deep breath to steady herself. Upon entering that room, she'd either accuse an innocent man or stand toe-to-toe with a killer. Neither was ideal, but at least she had backup on the way.

After a final steadying breath, she stepped up to the office door and knocked.

"Come in!" his low, curt voice called through the door.

Liz grasped the doorknob. Flashes of a dozen people touching that same door ran through her mind. *Strange*, Liz thought as she turned the knob. *Normally, I pick up visions from only the last one or two people who have touched something.*

"Mr. Moore? I'm here, as promised, to learn the date of that argument you witn—" Liz stopped in her tracks.

Her breath caught in her throat as her mind railed against the psychic assault slamming into her.

There was no doubt. She was standing in the room where Brittany Cabot was murdered.

Chapter Thirty-Four

"Ms. Pond, are you all right?" William Moore asked, standing up from the large, leather chair at his desk, his brow furrowing.

Liz pressed a hand against the doorframe to catch her breath. Her eyes closed. Waves of rage and terror eased their attack on her psyche.

She forced a smile onto her face and opened her eyes. "Yes, sorry. I've had an inner ear issue going on today," she lied. "I lost my balance for a moment there."

"If you're sure, please, come in. The last thing I want is to be around any more sick people. I swear this flu is running through the staff like wildfire! I have that information for you." He picked up an index card from his desk and held it out to her.

Liz entered the room, leaving the door open behind her. Unsteady, she placed her jacket, scarf, and purse on the low-profile chair by the door. A long, matching couch ran along the windows to her right. Pedestrians on the

River Walk strolled outside, disrupting the manager's view. She crossed the room, her mind still reeling from the barrage of emotions that lingered in this space.

"You have a beautiful office, sir," she commented, looking warily around. In contrast to the stylish, yet utilitarian feel of the hotel lobby, Liz got the feeling she had just entered an office belonging to a CEO rather than a hotel manager. She kept the desk of dark cherry-stained wood between them as she reached for the card.

Her hand brushed across the front of the desk, and another flash appeared in her mind, Brittany standing in this very spot opposite William Moore. Even in the vision, Liz could feel the fury pour off him as he gripped the back of his desk chair so tight that all his knuckles were bright white against his fair skin. Just as fast, the vision disappeared into the mist.

She forced another smile as she accepted the card from his hand without touching him, careful to not add any fodder to the psychic bombardment she was experiencing.

"Thank you for this. I like to follow up on all the details, big or small." Liz's eyes ran along the bookshelves, matching the desk in color and design, lining the wall behind the hotel manager. The shelves housed a small collection of what appeared to be antique books and crystal glasses of different types and styles. A small wet bar was full of whiskey bottles in various shapes and sizes.

"Thank you. If that's all, the wedding party is due to arrive soon." Mr. Moore gestured to the door.

"I have no doubt that your impeccably trained staff will be able to handle things," Liz commented distractedly, as she pushed back the barrage of emotions. She couldn't take her eyes off the collection of bottles. She wandered over to the shelf, touching each one, starting with the tallest at the back of the silver tray the bottles rested on.

"Is everything ready for the reception?" A brief vision of Mr. Moore pouring a drink appeared in her mind. It was so startlingly clear, she could even see his reflection in the glass doors opposite her face.

"Yes, everything is ready. Do you mind, Ms. Pond? What, may I ask, are you doing?" He stepped toward her.

Liz's hand dropped onto a short, fat, hexagon-shaped bottle. A skeleton face smiled up at her from the cap. The dark, heavy glass was cool against her skin.

"You won't be helping with the reception, Mr. Moore," she said, struggling to see past the blinding flash of pain and the overpowering white-hot rage that overwhelmed her senses as soon as her hand touched the small bottle. "Why did you kill Brittany Cabot?" Her voice was calm as she leveled her gaze at him. Her hand stayed on the small bottle, the psychic effect easing on her mind. She watched the color drain from his face.

Mr. Moore's color returned with lightning speed, pale to bright red in a blink of an eye. "I did no such thing!"

Liz looked him confidently in the eye, one eyebrow raising as the denial left his lips. "Really? I learned a few things about Brittany Cabot during our investigation. Like how much she disliked working for you originally."

The manager nodded. "Yes, well, not everyone appreciates discipline and hard work."

"I can understand that. Then, last summer, something happened. Suddenly, she had nothing but good things to say about you," Liz responded, and her finger tapped the small bottle. "Do you know the reason for the change?"

Mr. Moore's gaze locked onto Liz's hand. "I can't read my employees' minds, Ms. Pond."

"I believe you're lying to me, Mr. Moore. I think you know *precisely* why Brittany changed her opinion of you.

And it had everything to do with Charles McIsaac's visits to the hotel," Liz stated simply.

The manager's face registered his surprise. "How did you...?" He caught himself. "You have been a busy girl. Yes, you are correct about Mr. McIsaac. He has been coming here to conduct business for about a year, which is when I began to work for him, keeping his visits a secret from the rest of the hotel staff, meeting his every need. I thought I was done for when Ms. Cabot sweet-talked her way up to the penthouse suites last summer. I'm still shocked Mr. McIsaac didn't do anything to me for my failure. That's when I realized I'd become a valued employee to him."

"You're in the mob?" Liz gulped, almost choking in her effort to keep an amused laugh from escaping her lips.

The manager nodded as he calmly continued. "When Ms. Cabot started demanding cash from me to keep his presence secret last summer, I had no choice but to pay to make up for my previous failure to Mr. McIsaac. Then last month—" he nodded to the index card in Liz's hand, "—her roommate kicked her out after their argument, and what does she do? She comes to me, demanding even more money!" He approached Liz, his back to the open office door.

Liz kept her gaze steady on the manager. "And you decided that you had enough."

"That girl." He shook his head slowly. "Yes, I'd had enough. I saw red, and the next thing I knew..." He paused, his left hand gripping into a fist at his side. "She was on the ground in front of me. I hit her—"

"With this bottle," Liz added, tapping the dark brown glass with her index finger.

His eyes flew to her face, his eyes opened wide. "I didn't mean to. Really, I didn't. I was just so angry!" His gaze locked on the bottle as Liz's hand slipped off it.

Liz's desire to put distance between herself and the murderer was overpowering.

"I still can't believe it didn't break," he commented quietly, his gaze not moving.

Liz backed away slowly, keeping her eyes on the manager. "How did you get her from here to the Navarro Street bridge, where I found her in the river?"

"That was you?" Mr. Moore asked, raising his eyebrows, as he finally looked away from the murder weapon. "I didn't know. I used a laundry cart. The staff is forever forgetting them around the hotel. This time it worked to my advantage. One was left outside the pool doors around the corner."

She found the calm, matter-of-fact way he explained his actions unnerving. *Where is A. J.?* Liz glanced at the empty doorway.

"And how did you get the cart outside? Rolling it out the front door isn't exactly inconspicuous," Liz asked, pausing by a chair.

Mr. Moore nodded to Liz, but his gaze was over her shoulder.

She dared a glance. A pair of French-style doors blended perfectly with the wall of windows. The doors offered a view of the back of the staircase to the Navarro Street bridge above. A clear path under the stairs led to the sidewalk under the bridge, which headed directly to the crime scene where Brittany's body was discovered.

"What about the weights, the cord?" She turned back to the killer, eager for all the answers. *If I can just keep him talking.* Liz hoped he wouldn't figure out that she was stalling for time.

The manager scoffed. "The weights were easy. Mr. Stephens has to put in a requisition every few months to replace some random pair. I simply let myself into the fitness center and helped myself. I can go or do anything around here under the guise of customer service." He still stood next to the bottles, straightening them. He picked up the hexagonal-shaped bottle in one hand, studying it thoughtfully. "I cut the cord from the blinds on the window. They needed to be replaced anyway." He talked as he crossed the room slowly, purposefully, to the windows, closing the blinds one at a time as he moved toward Liz, the small whiskey bottle gripped in his fist. "It really looked like I would get away with it." His gaze leveled on Liz. "I may still."

He was too calm. It was disconcerting for Liz to feel that incredible calmness from him and simultaneously feel her own building fear.

Liz backed away. She glanced across the room, where she had set her belongings on the chair.

The firearm in her purse was well out of reach.

Fear started to creep through her limbs. Running past the manager wasn't an option. He'd easily intercept her. She bumped into the French doors behind her. Hoping they were unlocked, she spun around and grabbed the knobs, one in each hand, and, in a flash, the world changed from day to night.

Chapter Thirty-Five

Liz looked around the startlingly vivid vision. She was still in the manager's office, but in front of the couch instead of by the French doors. Other than the change in light, the darkened room looked the same. The blinds covering the windows behind her were closed. And she was alone.

The office door opened, and she watched as Mr. Moore stormed in, the door slamming into the chair next to it, flipping on the light switch as he passed.

Liz flinched, believing he'd see her, which, of course, he didn't.

"No, Ms. Cabot. We're done." He stepped behind the desk, slamming his hands onto the back of his chair.

Brittany Cabot, young and beautiful, breezed through the door, unperturbed. She closed the door quietly behind her. "Really? How happy will the mobster upstairs be if I announce his visits to the world? Do you think you'll still have a job if the hotel owners find out you are not only allowing a criminal to stay here but helping him conceal his visits while he conducts 'business'?" A snarl ruined Brittany's pretty face. "Aiding and abetting is the legal term for it, I believe. Will you enjoy prison?" The scowl transformed into a sickly sweet smile.

Mr. Moore stomped to the wet bar, where he pulled the stopper out of a short, dark, hexagon-shaped bottle. The furious manager poured a splash of the amber liquid into a glass on the tray. Grabbing it, he swallowed the alcohol in a single gulp.

He turned to face Brittany, the bottle gripped in his right hand, the glass in his left.

"Aren't you going to offer me a drink?" Brittany asked, swishing past the dark wooden desk. "We're going to be in business together for a long time. As long as you keep your pet crime boss happy." She stopped, placing a hand on one hip. She studied the fingernails on her other hand. "My continued silence is all you'll need to keep the money rolling in. And keep all this." She gestured to the collection of expensive office furniture.

Liz gasped when, as quick as lightning, Mr. Moore raised the bottle above his head and brought it down against the side of Brittany's head with a solid thud. She crumpled to the floor at his feet, her features frozen, her eyes wide open. Alcohol splattered onto the hardwood floor, and Brittany's uniform absorbed some of it.

He looked at the intact bottle in his hand, his eyes wide.

Liz couldn't tell if he was more surprised at what he did or at the fact that the bottle hadn't broken.

He stood perfectly still, straightened his suit, and set the empty glass on the tray. He pulled a handkerchief out of his pocket to dry his hand and sleeve, then wiped the bottle.

Liz stepped closer and looked at the white cloth. No blood stained the fabric.

He crossed to his desk, reaching for the phone with a shaking hand. He stopped, clenching his hand into a tight fist. He looked down at Brittany's lifeless body on the floor.

Watching the events unfold in the vision was unnerving. But, the incredible composure William Moore displayed was nothing short of disturbing.

Liz watched as the manager calmly did as he had described to her. He straightened his dark suit jacket and calmly left the room, quietly closing the door behind him.

Alone in the office, she avoided looking down at Brittany's lifeless body by her feet. She wandered around the room, trying to see anything that stood out that she could use as a clue to tie him to the murder in the real world. It wouldn't do to walk in here with A. J. and point to the whiskey bottle without cause. That would only raise questions Liz wasn't comfortable answering.

When Mr. Moore returned minutes later, he was pushing a large laundry cart. He left a second time, returning with a heavy pair of weights. He dropped them on the couch, and the cushions sagged under their weight. Breathing heavily, he wiped his forehead with the back of his hand.

Pulling a pair of scissors out of a desk drawer, he kicked off his shoes before standing on a chair to cut the drawcords unevenly from the blinds. He even made sure to fray the ends, so it looked like the cords had broken.

Unseen, Liz approached him as he tilted the cart forward, bracing the wheels against the French doors. He wrestled Brittany's body into it. Unnoticed by Moore, one of Brittany's slip-on shoes fell off her foot, and he kicked it under the chair next to the cart. It disappeared from view.

Bingo! The clue she'd been waiting for. The proof that Brittany had been in the manager's office the night she died. *I hope it's still there!*

He retrieved the weights from the couch, one at a time, and tied them to Brittany's waist with the drawcords before returning the cart to its upright position. Breathing heavily, he stood by the windows, pulling down a slat in the closed blinds to watch the foot traffic on the River Walk.

Time inside a vision passed differently, so Liz honestly didn't know how long he waited by that window before he finally moved.

Liz followed Moore when he opened the doors and slipped outside. He looked up and down the River Walk and on the other side of the still river. Silence. He was alone. For the moment. Moving quickly now, he returned to the office, unlatching the second door and swinging it silently open. There was just enough space for him to roll the cart straight out of the exit, past a small café set. He paused when he and the cart were out of sight under the archway of the curving staircase to the bridge above.

The silence around them was deafening and unusual for the city. Liz wondered what time it was inside the vision.

The manager dashed with the cart along the smooth sidewalk until he was safely out of sight under the Navarro Street bridge a short distance away.

Liz watched as he took a quick breath, glancing around. From her unseen vantage point, his calm demeanor was crumbling, if the wild look in his eyes was any indication.

The strung lights overhead flickered off and on, throwing dark, dancing shadows around him and his grisly cargo. William Moore walked determinedly along the length of the low black chain that ran along the sidewalk stopping when he reached the opening at the edge of the bridge. He stopped the cart, and tipped it forward as far as possible. Brittany's body rolled to the cart's edge, but the weights blocked her fall. Holding the cart in its awkward position with one hand, Mr. Moore reached in and dragged the barbells to the edge. When the weights hit the water with a splash, they pulled Brittany's lifeless body out of the cart and down until she disappeared from view into the inky blackness.

"Freeze!"

The scene at the river's edge vanished in an instant, and the door knobs were again gripped in Liz's white-knuckled hands. Only seconds had passed while the vision of the murder had unfolded in her mind. She turned around and saw Mr. Moore standing directly behind her, his arm frozen in place above his head. The same small whiskey bottle he had used to kill Brittany gripped in his raised right hand.

Liz's eyes opened wider as her focus shifted. She looked past her potential killer and saw A. J., feet braced apart, both hands on his weapon, aiming directly at her.

Or, more accurately, at Mr. Moore.

The vision she had at dinner the other night came into view in the real world. *Whew.*

Liz slipped away from Mr. Moore, acutely aware of how close she had come to being William Moore's second victim.

Chapter Thirty-Six

Liz slid along the doors, keeping her eyes on William Moore. She bumped into the end of the couch.

Mr. Moore slowly lowered his arm to his side. The bottle fell from his grasp and bounced awkwardly on the rug by his feet.

"Liz, come stand behind me," Detective Sowell commanded. "William Moore, you are under arrest for the murder of Brittany Cabot." A. J. holstered his gun and pulled out his handcuffs from the small leather case attached to his belt. "Liz, are you all right?" he asked, not taking his attention off the suspect as he approached Moore.

She nodded. "I'm okay. I have never been so happy to see you though!"

"Maybe you should sit down. You're as white as a sheet. We'll talk in a minute. Next time, wait for me," A. J. said, his voice low. He crossed the room and cuffed his suspect. "William Moore, you have the right to remain silent..."

Liz tuned out the rest. The case was solved. Her abilities were back, and then some, but she'd deal with that later. Mr. Moore had been prepared to kill her. He might have succeeded if A. J. had been even a few minutes later.

Her mind ran wild. *How long was that vision? Never had a vision seemed so detailed nor so accurate. It can't have been too long, but*—Liz stared at the table in front of her—*it was enough time for him to sneak up behind me. To raise the bottle.* A shiver ran down her spine.

Liz shook her head slowly to clear her mind. "It was pointless, by the way," she said quietly, as A. J. brought his prisoner to sit in the chair by the door, moving Liz's belongings to the couch next to her.

"What?" A. J. asked, his eyebrows crinkling.

Liz looked past the detective, her gaze on the prisoner. "Killing Brittany." She gulped. "Trying to kill me. It was pointless. You weren't hiding any criminal activity. And you are definitely not in the mob. Mr. McIsaac didn't want anyone to know he was in the city, nothing more. Oh, and about the money? He tipped Jim Stephens the same amount."

Moore's mouth dropped open. His eyebrows nearly disappeared into his hairline. "What?"

Liz kept the FBI's secret and chose to tell the most straightforward part of the story. "Chuck's a generous tipper, that's all." She looked at A. J. "It's funny what money can do to people. For some, they turn to blackmail and murder. Others, like Jim, use it to better their situation and improve themselves." Liz stood unsteadily.

"I don't understand. Why do you keep talking about Jim Stephens?" Moore asked, his eyebrows crinkling above his nose.

Liz gave him a shaky half-smile. "Jim broke your alibi. He was taking the class you claimed to be in last December. Jim was one of five students in the class and the only male. He's been using the tips from Mr. McIsaac to pay for his tuition. It's a shame that you...and Brittany...didn't use the money to, well," Liz faltered. "Let's just say things didn't have to go the way they did."

Moore clamped his mouth shut, his lips forming a hard line across his face.

Liz's gaze drifted to A. J. standing guard next to his prisoner when she remembered the shoe from the vision. "Oh!" She crossed the room, stopping in front of the chair by the French doors. She looked behind it and slid the planter out of the way. It was still there. She dragged the heavy chair to one side. "A. J., I think you'll find that this is Brittany's missing shoe. Not quite Cinderella's glass slipper, but if the shoe fits..."

Both A. J. and William Moore looked shocked.

"How did you know that was there?" A. J. asked, his surprise evident on his face.

Liz shrugged one shoulder, raising an eyebrow at A. J. "I saw it when I went for the door." A modest lie.

Officer Marcus Sanders led the way as several uniformed officers rushed through the open office door. "Sorry we're late, Detective Sowell. We ended up by the pool. Men." He pointed to the prisoner. The other uniformed officers stood guard next to the detainee. Officer Sanders turned his attention to Detective Sowell and Liz. He grinned, bright white teeth flashing. He gestured to Liz with a jerk of his chin. "Is she in trouble again?"

"Something tells me that trouble is a perpetual state with Liz Pond." A. J. gave Liz a crooked smile.

Moore's head dropped to his chest. "I thought I'd gotten away with it. No one came asking about her. No one saw me."

"Oh, someone saw you all right," A. J. interjected, as a crime scene tech entered the room. A. J. gestured to the shoe and the bottle on the floor. The tech went to work.

Moore's head snapped up from his spot between the uniformed officers. "What?"

"Who?" Liz asked simultaneously. "I didn't see—" She caught herself before she accidentally revealed too much.

"There was a homeless man on the other side of the river. He saw you dump her body," A. J. explained. "He told me this morning that he thought it was strange to see a gray-haired man in a suit pushing a laundry cart along the river late at night." He glanced at Liz. "George told me."

Liz's jaw dropped and her eyes opened wide. George. She'd come across him sleeping under that same bridge before. Liz had even left supplies for him there. "Why didn't he say anything to me?" she wondered out loud.

A. J. grimaced. "George told me that he didn't know it was real. I remembered that he'd sometimes take shelter under that bridge, so I looked for him. When we spoke over coffee and donuts this morning, George told me he thought it might have been his PTSD making him see things. But he described Brittany's uniform and identified Moore from a picture. Honestly, George seemed relieved that what he witnessed was real and not a hallucination. I would have told you all this on the phone earlier if you hadn't hung up on me." He gave Liz a pointed look.

Liz shuffled her feet and refused to meet the detective's gaze.

Moore sniffed in disbelief from his guarded position. "No one's going to believe the word of a homeless man."

A. J. looked Moore in the eye and waggled his thumb between him and Liz. "We do. And a jury will too. When that homeless man walks into court in his Marine dress uniform and wearing the Silver Star."

Moore bit his lip and stopped talking.

***

A. J. and Liz followed Officer Sanders and the prisoner down the hallway when A. J. asked quietly, "Liz, what happened? You were just standing there. Couldn't you tell he was right behind you?"

Liz shook her head. "I don't know. I remember thinking I needed to get out of there and grabbing the doorknobs. The next thing I know, I heard you yell." Not a total lie. "I guess I froze." Liz groaned internally. She hated making herself sound like the weak, scared female in need of rescue.

A. J. placed a comforting hand on her shoulder as they walked. "Was it the first time you were afraid for your life?"

A brief wave of A. J.'s concern for her washed over Liz, and she answered with a nearly imperceptible nod.

"It's okay. I've known rookie police officers who had the same reaction. Hell, it happened to me," he admitted quietly.

"Really, what happened?" Liz's eyes opened wide, curiosity taking over, but A. J. was already shaking his head.

"No way. Not in a million lifetimes. Too embarrassing." His hand dropped away from her shoulder.

"Please?" She clasped her hands together under her chin. She batted her eyelashes at him for good measure.

He just grinned, still shaking his head at her. He pretended to lock his lips, throwing away an imaginary key.

Chaos greeted them when they entered the lobby. Dozens and dozens of people poured through the main lobby doors. In the lead was a beaming bride and groom.

"Mr. Moore! Mr. Moore!" the bride called out, waving her bouquet in the air, leaving the groom in her wake. "I hope everything is ready. The wedding was beautiful. It went off without a hitch—" The young woman stopped talking, taking in the tall, uniformed officer in front of her. "Hello," she said brightly. "I just got married!"

Officer Sanders smiled awkwardly. "Uh, congratulations." He tightened his grip on his prisoner's arm.

"Thank you! Mr. Moore, please, we need your help! My Aunt May brought her new boyfriend with her, so we're going to need an extra place setting at her table, and—" She stopped talking. "What's going on here?" Her gaze moved over the small group.

Mr. Moore's eyes darted around the room, studying the crowd forming around them. His gaze fell on Rosemary. "Ms. Travers. Please assist the happy couple. Oh..." He stopped, belatedly realizing who he was addressing. His gaze fell to the ground. It was the first true sign of remorse he'd shown.

Rosemary's eyes opened wide. "No way!" She looked at Liz, her eyes huge in her fatigued face.

Liz kept her voice low. "I'll explain tomorrow, okay? Come by my office."

Mac appeared in the crowd, snapping photos with his phone. "Really?" he mouthed to Liz.

She nodded to him as the crowd of wedding guests jostled her, A. J., Officer Sanders, and Mr. Moore.

"What's going on?" a shrill voice called out above the crowd.

Everyone looked in the direction of the voice, and a path broke through the swarm of wedding guests.

"Mother!"

The mother of the bride rushed to her daughter's side. "I'm here, honey. I'm sure it's just a misunderstanding." A tall, stately woman dressed in pale pink looked at Mr. Moore. "Mr. Moore, is everything ready for my daughter and son-in-law's reception?"

"Excuse me, ma'am." Rosemary Travers stepped up, avoiding looking at her former employer. "Let me help. The ballroom is this way. Will you please follow me?" She steered clear of her roommate's murderer.

"Thank you, dear, this is *most* unusual!" The kindly woman acknowledged the police officers with a small wave as she followed Rosemary.

With the crowd moving toward the ballroom, the small group took advantage of the distraction and headed for the doors.

Mac called out, "Liz!"

She turned to find him. He was caught up in the flow of guests moving toward the ballroom.

"Call me!" She held up her hand, her thumb and pinky held wide, relying on the familiar hand gesture if he couldn't hear her.

He nodded and stopped fighting the crowd, disappearing into the ballroom with the wedding guests.

The arresting party went out the front doors without further delay.

Chapter Thirty-Seven

A quick phone call to Claire from the homicide unit at the downtown substation resulted in a small crowd arriving to check on Liz.

First, Claire, followed shortly by Audrey and Pam. Liz was in the middle of a group hug with all three women when someone cleared his throat.

Liz broke away. "Sorry, A. J. Let me introduce you." Liz took her mother's hand and drew forward the woman who was an older version of herself. "This is my mother, Audrey Pond. Mom, A. J. saved my life this morning," she added with a grin. "Sorry, A. J.!" Liz apologized as the detective was swept into a tight embrace.

"Uh, it's nice to meet you, Mrs. Pond." His arms awkwardly surrounded her slim waist.

Liz, Pam, and Claire stood back and giggled.

"Thank you! Thank you for saving her," Audrey gushed, sniffing as she released her grip on him. She wiped tears away with the back of her hand, keeping one arm around his shoulders. "How can I ever thank you?" She hugged him again, planting a big kiss on his cheek this time. "Wait, Liz, is this the young man you went out on a date with the other night?"

Both Liz and A. J. glowed bright red.

Audrey linked her arm through A. J.'s. "We need to get to know each other better."

"Mom!" Liz looked at Pam and Claire, her eyes huge and panicked. "It's high school all over again!" she exclaimed as her friends smothered their laughter behind their hands.

A. J. caught Liz's eye, a mischievous glint in his gaze. "No need to thank me. But, if Liz hadn't hung up on me, she never would have been alone in a room with a murderer to begin with." He grinned broadly as Liz's mother released him and turned on her daughter.

"What?" Her eyes narrowed, and Audrey stepped toward Liz. A clawed hand reached for her daughter's shoulder.

Liz's eyes grew huge. "Oh crap!" She dodged her mother's grasp and ducked behind the still giggling Pam and Claire.

A. J. laughed at the abrupt change in Audrey Pond's attitude toward her daughter. "Will she kill her?" he asked Pam.

"No," Pam answered, her lips pursed. Then her mouth moved to one side, "Well, maybe…"

Gerry walked in with Tom at his side.

"Dad. Thank God!" Liz ran to embrace her father and honorary uncle. "So glad you're here. I think, no, I know, Mom's about to kill me. I'm pretty sure she could get away with it too! Even here!" Liz's arms opened wide, gesturing to the busy police station around them.

Tom dropped his arm around Liz's shoulders steering her away, while Gerry worked to calm his upset wife.

A. J. leaned against a desk, his arms crossed, watching the chaos with an amused expression.

"A. J." Liz smacked his arm playfully, appearing at his side.

He grinned at her happy, glowing face.

"I can't believe you told on me—to my mother!" she exclaimed. She kept a grip on the back of Uncle Tommy's tweed jacket, keeping him positioned between her and her mother like a human shield.

"Grounded!" Her mother's voice carried across the room, causing police officers throughout the unit to laugh.

"You can't ground her, honey. She's an adult!" Gerry's calm voice followed.

"Wanna bet?" Audrey said, losing steam in her irritation with her daughter as she accepted an embrace from her husband.

A short breath escaped Liz when she saw her mother calming down. She released her grip on her uncle's jacket and tapped Tom on the shoulder.

He turned, an amused grin on his bearded face. He dropped his arm around Liz's shoulders again. "If I were you, I'd sleep with one eye open for a while, honey. Whew!"

"Oh, she'll be fine. I know my mom. She'll break into my apartment, shortsheet my bed a few times, and she'll feel better. Tom Whitlow, I'd like you to meet Detective A. J. Sowell. A. J., this is my Uncle Tommy. Pam's dad," she offered by way of introduction.

A. J. gave Tom a firm handshake. "Nice to meet you, sir."

"Likewise. Thank you for saving our girl." He glanced affectionately at Liz. "Sowell. You know, there was a Sowell connected to the Alamo. An Andrew Jackson Sowell, any relation?" Tom asked, studying A. J.'s face.

"Yes, sir," A. J. confirmed. "A many times removed great-grandfather. I'm named for him."

"Wonderful. I have so many questions." Tom left Liz's side and dropped his arm around A. J.'s shoulders, leading him away.

Liz knew the detective was about to be interrogated about his family history.

Pam and Claire clustered around Liz. "Are you sure you're okay?" her lifelong friend asked.

Liz nodded at Pam. "Completely. I didn't even realize how close I was to…" She shuddered. "Well, let's just say, A. J. has impeccable timing."

"Thank goodness for that!" Claire exclaimed. She hugged Liz again. "I'm so glad you're okay. Don't ever do that to me again!"

"Deal. Since you have all this gratitude, do you mind preparing the final invoice for Rosemary? She's coming by the office tomorrow morning to hear the full story. Two birds, one stone, that kind of thing."

"Consider it done," Claire agreed.

Gerry led his calmer wife forward. Audrey gripped her daughter in another hug, and before they knew it, they were embraced by Gerry, then Pam, Claire, and Tom joined in. On a whim, Pam reached out and grabbed A. J. before he could escape, and he was brought into the awkward, messy, affectionate family hug.

The rest of Friday went by in a blur of paperwork, questions, and more questions. Liz and Audrey had a serious and tear-filled talk alone in Liz's apartment, during which Liz promised she'd never again, knowingly, put herself alone in a room with a killer.

***

On Saturday morning, Liz, Claire, and Rosemary sat together in the cozy waiting area of Liz's office.

"I still can't believe it was Mr. Moore! He seems so—I don't know, really?" Rosemary commented for the umpteenth time since hearing the full story.

The news played quietly on the small television on the wall. The bride and groom from the hotel had been at the center of every broadcast since the news broke. Not one reporter approached either Rosemary or Liz. No *television* reporters anyway. They each had already agreed to answer all Mac's questions that afternoon.

"I don't know how to thank you, Liz. Both of you." She gestured to include Claire.

"You're welcome, Rosemary," Liz offered a small smile. "I only wish I could have taken this case at the beginning so you wouldn't have had to wait so long for answers."

Claire stood to retrieve the invoice enclosed in an envelope from her desk. "I know it's probably inappropriate timing, but..." She held the bill out to Rosemary.

Rosemary accepted it without hesitation. "Worth every penny!" On a whim, she turned and hugged Liz sitting next to her. "Thank you! Thank you!"

Liz didn't hear anything more. A flash of vision took over her senses. She saw Rosemary crying as a naked baby was placed on her chest. Frank Stanley, dressed in scrubs, kissed her on the lips, one large hand resting gently on their child's tiny back.

Liz snapped back to the present when her client released her.

"...nothing to save her," Rosemary finished, unaware Liz hadn't heard a word.

Liz smiled and quietly slipped the envelope out of Rosemary's grasp. "You know something. We're not going to charge you anything more. Consider it a gift of peace of mind." Liz offered Rosemary a bright smile. *Or, a baby shower gift*, she thought.

"But," Rosemary resisted as Liz tore the envelope in half and set it on the coffee table. "Thank you!" she gushed. Then looked at her watch. "Oh, I've got to go. I promised Frank I'd meet him for lunch to share the news firsthand. I think he's going to propose!" Rosemary gushed, her eyes glittering.

"That's wonderful!" Liz and Claire said in unison.

Rosemary rushed out the door with another wave of thanks.

"So, why aren't we charging her? Really?" Claire asked, standing next to Liz, bumping her shoulder.

Liz smiled and sent a final wave to Rosemary as she walked away from the gate. "Let's just say she and Frank will need every penny they have—in about nine months!"

"No way! Wait, when she hugged you, did you have a vision of the future?" Claire pointed to the couch where they had been sitting only moments earlier.

Liz nodded. "I'd say there's no doubt. My abilities are 100 percent back!" Liz exclaimed happily. "Maybe 110 percent back. It's been a weird week!"

"So, does this mean you will keep being a private investigator?" Claire asked, clasping her hands under her chin.

Liz paused and glanced around her office. "Yeah. I'm going to keep being a private investigator. Do you still want to be my assistant?" Liz asked, smiling as Claire did a little cha-cha across the floor.

"Yes!" Claire sang, spinning in a circle in the center of the room.

"Will you finally let me pay you?" Liz asked, smiling at Claire's antics.

"No!" Claire sang again, dancing to her desk.

"Status quo, then." Liz shrugged and dropped to the couch, her feet resting on the table. "Works for me!"

The phone rang, and Claire answered it in her usual sing-song way. "Pond Investigations! How may I help you?" She pushed a button and replaced the receiver. "Hemingway is on line one for you!"

Liz groaned as she got to her feet.

Claire gave her a pointed look.

Liz held her hands up. "I'm being nicer to him, I promise! I'm answering his questions, aren't I?" She hummed happily as she disappeared around the corner to her desk. She picked up the receiver and said cheerily, "Hey Mac, what's up?"

Epilogue

Liz woke refreshed early the following day, after an unexpectedly quiet Saturday night locksmithing shift.

She dressed quickly, called her shift supervisor, and headed outside for her early morning run. She paused on the small balcony outside her closed door and breathed in fresh cool air. Her gaze moved to the river. Fresh, clean water was slowly refilling the cavernous, man-made riverbed.

"Perfect," she said out loud, nodding. She walked past the darkened yoga studio and down the spiral staircase to the River Walk level.

She stretched for a few minutes as the small convenience store started to open up for business.

"Morning, María!" Liz greeted the owner of the shop with a smile. The older woman wheeled a cart loaded with various types of hats out of the door, a sales ploy meant to entice patrons inside, where they could buy anything from a candy bar to a souvenir t-shirt.

"Morning, Liz. Going out for your run?" the shopkeeper asked, greeting Liz with a warm smile.

"Yes. Here, let me help you with those." Liz grabbed one of the bundles of newspapers left by the door. María picked up the others with a practiced heave.

Liz looked down at the papers in her arms. She knew the murder of Brittany Cabot was going to be front-page news. Sure enough, a picture of Brittany stared up at her from the newspaper on top of the stack. A faint grin crossed her lips when she saw Mac Murphy's name in the byline.

But, off to the side, a bold headline caught Liz's attention. *Missing Woman Found in Barn. Murder and Arson suspected.*

A cold chill ran down her spine.

"Um, María, I know you're not quite open yet, but would you mind if I bought a paper?"

"No, *mija*, come on." María dropped the bundle onto the countertop before she circled the counter to retrieve scissors. In moments a copy of the Sunday morning *San Antonio Dispatch* was placed in Liz's shaking hands.

"Are you okay, Liz?" the older woman asked, accepting the bills Liz held out to her. She rang up the sale and gave Liz the change.

All color had left Liz's face. She didn't answer María's question as she skimmed the article. Keywords popped out at her, abandoned barn, candles, tied to a chair.

Liz pulled her cell phone out of the zippered pocket of her jacket. She navigated to the contacts and dialed.

"Uh, thanks, María," she said distractedly, walking out of the shop, the newspaper gripped in her icy hand. The phone only had time for half a ring before he answered.

"I was just about to call you," A. J. said, his voice hoarse. "Did you see the news?"

"It's the same person who killed Regina Masterson, isn't it, A. J.?" Liz asked quietly. She shoved the newspaper under one arm and pulled out her keys as she returned to the gate at the bottom of her stairs.

"It looks that way. I'm coming over."

"I'll make coffee." Liz disconnected the call.

She stopped on the balcony and turned around. She watched the fresh water slowly fill the river as a low sigh escaped her. The perfect morning wasn't so perfect anymore.

About the Author

Jenni Stand lives in Texas and is achieving her lifelong dream of becoming a published author. She was born and raised on Prince Edward Island in Canada, and she now lives in Texas with her husband, daughter, and slightly spastic dog. She has always wanted to be a writer, partially due to being surrounded by everything connected with Anne of Green Gables and Lucy Maud Montgomery and partially due  to her love of reading. Growing up, she always had her nose in a mystery book, whether it was Nancy Drew, The Hardy Boys or Trixie Belden. Plus, the eighties was the best decade for some of the best mystery series on television. Lately she's been enjoying Agatha Christie. It's fun getting to read her books for the very first time.

After years of trying to write a book without success, Jenni was one of the earliest students of Ellie Alexander's Mystery Writing Masterclass. Since joining, Jenni wrote her first book, *Mad Money & Murder: A Pond Investigations Mystery*. She has already written the first draft of the second book in the series titled *Death is in the Cards*. Jenni has plotted book three of the series titled *Sage's Bluff*.

If she doesn't have a pen in her hand, it's usually holding either a crochet hook or a knitting needle instead.

She is an Affiliate Member of the Mystery Writers of America.

COMING 2025

DEATH
IS IN THE
CARDS

A POND INVESTIGATIONS MYSTERY

After the events of *Mad Money & Murder*, Liz Pond's private investigation agency has resumed its daily routine in historic San Antonio, Texas.

Coaxed by a friend, Liz agrees to operate a fortune teller booth as a part of a local charity fundraiser. However, the people coordinating the event don't know that they are getting a real psychic when she volunteered for the job.

Wearing flashy, ornate attire, Liz spends her morning reading fortunes for the lovelorn and hopeful. In the afternoon, a rowdy group of young men approaches her tent, but only one of them is brave enough to step forward and agrees to have his fortune told. All teasing falls away, and the mood turns serious after the Death card makes an appearance. Liz is unconcerned until she shakes the young man's hand, and a vision of his murder fills her mind. She tries to stop him, but his friends lead him out of sight too quickly. Before she can do anything to warn the potential murder victim, she is struck on the side of her head by a wayward softball. The injury results in a concussion and a little something extra. Her ESP abilities spin completely out of control. In response, her family and friends surround her to help protect her secret, but with a potential murder on the horizon, it looks like Liz needs to bring one more person into her circle of trust. How will Detective A. J. Sowell handle the news that Liz isn't only a traditional private investigator?

Made in the USA
Columbia, SC
28 July 2024

39323930R00178